What's her Secret?

UNFINISHED BUSINESS

Alice —
Pretty girl in
the yellow dress!
Rock on —

ISABELLE DRAKE

Unfinished Business
ISBN # 978-1-78430-398-3
©Copyright Isabelle Drake 2014
Cover Art by Posh Gosh ©Copyright December 2014
Interior text design by Claire Siemaszkiewicz
Totally Bound Publishing

Published in 2014 by Totally Bound Publishing, Newland House, The Point, Weaver Road, Lincoln, LN6 3QN, United Kingdom.

Totally Bound Publishing is a subsidiary of Totally Entwined Group Limited.

UNFINISHED BUSINESS

Dedication

For Melissa Ford Lucken, who understands things
such as these better than most.

Acknowledgements

With thanks to Dana Nussio, for laughing out loud at
the right times, and
Sarah Smeaton, for believing in this story from start to
finish.

Chapter One

Black Vinyl: Hard Pressed and Ready to Go

It's Thursday night and I'm hanging out at a record store. It's the kind of place you'd only find in Detroit. Three months ago The Twelve Inch Groove didn't exist. It was storage area in the back of the bowling alley. I don't mean just any bowling alley. I mean the Midtown bowling alley that also has an upscale restaurant on one side, a bar filled with regulars up front and a club upstairs where anybody from Whitey Morgan to DJ Assault will be on stage. Two weeks of cleaning and moving crap around, and bammo, it's a store.

Sure, you have to weave through the bowlers to get here but as long as you keep off the lanes and don't mess with the barrel-chested guys hurrying to get their next pitcher of Coors before their turn rolls around, traipsing through is no big deal.

"You like this track?"

On my left is what looks to be a walking ad for Goodwill. Baggy pants, huge Red Wings shirt, but short, clean-cut bleached hair. Two-tone Sperrys. It's like he can't make up his mind. Can't commit.

On second thought, maybe I have something in common with the guy. Commitment and I aren't on speaking terms, apparently. I pay attention to the music blaring from the speakers. "I think it's from *Criminal Minded*."

"BDP. Ooooold Skooooool." He smiles, obviously happy with the way he can stretch out words.

Nice teeth though.

I flip through the Retro Classics, wondering if it's possible to develop any sort of relationship based on a good set of teeth. Seems doubtful but who knows? Maybe. Anything is possible in Motown. Especially in the spring when everyone is emerging from the winter darkness like—well in this guy's case—trolls from under a mud-coated, concrete overpass.

He starts talking again, this time about the horrors of new rappers and how they're all sellouts. Lil Wayne for example. "Take that *Lollipop* song. Stupidest damn song on the whole fuckin' radio. He should've been long gone after that shit. But he's not. He's still here. Gettin' paid."

I do not need to degrade myself with this sort of stupidity, talking about rappers as though them getting paid has anything to do with me. Inside my head I hear myself whining. Not about the guy's behavior—predictable. But about my own—pointless. My subconscious is complaining about the sad state of my affairs and the way I spend too much time hanging out in the sort of places that seem like going there is a good idea but once there, after looking around, it's obvious being there isn't so hot after all. Do I leave these places? No. I draw on my inner self, that practical rural Midwestern part of me that I'm always trying to hide, and I make do.

Hayley, I say to myself, there has to be more to life than this. Deep inside I accept that there has to be a way for me to get my shit together. No, I've never had my shit together before but it could happen. Right? Grasping for a sense of purpose, I push away from the classics and say "See ya" to the guy.

"Sweetness," the guy pulls out a Gap Band promo twelve-inch doesn't notice that I'm leaving. How flattering.

I head to the vending machine for a little something but spot a mob milling around it so I detour to the ladies' room that the bowling alley and record store share with the bar. There are a couple of couches in there, separate from the stalls so it's pretty common to find people randomly hanging. I go to the mirror. The girl staring back at me looks pretty much like she did an hour ago. I coat my lips with more gloss anyway.

"That's the stupidest thing I ever heard. Of course you can wear plaids that don't match."

That from Scotty, the notorious hairdresser to the stars — stars being the local news anchors and those girls at the auto show who strut around Cobo Hall and stretch across the new model cars. He pats the redhead next to him and adds, "It's just a matter of attitude. It's all in how you do it."

The bowling alley regulars are getting used to finding Scotty perched on the counter in front of the mirror. Actually, I think they're a bit excited about the whole thing and are starting to appreciate the alternative flair that having a guy hanging out in the ladies' room gives The Woodward Lanes. The girl next to him is an exception — she isn't sold yet. But she will be. What she doesn't know is that in the end, Scotty somehow always manages to be right.

"I have four guys signed up already, Hayley. Are you sure you don't want to get in on this with me?" My friend Josie has appeared and is sitting on the sink, chomping on a Twizzlers. She's one of those beautiful, sexy girls that pretty much always look awesome.

I slip my lip gloss into my purse. "I'm positive," I say.

Josie recently cooked up what she calls a perfect business opportunity. Perfectly ridiculous, I said a couple of nights ago when she'd cornered me.

"Let me explain it to you first, before you say no," she insisted.

I reluctantly agreed to listen to her plan when she unscrewed the cap of a pleasantly large bottle of our fine friend Carlo Rossi. From what I remember, it's this deal where she videos guys talking about themselves and saying what kind of girl they want to go out with. Then she offers the recordings to girls. The point—to hook them up with guys without the total overexposure of the Internet sites.

All this for a price, of course.

The details are kind of fuzzy because it took the whole bottle of wine for her to explain everything. The more she talked, the more sure I became. I was not cut out for the digital dating business world. All this explains why I shake my head when she asks, again, if I am totally sure I do not want in. Even if it means missing out on all the money.

"I don't care about making money." That is a bit of a lie but it sounds good.

Josie grabs my arm and pulls me over to the lumpy couch vacated by two giggling girls who'd obviously been helping their parents with those pitchers of Coors. After we watch them totter out, she turns back to me. "True or false—it is impossible to find a decent guy to date."

I look around the bathroom. Unrelenting, Scotty is still trying to get the resistant girl to come over to the risky side of dressing without boundaries. I hear the drone of that Goodwill dude. The answer pops out, "True."

Josie swallows the last of her Twizzlers then pushes her blonde curls out of her face. "True or false—guys love to talk about themselves."

I don't even have to think that one over. "True."

Her face is triumphant as she springs the last one on me. "True or false—girls are willing to try almost anything to meet the elusive Mr. Right."

Like hang out in a record store that's so bootleg it's in the back of a bowling alley?

Like sit in the same crappy donut shop every morning for a month, waiting and wishing, that just once her life could be like a movie—or at least a commercial?

I fight against these truths but can't come up with anything. So I offer an opinion. "Not everyone is looking for a boyfriend."

"Of course not, some girls already have one." Josie frowns and looks at me, as though seeing the truth for the first time. The truth that I don't have a boyfriend.

There are other truths she doesn't see but those are definitely staying hidden from her and everyone else in the city of Detroit.

Chapter Two

Jobs and Money: Got to Get Paid

If my so-called boss, Caroline, has a last name, I don't know what it is. Everyone at North Pointe Farms Apartments simply calls her Caroline, as if that says it all. I could think of a couple of words to add to her name but what would be the point? I know I can't stand her, she knows I can't stand her — she must? — and neither of us cares. So every time the phone rings, and it's a call for her, I only write Caroline across the top of the message. If the call is for Bob Hastings, the old dude who takes care of security, I write Mr. Hastings. If it's for Tony, the macho guy who fixes stuff, I write Tony Cattalioni.

What does this have to do with anything? Not much, except it gives me something to think about while I'm sitting at the desk that's been my home away from home since I gave up on college. Friday afternoon around three I'm sitting there, thinking about how much I despise Caroline, when my phone hums.

It's Josie. "It's a good thing you didn't want to be a partner because I just finished recording this one guy." She moans obnoxiously. "You've got to see *this*. Tonight."

I don't like the way she put emphasis on *this*. And I don't like the way she's in such a hurry. What's the rush?

She doesn't give me a chance to say anything.

"Want me to come by at eight or nine?"

Behind her voice is the high-pitched chatter of women getting their hair done. Being a hook-up queen is not Josie's real thing, she's actually a hairstylist—that's how we know Scotty but that's a whole story in itself.

"Ummm," I stall. I need an escape route. Something to keep me from the clutches of the self-proclaimed dating guru. "What about Riana? Maybe she's got to see that."

"Riana?"

I feel powerful and creative and maybe a bit bad for throwing my friend into the net but because she's been saving my ass for a while now, I come back with, "Yeah. Riana."

A sigh comes out of the telephone. "I don't think Peter would appreciate your attitude. Besides, this guy is not for her."

With that settled, I let curiosity have its way with me. "What does he look like?"

"Oh, no. I'm not telling you a thing. Eight or nine?"

Not willing to let Josie call all the shots, I negotiate. "Eight-thirty—and I'm calling Riana—as back up."

"Oh please. What about Nick? You going to call him too?"

If I invite him, Josie will give me a hard time about lying to myself about us just being friends and me using him as my crutch. Whatever that means. "No, I'm not going to call him."

"Riana isn't going to bring Peter, is she?"

Argh. The stupid boyfriend. Really, I love Riana. But that vain, hypercompetitive guy, he could suck the fun out of...well, anything. "If she says she's going to bring him I'll make up some reason why he can't come."

"Good. It'll just be us girls."

We shake on the deal by saying okay and goodbye.

"Are there any messages for me?"

I look up to see Caroline marching toward my desk. Why can't she stay in her office — which has a door — and leave me alone in my 'office', which is actually a desk sitting in the middle of the clubhouse that doubles as the rental office?

"Here you are." I hand her a mini-stack of messages carefully printed on pink sheets of paper.

"Anything for Bob or Tony?"

"Four for Mr. Hastings, one for Tony."

Her face puckers. "Four?"

"Three from Mrs. Klonski. She says Snickers was barking for two hours last night. She's convinced someone is stalking her dog. She's worried someone is trying to steal her precious pooch."

"We'd never get that lucky," Caroline snarls. "I wish that stupid dog would die already."

I'm not shocked by her nasty attitude. I've been listening to her say the same sort of thing for the last six weeks.

The big scandal around North Pointe Farms — one of them anyway — is that Mrs. Klonski is allowed to have Snickers because she is the only tenant left from the dark days — the time before the careful landscaping, the time before Bob Hastings' charming security booth. The time when North Pointe Farms was Motown Manor.

There is nothing to say about Caroline's death wish for poor, little Snickers. So I say nothing. Instead, I watch the way her lip curls as she reads communications meant for other people.

After she reads Mr. Hastings' four messages and Tony's one message, she hands them back to me and scans my desk as if she has some sort of extraordinary vision that can detect the evidence of wasted time. Finding nothing to let on that I've spent most of the day studying reviews of self-improvement books — who knew so much information was so easy to get? And that self-help books had such great covers? — she tucks her messages into her pocket and creeps back to her private office.

Sometimes I wonder if Caroline rides a bicycle to work. One with a brown wicker basket strapped to the back. I wonder if some day she'll nab Snickers and stuff him into the basket then pedal off.

If that does happen, and a tornado spouts up and inhales her, I want to see it.

But first I need to see whatever, I mean *whomever*, has Josie so worked up.

Chapter Three

Book Smarts

Josie is never late and she is never early. Riana is usually early, so at eight o'clock when there's a knock at my door, I yell, "Come in, Riana."

She finds me at the sink scrubbing a pot with burned chili at the bottom. Her brown hair is pulled back and her body is wrapped in sweats.

She shrugs and says, "I was too tired to take a shower so I dumped a bunch of powder down my shirt."

I glance down at what I have on—bike shorts and a vintage—aka nasty old—Insane Clown Posse T-shirt my brother gave me about five years ago. For Christmas no less.

Riana is one of those annoying people who actually does the dumb things she writes down on New Year's Eve—so she's training for a bike thing, one of those two-day deals that raises money for something. "Is your butt going to make it three more months?"

"Very funny," she says right away. Then more quietly, "I sure hope so."

The bottom of the pot finally begins to show through the black sludge. "You don't have to do it, you know. It's not like you've got anything to prove." I scrub harder, knowing the end is near.

"Yes, I do. Juvenile diabetes research is underfunded, and besides, I want to." After a couple of long seconds she adds softly, "Even though Peter says it's stupid, I'm going to do it."

I want to say what I think of Peter, that he doesn't deserve her, that he's boring and a jerk, but I don't. Last time I tried that she was not happy with me.

I turn my full attention back to the matter at hand, or rather in hand, and continue scrubbing off the last of the crusty stuff. Riana digs through the stack of magazines and unopened mail that lives on my kitchen table. She shoves aside the bank statements from the account back home and pulls out the book I'd buried in the pile.

"*Sex and the Single Girl* by Helen Gurley Brown?"

I ignore her chuckling. "Don't diss Helen. She's cool."

"Um. Okay. But the book is—"

"Old. I know. So what?"

I hear the rustle of pages and try to keep my mouth shut but I can't, because knowing Riana, she'll have the whole thing read within fifteen minutes and realize I'm trying to figure out how to be a cool urban girl, so I spin around and blurt, "Read the end. I already blew it."

"What? Does it tell you not to watch videos of lonely guys?"

"Ha. Ha."

"Oh." I turn back to the sink while Riana keeps talking. "'A girl may surrender two hours after meeting a guy?' They thought that back then too?"

"Sure. Why not?"

"Yeah. Why not?"

"You don't think so?"

"Mmmmm…" She closes the book and looks at the retro cover. "Sure. Sometimes a woman might just want sex. You know, like guys."

"Exactly."

Out of the corner of my eye, I see her slip the book back under the stack of magazines. The window of the oddly shaped, small space I pretend is my living room slides open and Josie stumbles through, a brown grocery bag in her arms, while a big fat jug of our fine friend Carlo tangles dangerously from the index finger of her right hand.

She collapses across the couch with a huff. The bag flops onto the floor and after three gleaming silver discs spin out, a bag of cheese popcorn rolls across them. "Why do you have to live at the top of a fire escape?"

"You didn't have to come up that way," I say, pushing the window shut. "You could've come up the front like a normal person."

Josie makes a noise in the back of her throat. "You know I hate that guy below you. What is his deal, really?"

Riana grabs the wine off the floor and sets it on the table. She waves her hands in circles. "Please, let's not talk about him."

The portly bottle squats on the table, waiting. "I'll get the glasses," I say.

Riana picks up the popcorn, sets it next to the wine then stacks the discs on top of the TV. Josie settles herself on the couch with the remote firmly in her grasp.

After I pour the wine, we all lean back and stare at the TV, which is still turned off.

For some reason, even though I really am curious, I put off asking about the discs. Like, why are there three? And, do these guys know you're showing them to your friends?

Riana gazes thoughtfully into her wine. "Carlo is a fine fellow indeed."

When I first met Riana over seven months ago, we were both working at a bakery on Cass. Now she goes to Wayne State University full-time and works with a bunch of stiff attorneys at Beck, Patterson and Willis. In other settings, very unlike my not-totally-ratty apartment, she is completely professional and efficient. I've been to the office where she works. There's enough wood paneling there to make a beaver jealous. And they all love her because she does an amazing job filing crap and figuring stuff out. Her only flaw is Peter. The Stupid Boyfriend. *'You don't know him like I do.'* Whatever.

Anyway, now, as she happily downs her wine and tosses cheese popcorn into her mouth, she's hiding the fact that she actually is a very together person. But that's okay. We all hide stuff about ourselves. Right?

"Guys one and two are the warm-ups," Josie says to me. "We'll save number three for last."

"So, Josie," I try to sound casual, like I haven't been wondering this very question since it had occurred to me at three-forty-three that afternoon. "Why is it you don't want guy three for yourself?"

"You'll know when you see him." She grabs a handful of popcorn then sets it on the table in front of her. The orange pieces tumble around, making a mess on the cover of my new *Glamour*. "Besides, I'm doing this as a business. There has to be some ethical problem with taking money from a guy then going out with him."

Riana laughs.

The bottom of my glass greets me so I fill it back up. "Okay, Josie, let's have at it."

Riana, who is still chuckling, hops up and shoves guy number one into the player. He's on the steps of Josie's apartment.

"I guess I'm your average guy," he says. *"Right now I'm a senior at Wayne so I guess I'll be graduating this May – if I make it through finals and all that."*

I make a point of studying his face. Brown hair, brown eyes, cute smile. "He's right," I said. "He's the basic model. Okay enough to look at but not much to say. No add-ons."

Riana scoots forward and stares at the screen. "Maybe he was nervous."

"No, I bet he's always like that."

Josie's voice comes from inside the TV, *"Where do you work?"*

"Oh, yeah. I work at Riverfront Coffee. I'm the manager."

He goes on about keeping the coffee beans stocked and some other stuff like firing losers who come in late. Riana talks over him to ask Josie, "Do you have these guys sign contracts?"

After Josie shakes her head, Riana comes back with, "I don't get how you've got this worked out." Her eyebrows pull together as she points at Josie. "You ask the guy if he wants to be recorded. He says okay. You make the disc and for a fee you promise to show him to different girls."

"Yep."

"What's up with the discs? Kind of retro, aren't they?"

"I have them on thumb drives too. Either way, I control the merchandise."

"The guys take your word on everything?"

"Yep."

"No contract?"

"Nope."

"How do they get hooked up?"

"If a girl sees a guy she's interested in, she tells me and I tell him."

"The guys are okay with that? They don't get to see?"

Josie sets her wine down. "First thing, girls are too busy to sit around talking about themselves. And second thing, guys will go out with any girl who's interested in them. If I say she looks okay, they'll believe me."

I cut in to support that theory, "That's true. Guys will go out with anybody who wants to go out with them."

Riana isn't sold yet. "What does she pay? The girl?"

Josie smiles at the basic guy chattering on about his plans to see the Grand Canyon this summer then turns to Riana and me. "Would you pay? Would any of us pay?" She twists her face up. "I don't think so." She takes a long sip to empty her glass. "Girls don't pay."

Personally, I like that system. Girls have enough hassles, they shouldn't have to pay to have some creepy guy stare at them and listen to their darkest secrets.

Mr. Grand Canyon finishes up by saying he's looking for a regular girl. *"Not one who's going to psychoanalyze me, us, you know, our relationship."*

All three of us burst out laughing.

Guy number two has jet black hair and blue eyes. For some reason, he also has a tan even though Josie made the tape a couple of days ago. I wonder if he has a condo in Miami but don't ask because he also looks like he's thirty.

We drink our wine and stuff our faces. Why can't anyone invent cheese popcorn that doesn't make people's fingers turn that awful, yellow-orange color? They'd be a millionaire.

Guy number two finishes up with, *"She'd have to be somebody who likes to have fun and do fun stuff."*

Riana hits eject, pulls him out then sets him on top of guy number one. She slips in the long-awaited guy number three.

I expect Josie to offer an enticing intro about what a hottie guy number three is but she doesn't. Instead she aims the remote and hits play from her post on the couch.

Right away I see what she meant.

The guy is a big square of muscle with a Greek god face. Beautiful but built like a Mack truck. His chest is wide, wide, wide. I take a good look at his hair. It's a little bit red, kind of a strawberry blond, actually.

He lifts his hand to emphasize something he's saying. I stare hard at the huge square thing with clean, blunt fingernails. My mouth goes dry then I actually salivate. I gurgle out, "Look at his hands."

Josie nods.

Heat rushes to my head and mixes with the warmth Carlo's touch already started. My stomach loops into a knot.

"His hands!" Riana laughs.

I realize I haven't been listening to a word the guy's been saying. I snatch the remote from Josie and hit replay. While the disc is whirling, my two best friends discuss my hand fetish. I don't care. They're my friends. I know stuff about them. Weird stuff. Stuff a hell of a lot weirder than having a thing for hands.

"What's this guy's name by the way?"

Josie makes an apologetic face. "Clifford."

Clifford. Cliff. Cliffy?

No getting around it. Dude's name is Clifford.

I turn back to the screen and hit pause. He is frozen in time with his big mitt above his lap. Maybe I want him to drop that thing in my lap.

Maybe?

Ha.

Hell, I don't care if his name is Sandy.

"He's big," Riana announces for no apparent reason. "Big Clifford."

I hit play and he starts talking.

"Some girls don't want to go out with a guy like me." There's a long pause. A thoughtful one? "They don't like guys so big" — he points to himself with his sexy hands — "I gotta be big, you know, or I'll lose my scholarship."

"Big Clifford," says Riana.

He says something about football and pushes his strawberry hair away from his bottle green eyes.

Riana hiccups. "Clifford the Big Red Dog."

Chapter Four

What Does He Really Want?: Confessions from Real Men

It's never a good idea to start drinking while you are wearing an ICP T-shirt and gym shorts because after a while of laughing and flipping through channels, you decide you look as cute as any girl in any video dressed exactly the way you are. You don't need all that makeup and sea-salt hair texturizer. I'm ashamed to admit that's what's going on with me about the time Nick calls.

"You guys done with your videos?" he wants to know.

I bristle a bit at his tone. What's it to him if I'm sitting around watching random guys talk about themselves? "Yes." I lift my nose in the air even though he can't see me. "We're done."

"Bring Josie and Riana over. The guys are here."

Even though I'm glad he called, I'm still feeling feisty about his attitude so I offer a deal. "We'll come over if you have some wine because we're on empty."

shorts. Maybe forgetting all about skinny jeans and yoga pants is the way to find my true self. Maybe if I forget about looking my best at all times, I'll be free. I could cast my fashion cares away and wear practical things like, like… What do practical people wear?

My mother is practical. She has a sweatshirt with cats wearing cowboy hats on the front, which shows the cats' butts on the back. The kitties wear cowboy boots on both sides.

A shudder of horror ripples through me.

"You coming in?"

This from Josie who I realize has already gone inside then come back out to find me staring at the door.

I shake off the image of me cozy and satisfied in a kitty-butt sweatshirt and follow Josie. Wilson and Nick are on the crushed velvet couch. Sam is stretched out on the shag rug. Josie drops into a La-Z-Boy chair.

Wilson shifts into a semi-upright position, making some space between him and Nick. The harvest gold couch looks strangely welcoming so I plop down between the dudes. I grin at Wilson then at Sam, as if to say, *Here I am, aren't I great?*

The move is not my usual I-don't-give-a-shit style but I'm cute in my non-fashion conscious — practical? — outfit. Besides, maybe being bold is what I need to do in life. Let the cat out of the bag so to speak. Oh. I guess I already did, and it, along with all its cowboy booted friends, chased me out of town. A wave of queasiness swirls through me.

Lucky for me, Riana and Marc bust through the door in a fit of laughter right then. Soon enough, we're all comfortably drinking and chatting.

After we get done complaining about the annoying walking tours of Midtown and how the groups of people are always getting in the way, Marc changes up the conversation. "I hate it when I ask a girl how many guys she's been with and she can't give me an exact number. I want to know what I'm getting myself into."

Josie turns to Marc. "Do you know an exact number?"

"No," he scoffs, "it's different for guys."

"Do halves count as wholes?" Riana asks as she stares at the ceiling. "For the total count I mean."

"Half?" Josie and Marc say in stunned unison.

"When you start but don't finish."

Josie nods, gradually understanding.

Even in the dim light I see Marc's face pale. "Why wouldn't you finish?"

"It depends on whose fault it is." That from Josie, who is the sort to toss a guy off her if he isn't performing up to par.

"Why does it have to be somebody's fault?" Wilson wants to know.

A drunkenly thoughtful pause staggers among us. Nobody wants to go there…to the land of faults. I especially don't because I lived there and it was hell. That's why I packed up and moved to Detroit where none of the blamers can find me. Never mind that I left something undone back home. Here in the city it's easy to pretend that other place doesn't exist and that one last piece of personal business is only a dark story I tell myself.

"Do girls really fake it?"

I turn to Sam, realizing that's the first thing he's said. He looks like he wishes he could snatch his words out of the air and stuff them back into his mouth. I feel a little sorry for him in the big sister, poor kid, kind of way.

Wilson hitches onto Sam's train of thought, "Don't ever ask a girl if you're the best."

"Yeah." Marc agrees. "She'll say something meaningless like, 'I don't think that way' or 'I don't compare guys'."

Wilson leans forward and I notice he has a long, black ponytail. "Yeah. The next thing you know, you're back to trying to figure out how many she's been with and where you rate in the lineup, and that sucks."

"Can't you tell? How you rate?" Marc looks over at Wilson, then leans back and nods — to himself I'm guessing. "I know when I'm giving a girl a really good time."

"What if she's faking it?"

Poor Sam.

Silence seeps into the conversation again, either because we feel sorry for Sam and his obviously struggling male ego or because the whole faking it conversation is a no-go. Nick isn't involved in this whole conversation. He's staring off into space. Thinking about some math problem, probably.

Needing to do something with my attention, I gaze over to Wilson's shiny locks.

Long hair.

How about that.

Sexy?

Out of habit, I check out his hands.

I can't get a clear view because one arm is behind his head and one hand is wrapped around a beer bottle. The fingers look promising though. Sort of.

Wilson glances over. He doesn't smile but something passes between us. At least I think it does. But what do I know? It's not like I have all that much experience with city guys. Before I decide whether or not it actually did or whether or not I should do anything about it, Riana, who has been acting as hostess by refilling our wine glasses, wilts onto the olive green carpet. "Do guys really fantasize about doing it with two girls?" she asks.

The query floats around the room like a dark cloud with absolutely no silver lining. The fog of thought is dark because, one—we girls all know guys think about that and we hate them for it, and two—the guys want it bad, know we know it, and hate us because we are not willing to subject ourselves to that kind of stupidity. Well, unless it's our idea. That's totally different.

We all make up scenarios in our minds, whether we want to—the guys—or not—us girls. Me and Wilson and Josie? She'd take over everything and get all the credit. Me and Wilson and Riana? She's so sweet I'd look like a bitch.

I turn to Nick. This time he's looking right at me, the dark brown of his eyes even darker in that dim light. For no good reason I look down at his mouth. He smiles. I try to remember what we were all talking about but I have absolutely no idea.

Out of nowhere, he reaches over and sets his hand on my thigh. A bolt of electricity skittles up my leg and a crooked smile wobbles across my mouth. Awkward doesn't begin to describe the way I feel. Right then, Riana meanders over and hauls me up. Hoping I'll thank her later, I let her pull me away from Nick. Josie follows us out of the door.

Chapter Five

Celebrate

Shh.

Ssssshhhhh.

My brain thinks that but my body acts on its own.

"Hayley?"

I wake up realizing that I'm holding the phone to my ear. My brain careens dangerously inside my skull so I hold my head very still and whisper hello.

"Hayley, it's me."

Behind the sweet, enthusiastic voice greeting me, I hear my Aunt Sandy rattling around in the background. Oh yes, it's my eleven-year-old cousin calling from an actual wall phone at the farm he calls home.

"Hey, Frankie," I say softly, trying not to wake myself any more than necessary as I ease my head back onto my pillow.

"Big Friday night? Out drinking again?" he asks.

"Huh?"

"Mom says that's all people do in the city. Drink, go to bars, and spend too much money on fancy coffee so they can do it all over again."

Although I have no response to that statement of fact, apparently my aunt does, because Frankie's hollering something at his mother that sounds like, "She doesn't care what you and Aunt Maggie say. She thinks it's funny."

Nothing is funny right now, kid.

"Anyway" — he is back to me — "I've got a new limerick and you're really going to love it."

I swallow against the sour taste in my throat.

Like early mornings and calls from eleven-year-old cousins, limericks and hangovers don't mix.

There is a muffled yell, then, "Don't worry, Mom, it's not the one about Bart. Mom thinks I'm going to tell you this other one I made up about a boy named Bart."

A smile creeps onto my face. He's a weird one, my cousin Frankie. "I can guess the rest of that one."

He laughs the clear, happy, chuckle of a pre-teen boy who is living the honest life out in the sweet, clean countryside. He is safe from the drunks swilling down four-dollar cappuccinos. "You could try to guess the rest, Hayley, but you'd never even get close."

I do not ever remember getting so excited about a rude poem when I was eleven.

Realizing that the only way to get the phone back on my bedside table where it belongs, I sigh and agree with, "Okay, Frankie. Lemme hear it."

He giggles then clears his throat as if he is about to recite Shakespeare.

"There once was a pretty young model,
Who was often drawn to the bottle.
She'd drink and she'd drink,

Till she puked in the sink.
Then off to the next bar she'd tottle."

A reluctant chuckle escapes my throat and wakes me up.

"See, I told you it was a good one."

"Okay, Frankie. That's a good one. It's so good I'm going to tell it to my friends."

There is another muffled yell, then, "Mom and me gotta go over to your house and help clean out the chicken house."

I hear the agony in his voice, and I understand completely. I know what it is to be a kid and scraping up rotting cedar shavings dotted with chicken shit while your mother pretends to be Naomi Judd to your Wynonna. Maybe Frankie won't have to be Wynonna. Maybe he'll get to be Clint Black. "Call me again, Frankie. Just try to make it after ten next time."

He laughs as he hangs up.

I hang up. *Night, night Mr. Phone.*

With the blanket pulled tightly around me, I snuggle back against the pillow and wonder about Nick's hand on my thigh.

Hmmmm.

What did that mean, exactly?

The stupid phone hums. Again. I silence it by answering.

"It's all set."

How can Josie be so awake this early in the morning? Isn't there a law against that? "What's all set?"

"You and Clifford. I called him this morning and gave him your number." She says something to somebody about color bottle B-23. How can she be at work already? "Don't worry, I told him to call after ten."

Clifford?

Oh right. Him.

The fact that Josie remembered — although did not observe — my policy about early morning phone calls does nothing to quell the sensation of frustration churning in my stomach. Or is that confusion? Or the after-effects of the wine? Defeated, I grumble, "Okay."

Instead of speaking to me, she mumbles something to one of the other stylists about capes.

The horrifying image of Clifford arriving at my door with a red cape hugging his shoulders and a fat C stamped on his broad chest infiltrates my mind. "I gotta go, Josie."

"Okay," she's back to me. "Let me know when he calls so I can send him a bill."

Hmmmmm.

A bill.

For calling me.

Maybe it isn't such a good idea. I open my mouth but Josie pipes up with a quick goodbye and a speedy hang up.

Guess I won't be calling my mom today like I usually do on Saturdays. Hi, Mom. No, nothing's new. Dates? Oh no. Unless you count some guy who's paying to go out with me. No, calm down Mom. It's not like that. I'm not getting the money. See? So it's okay.

I don't even think so.

With the possibility of Clifford's call lingering in the air, I accept that sleep will not be coming back. I rotate until I'm out of bed and wobble to the kitchen. *Must drink coffee. Need proper food.*

My stomach rolls around inside my body like a water balloon. I regret feeling self-righteous — and fat — last Wednesday, because if that hadn't happened

34

I'd have three chocolate donuts waiting for me in the kitchen. No, I wouldn't have cared that they were stale.

Immediate action is necessary. I go back to my bedroom and sit on my bed. My phone buzzes when Josie sends me a text.

You don't sound so good, BTW. Perk up before he calls.

I'm not yet in the mood for her attitude. I reply with my custom designed Hangover Recovery Plan.

1. Gently wash face while the coffee is brewing.
2. Drink coffee and review clip of The Big Red Dog.
3. Take off the ICP T-shirt and bike shorts I slept in.
4. Find some clothing that won't squish my stomach.
5. Walk down to Pastry Pete's, get donuts.
6. Scarf down donuts on the way back.
7. Take the back way up to avoid Him.
8. Lie down and hope to either throw up or fall asleep.

* * * *

My future looks better already. After accomplishing tasks one to four, I grab the wad of dollars off the coffee table and stuff it into my pocket. I find my smile and sense of humor next to sad, empty Carlo so I grab them too.

Urgh. My phone hums. Again.

I answer with the freshly recovered smile snugly in place. "Hayley's Happy House of Hangovers."

A low voice curls through the phone. "Um… Uh… Is this Hayley?"

Clifford. The dog.

Those hands.

"Yeah, hi. This is Hayley."

"I got your number from that girl, Josie."

My mind is so blank all I can come up with is, "Yeah, I know."

"Okay if I come get you at six-fifteen on Wednesday?" he wants to know.

Why Wednesday?

Why six-fifteen?

I have no idea.

But I say, "Sure, that'd be great."

His response, "Cool. She already gave me your address," is followed by silence that hums between us.

The awkwardness lingers until I say, "See you then."

That prompts a matching pair of goodbyes and we hang up.

Chapter Six

Holiday Survival: Keep the Joy

Why didn't someone tell me it was St. Patrick's Day? It's important to be ready for these things in advance. Had I known this significant holiday was approaching I would've prepared. If someone had been kind enough to remind me I would have...would have... *Would've...?*

I glance down at the thin, green beer in my formerly frosted mug. I would've drunk less wine at Nick's last night.

That way I wouldn't have this cloud of guilt fogging my vision. Girls who are trying to get their lives together shouldn't drink too much three nights in a row. It's tricky enough business trying to see through one's drunken haze without the nuisance of an emotional cloud of guilt making things worse.

Come to think of it, I'm not hearing so well either.

"Whaddya say, Riana?"

Riana arches across the tattered booth she, Nick and I have been using as our home base for the past two hours. "It says here"—she stabs at the helpfully informational, green flyer that was handed to us on the way in—"that there's going to be a limerick contest."

A contest.

I twist my mouth thoughtfully, as if I can taste the question lurking there. "What's the prize?"

Her eyebrows pull together as she positions the sheet closer to her face and peers at me across the top of it. "Dinner for two. The Rooney McNamara special!"

I try to ask, "Do you suppose that's corned beef and cabbage or some other traditional Irish dish?" Unfortunately, what comes out sounds more like, "Dahya sink thats cornbeefan cabbish?"

Before Riana translates, Nick slides in next to me, bumps my shoulder with his and grumbles, "Jukebox is broken."

A sappy grin tilts across my face as I grab his left arm. "I'm so glad you're out with us tonight, Nicky-boy." I hold up my hand so my forefinger and thumb are about an inch apart. "I might be a little sorry you lost the toss, seein' as you're the only one of us who's actually Irish. Or part Irish. Whatever."

Riana frowns and pats the arm I'm clinging to. "You ought to be getting drunk on this nasty beer."

"Clear the air, girls. It's starting to look like one of those weep fests." He shakes his head. "I guess I should be glad Josie isn't here."

I shift to Riana. "Are you feeling all stupid and weepy?"

She ignores my question and stabs at the air near Nick. "The contest! Nick! You have to know a limerick!"

Looking thoughtful, he takes a long drink of his Gatorade.

"I know a limerick," I mumble, half-hoping neither of them heard me and half-hoping they'll think I'm wonderful.

Unfortunately, after the words are out of my mouth, their heads swivel simultaneously like puppets. Creepy, slow moving puppets. Not at all a response I was hoping for. Or one I'd even considered. *Please God, don't let them blink at the same time, because then I'll have to scrabble over the table and bolt for the door.*

Oh, relief. Nick is talking.

I stare at him for a minute because his teeth really are so nice and straight. "Huh?"

He waves his hand between Riana and him. "Tell us the limerick."

Nice hands, too. Why haven't I ever noticed that before? "Limerick?"

"To win the Irish dinners," Riana says as if I'm some dolt who can't remember bits of conversation from one piece to the next. "The contest, Hayley."

Oh yeah. I ask them, "Do we even want that cabbish?"

Nick opens his mouth but the voice that comes out is cheerfully musical. I didn't know Nick could do an Irish accent.

Oh. He can't do an accent, it's some round, little man wearing a green cap. He has suspenders and lime green striped pants. It's a leprechaun? Can't be. Yet there he is, right there in the front of the bar, standing on a tiny stage.

The leprechaun keeps talking and it sounds great. The right thing to put a person in the mood for a real old-world St. Paddy's Day. The crowd is so noisy, I can't really make out what the little guy is saying but it doesn't matter. *Rolling, rolling jolly words.* He laughs and his world laughs with him. *More jolly words, something else…* "Limericks."

Nick shoots to his feet and does a weird saluting thing. There's a warm round of applause. What nice people to clap for my friend. Maybe they like his smile too. And his arms. I bet they like his arms as much as I do. I peek at him from the corners of my eyes. His back is nice too.

While I'm giving him the once-over, Nick grabs my arm and rudely jerks me to my feet. After I totter a bit, I turn to glare at him but notice that everyone in the room is staring at me. Expectantly. Actually, I have to admit, I feel their expectation more than see it, because mostly their faces are obscured by that damn guilt cloud.

The next thing I know, the nice leprechaun is taking my hand and leading me through the tables crammed with muddy brown and bright green people. He squares me in front of a microphone and nods.

Silence greets me.

I blink, puppet-like, and frighten myself as my head pivots stiffly above my neck.

A shout comes from my table.

"Say the limerick, Hayley."

What would I do without Nick? I understand now. I'm trying to win some cornbeffan cabbish.

Here's a chance to do something different. Step out of my comfort zone and learn about myself. Public speaking is not in my comfort zone, that's for damn sure. I hate it, as a matter of fact. So being at the microphone is a good thing. Right?

Appreciating this opportunity for growth, I smile at the crowd and scroll back through my brain for Frankie's words.

"There once was a pretty young model.
Who was often drawn to the bottle.
She'd drink and she'd drink,
Till…"

The crowd leans forward, willing me to go on. Sadly, all I can remember is something about four dollar cappuccinos. That doesn't fit. It doesn't even rhyme.

Here's my perfect chance to express myself, to grow as a person, to be a cool city girl, and all I can think about is overpriced coffee. A nasty, hot, liquid sensation creeps up my throat and floods my face.

"Go on, girlie," someone shouts from the crowd.

"Pull 'er off, Rooney. Give me a go."

The crowd has become hostile. To me!

I'm sorry I went looking for myself, because I found myself and I suck.

I didn't want to come up here. They made me. Only seconds ago they wanted me, but now?

When the leprechaun nudges me I reluctantly accept that the little man is not a leprechaun, he's Rooney McNamara, as in The Rooney McNamara special and Rooney McNamara owner of the pub. He cups the microphone with his pudgy hand. "Can you remember the rest, dear?"

I can't. I shake my head.

Standing dumbstruck before a horde of drunken Midwesterners on St. Patrick's Day is fairly degrading. I don't recommend it.

Humiliation sweeps over me as the old man gives me a push and sends me hobbling back through the crowd. The mob starts shouting again and the noise rings in my ears as I swim between the chairs. This sort of public shaming is much too familiar.

Maybe Nick was right about us being weepy and pathetic, because I don't feel so happy.

Riana rushes up with her arms out stretched. "Oh, honey," she coos, taking me and guiding me back to our booth where Nick is piling our coats into his arms.

With the pall of failure hanging around us, we head outside to the parking lot. Defeated and without the prize.

"I shouldn't have made you go up there, Hayley. I'm sorry," Nick says as he climbs behind the wheel of his midnight blue pickup.

I scoot in from the other side and wiggle to the middle where I always sit. Riana crawls in after me. Now that we've left the scene of the accident, I don't feel quite so horrible. Honestly, though, I still feel pretty crappy. Thank goodness Nick is there to steady things out.

"I really have to get a grip on my life," I mumble.

Nick glances at me after he pulls out onto Seven Mile Road but he doesn't say anything.

I rest my head on his shoulder, and Riana rests her head on mine. The lights of Woodward flash past as Nick drives south, toward Palmer Park. He's a good driver, Nick is. He's good at everything. Good, solid, Nick. Always there. Ever since he started coming into the bakery where I worked when I first got to the city.

Thinking about Nick makes me so happy I laugh. He was so cute with his coffee and notebooks and old school nerdy stuff.

He glances away from the road to me. "What?"

"Do you still do those calculator puzzles?"

He gives me a wry look. "Yes, I do. It's why I get the scholarships."

I stop giggling and look him over. He sees my scrutiny and turns his face back to the road but I can still feel his attention on me. And I remember the way it felt when he put his hand on my leg. I start wondering, when will he do it again?

Not if.

When.

That definitely gives me some things to think about. Starting with what I'll do when he does. We ride along without saying any more until he pulls up in front of Riana's apartment. She grabs my hand. "Come on in, I'll make us some nice tea."

"Coming?" I ask Nick.

He shrugs.

We all pile out of the truck and, because our invisible bar blankets have evaporated, retreat into our coats and hunch over like turtles. After Nick double-checks the lock on the toolbox in the bed of his pickup, we scuttle up the walk.

Palmer Park may have been a truly pleasant neighborhood once upon a time. Maybe during the fifties? The architecture of the pale brick buildings reminds me of those houses on Sesame Street. The ones where people sit out front talking and watching the world go by while neighbors lean out of windows and say hi.

Riana's apartment is exactly like that—wide windows and squat brick steps, only it isn't safe to sit out front and chit-chat with people who happen by. For one thing, there won't be anybody reasonable strolling along. For another, if somebody did poke their head out and start calling hello, somebody else would call the cops. Not that they'd come.

"Stop being so negative."

I grab the entrance door, yank it open, slant against it and frown at Nick. "I haven't said a thing."

"That look on your face. I can tell it's coming."

I lift my chin and reply in my best, most petulant, childlike voice, "I'll be negative if I want to."

He rolls his eyes and pushes me through the doorway.

"Teatime," Riana trills as she sways down the hall.

I should lighten up, it is a holiday after all. So what if I made a complete fool of myself in front of those drunken Irish wannabes. To show him how wrong he is, I throw Nick a smile then skip down the hall to Riana's door.

Only Riana is not digging for her keys or pushing her door open. She's hugging Josie—where did she come from?—and rubbing her back, murmuring, "It'll be okay, honey. You've been through it before and it's usually not quite as bad as you think it's going to be. Right?"

Josie sniffles and rubs her face. "I guess so."

"Oh, no. No way. I am not doing this." Nick is backing up and lifting his palms as though he's warding off a trio of vampires. "I knew it was coming to this. You girls go ahead with your...your...thing." He throws his hands in the air then flattens his fingers across his chest. "I'm going home."

Right before he turns the corner to disappear, he spins around and points at us. "No driving. None of you. Got it?"

Riana leans between Josie and me to yell, "We're going to have some nice tea."

"Fine but no driving. You all sleep here," he hollers from around the corner.

"Who made him the big boss?" I grumble.

"They're like that," Josie stammers. "Those kinds of people. They think they can boss everyone else around because they're so special." Unfortunately she's beginning to snarl. "Those special, important, fuckheads."

Oh dear.

Maybe I should have left with Nick. Angry Josie can be a bit scary. *Please, please don't let her and Riana start doing that puppet thing with their heads.* I've sobered up enough so that I'd notice it for sure.

Riana's cheery expression doesn't fool me. I know for a fact that she's frightened by angry Josie too. "In we go," she says, smiling and patting us both on the shoulder.

After she locks and bolts the door behind us, Riana toddles to the kitchen. Josie takes a long, shaky breath then slumps on the couch and stares with smudgy makeup eyes at the blinking lights of the Seven Wood Café across the street. I wonder what to say next.

'So Josie what's up?' Too wide open.

'Besides Nick, who's a special, important, fuckhead?' Too sarcastic.

Riana steps into the room, and I look at her beseechingly.

"It's her sister," she says then ducks back out.

Oh.

My shoulders drop back into place and my fingers uncurl. Josie's dysfunctional relationship with her sister. That I can deal with.

Because Riana's right. We've been through it before and even though it usually does turn out as bad as we think.

"What's she done now?"

"It isn't what she has done," Josie replies combing her bright red nails through her tangled hair. "It's what she's going to do."

Riana bustles into the room with a tray of cookies and the yet-to-be-filled tea cups. The matching cream and sugar set I gave her are tucked in the corner of the tray under a pile of cloth napkins. How can she go from chugging watered-down beer in some lame ass Irish pub to this in less than thirty minutes?

"She's going to write an article," Riana says to me as she sets the tray on the table in front of the couch.

Josie rubs away the last smears of mascara then grabs one of the cookies and snaps it in half. "On modern dating, you know, Detroit style."

Maybe if I ate one of those cookies I'd be able to think better. Clear my head. Chocolate chip even. Sure to bring out the best in anyone. Hopefully, that includes Josie.

I stuff one into my mouth.

Yummy. But it isn't working yet. "I don't get it. What's the big deal?"

"She started asking me all this stuff about how people hook up these days, like she has no idea — what does she live in, a convent? Anyway, I ended up telling her about my whole thing and now she wants to use it in her article." She pops half of a cookie into her mouth and proceeds to talk around it. "Somehow, it'll end up being her idea."

There's no point in denying that because there's a good chance it'll happen. Josie's sister is a human sponge. The selective kind. She only soaks up excellence. Anything that will either make her look better than those around her or will make her achieve some sort of unparalleled success.

Because I can't cheer Josie up by saying don't worry about it, I try to shift the topic onto a different track. "I'm surprised she even has friends. Who'd want to hang around somebody like that?"

Riana returns with the pot of tea. "Other sponges. They all stick together. You know, trading pointers on the best way to use people." She pours the tea, mumbling to herself, "That must work somehow."

I take a tiny ladylike sip, set my cup down then dump a big spoonful of sugar into it. "Vampires have friends, don't they?"

"Ever meet her friend Suzie?" Josie asks us over the rim of her teacup. "I can see that bitch sucking the life out of anyone who gets in her way."

"Speaking of things that aren't funny." Riana turns to me. "Did you ever remember the end of that limerick?"

I'd forgotten all about *that*.

Josie perks up. "Limerick?"

Riana fills her in on The Degrading Limerick Fiasco. Including the beginning of that daft poem and our hasty exit. I'm glad I didn't say anything about Rooney being a leprechaun, because now that the second-rate beer is wearing off, I realize it would've sounded really pathetic.

"So what is the end?" Josie asks.

For some reason, Riana really wants to know, too.

Suddenly, I need to know.

It's as if remembering the end of the poem will make everything okay for us. Riana will wake up and realize Peter is not worth her time, Josie's sister will vanish and my life will instantly have some sort of meaning.

Riana prompts me with, "She'd drink and she'd drink till…"

My brain remains stubbornly blank so she asks, "What rhymes with drink?"

"Sink!" *Why didn't I think of that?*
"She'd drink and she'd drink,
Till she puked in the sink,
Then off to next bar she'd tottle!"

Chapter Seven

Decode His Touch: Read His Mind

"Something big is brewing, Hayley."

It's three days later on Wednesday morning and Mr. Hastings is hanging out of his security booth at the complex's entrance, pointing at the clubhouse. "You know that Caroline." He peers up at the brim of his navy blue cap. "She's a pretty gal. Not real talkative, though."

Sure, I know that Caroline but I never thought of her as attractive. Maybe in a stiff hair sprayed, fake eye-lashed, full-figured Kim Kardashian kind of way. From a distance.

Not in any hurry to get behind my desk, I rest my arms on my car door and ask, "Why do you think something's going on?"

He leans forward as his eyes widen and his wiry, gray eyebrows disappear under the brim of his hat. "Mr. Neville is here."

Right away I understand what he means. Mr. Neville, The Big Boss as Bob likes to call him, never shows up at North Pointe before noon and usually it's after two.

Immediately, I imagine Caroline stuffing the framed pictures of her college friends along with her oversized Michigan State diploma into a box as she sniffles and cries about it being unfair.

I smile at Bob. "Do you think it's something really bad?"

"I hope not." He shakes his head. "I don't think so. No reason to think that really, it's just the impression I got."

That picture in my head morphs into Caroline toasting her success at North Pointe because she got a big fat raise.

Now that would be unfair.

"I guess I'll find out when I get there."

Mr. Hastings straightens and grins. He smacks the top of the half door by his stool. "I hope it's good news, Hayley, and I hope it has something to do with you."

Why can't all old guys be like Mr. Hastings? All cheerful and encouraging? "Thanks."

I step lightly on the gas pedal and coast up the tree-lined hill. There's a nice pool to the left and the whole place is surrounded by pines. There are hundreds of daffodils clumped around the shrubs and sidewalks. The clusters of yellow and white are actually very appealing. Working at North Pointe wouldn't be so bad. If only I actually understood what my job is supposed to be about. And there was no Caroline.

Did I mention that Mr. Neville is handsome? His first name can throw a person though. Oliver. What were his parents thinking? Do they ever call him Ollie? I snicker as I park my car and get out.

Ollie. *Ollie. Ollie.*

Mr. Neville doesn't sound so bad. A little smooth and European. He wears these great three-piece suits and is always tan and vital looking. Like some sexy, older guy who just stepped off his yacht and shrugged into his suit and tie.

Not my usual type but for variety I enjoy him. Why not? The only time I see him is at work and I am getting paid to be there. He's certainly a lot easier on the eyes than Caroline.

Caroline is a pretty sort?

I honestly hadn't noticed.

I tuck my getting-more-rumpled-each-day copy of *Sex and the Single Girl* into my glove box and grab my lunch from the back seat, then stroll between the yellow and white up to the pretty French doors of the clubhouse. I slip inside and, after I dig out the second half of a donut I didn't finish on the way to work, stash my lunch in the cozy kitchenette.

As soon as I cram said donut into one of my desk drawers next to a bag of what may be stale pretzels and between some clusters of wadded paper, Mr. Neville saunters up. Caroline is floating behind him like a half-filled helium balloon that's been tied to his back too long. By leaning to the right, I'm able to avoid looking at her so I can fill my view with his suited shoulders and aristocratic face.

"Hayley!" he says. "Did you know that as of this May, North Pointe Farms will be celebrating fifteen years of luxurious living?"

Instead of saying the first thing that pops into my mind — *No, I had no idea and why would I care?* I tip my head thoughtfully and say, "No, I didn't realize…" *And the buildings look so young* — probably not the response he's wanting. *The plants are still alive* — no that's not quite right either, is it? I go with a non-committal, "That's great!"

"It is great." He folds his arms across his chest and beams.

Caroline pats her glossy black hair. It doesn't budge. "Oliver and I were just talking about it. It's so great that our tenants love this place."

"Especially Mrs. Klonski," I spurt.

Caroline's fake smile stiffens but Mr. Neville's real one broadens. "She's been here longer than anyone, hasn't she?"

Loving this delicious moment, I add, "That's right. She's been here so long that she's the only one who's allowed to have a dog."

Mr. Neville runs his hand across his smooth jaw. "How old is that dog?"

"Good question." A low-watt bulb appears over Caroline's head. "I remember hearing somewhere that those little dogs can live a long time."

"Much longer than fifteen years?"

The disbelief in his voice makes me assume Mr. Neville and Caroline share a dislike of sweet, loveable creatures.

For a horrifying moment they have the exact same expression loitering on their faces. Sort of a Cruella de Vil meets Bill O'Reilly thing. Trust me, it is not a combination one should have to witness before lunch.

"You ready?" he says, turning to Caroline.

She snaps to attention with a flight attendant smile. "Sure am."

He nods at her, then at me. "You take care of things here, Hayley. I'll have Caroline back after lunch."

After lunch?

Caroline won't be back until after lunch?

Before I can say *don't hurry back*, they're out of the door and on their way to…?

Who cares! They're gone!

Hmmmmmm…should I eat that half of a donut now? I decide to enjoy a peaceful, Caroline-free cup of coffee instead.

After I check to be sure that they are really gone, I start the coffee and pull out my phone. Josie answers on the second ring. Between bursts of laughter, she manages to say, "Good morning from Fairlane Fabulous!"

"Can you talk?" I ask.

She keeps laughing for a minute, then finally speaks. "Until my nine-thirty shows up."

"Caroline's gone until after lunch." Because Josie keeps giggling, it's hard for me to stay excited about being alone in the empty clubhouse while she's there with a bunch of girls and they're all having the time of their life. Maybe she can clue me in so I can be laughing and having a grand time too. "What's so funny?"

She guffaws several more times then says, "You'll never believe this."

"Try me."

"This girl, Veronica, she works here as a shampoo girl, well, her boyfriend works at this pet shop on Woodward and —" She interrupts herself with her own laughter followed by, "Shut up, she won't tell anyone."

Friends are supposed to make you feel happy aren't they? This is not making me feel happy. This is making me feel left out and lonely. "Want me to call back later?"

Josie sucks in a long breath. "No, I'm together now.

"So. I told the girls here about the article my sister is doing and we started going through our dating horror stories, you know, the stuff you think you'll never want to tell anybody but eventually you figure you might as well tell someone and laugh about it so the whole thing can go away?"

Did she say that all at once?

"So. Anyway. Veronica went to get her boyfriend from work one night after he closed up. He's some kind of environmentalist weirdo, you know, really into animals and all that natural stuff. He asked her if she'd strip down so he could put a snake on her shoulders so they could do it like that—standing up right there in the shop with the snake crawling all over her. Like she was Courtney Love or something.

"She figured okay, if it gets him turned on, why not? They did it and—" Josie starts laughing again.

For some reason, I'm getting more annoyed by the second. I don't care about some naked girl with a snake.

Josie takes another deep breath then finishes, "The manager came back because he forgot his phone and when he got there they were running around the shop totally naked—except for their socks—trying to catch the snake. Because it had gotten loose. But because they had their socks on, they were sliding all over the place and falling down."

When I don't start laughing she fills in the silence. "Seriously," she says in a small voice, "it was way funnier when she told it."

Now I'm starting to feel like the lame cousin from out of town who always ruins the party because she hates to be around other people who are having fun living their lives. I manage a chuckle. "That is pretty funny, I guess. What happened next?"

"Oh, gotta go, my nine-thirty's here. I'll call you when I get a break, okay? Might be a while, we're pretty busy today."

"Okay, I'll be here." What else can I say? Thanks for ruining my good mood by laughing and being so cheerful? How bitchy is that?

By this time the coffee machine is sputtering and spitting the last couple of drops into the glass pot so I go pour myself a cup then shuffle back to my desk.

What to do?

Pick up my phone and stare at it?

Text Nick?

What would I say? *When are you going to put your hand on me again?*

I set my phone back down.

There's a stack of late rent payments on my desk that need to be sorted then left for Caroline to deposit. While that is actual work, it's pretty easy. The unpleasant part comes when I figure out who still hasn't paid their rent and have to print out those 'nice' reminders.

The other choice is returning calls from people who are apartment hunting and want to see some of our models. *Urgh. Talking to strangers on the phone. Yuck.* That'll have to wait until after coffee.

I grab the stack of payments as Tony Cattalioni struts in.

For an unfortunate minute his head jerks over his shoulders making him look like a rooster checking out the hen yard. "Where's Caroline? She around?"

"She went somewhere with Oliver." Of course I'd never call Mr. Neville that to his face but with Tony it's fun to pretend Ollie and I are chums.

"When is she coming back?"

I scoot forward and eye him slyly. "Why do you want to know?"

He glances past my shoulder into Caroline's empty office. "I need to get on the net for a couple minutes."

I lift one eyebrow.

"To check my mail."

Why can't he use his phone like a normal person?

I'd ask, but I'm bored with the whole giving Tony a hard time thing so I fess up. "She won't be back until after lunch. Go ahead." I jerk my thumb toward her computer. "I'll cover for you if she resurfaces unexpectedly."

When he smiles pleasantly, I reconsider my treatment of North Pointe's maintenance man. Even in his brown shirt and pants he's put together better than most other guys. He strolls past with long, quick strides, and a woodsy scent drifts under my nose.

"Hey, Tony," I hear myself say. "Do you think Caroline is pretty?"

"Caroline?" he chokes out. His mouth twitches and he seems a bit panicky. Like he can't unscramble the letters on *Wheel of Fortune*. "Why are you asking me?"

I lean back in my chair and shrug innocently. "You're a guy. You'd know."

The angst falls from his face onto his feet, which start wiggling.

"She's okay, I guess." Looking almost as if he's going to cry, he shifts to the side, moving two steps closer to Caroline's sanctuary. "I really gotta get on the net."

"Yeah. Right." Embarrassment and shame skim over my arms. How was I supposed to know he was so sensitive? I make a promise to myself not to give him such a hard time any more. "No problem."

A yucky silence floats into the clubhouse and threatens to squash us. Luckily the phone rings. I pick up the handset and thank the person on the other end for calling North Pointe Farms, where living is luxurious, as Tony dashes off to check that email.

"Hayley?"

My own mother has to double-check it's me?

"Hi, Mom."

"Are you too busy to talk?"

What do you know, I'm actually glad my mother has called, so I tell her I can talk.

"What time will you be coming on Saturday?"

My mental calendar refuses to come into focus. "Saturday?" I parrot back at her.

"Next Saturday. For the April Fool's Dance."

Oh. That.

The annual April Fool's Dance at the VFW hall. The one where the farmers get dressed up by donning boots that don't have cow shit coated to the bottom. Four hours of over-cooked chicken, soggy green beans and lively conversation about 4-H projects.

Last time I went, I was a totally different person.

"I don't know, Mom. Maybe it's better if I don't come."

There is a long pause then a sigh. "It's been months, honey. It'll be fine. He won't be there."

Realizing that there is no way out without having a serious conversation about *it*, and that at least there will be free beer, I ask, "What time is good for you and Dad?"

"The dance starts at seven. If you come early you can help your dad with the birds. He'd like that."

My dad is a machinist, not a farmer like everyone around us, but he's always had this thing about 'taking advantage of the fact that we live in the country' and 'being part of the country culture'. What do those beliefs have to do with me? A lot. For one thing, we raised chickens and ducks and turkeys and any other bird my dad could order from that little catalog that showed up in the rusty mailbox at the end of our gravel driveway. That thrill of peeling off the top of the cardboard box that the birds were shipped in to find out 'how many made it' can't be duplicated.

For another, in the end, all living in the country got me was a reason to leave it. But nobody wants to talk about that inconvenient truth. Certainly not my mom.

"And we'll see you around five?" she says, all cherry-like, oblivious as usual to my lingering pain.

A sinking in my stomach tells me I missed some vital bit of conversation. Instead of asking her to playback her words, I agree to the time.

"Your cousin Frankie had an exciting weekend. Did you hear about it?"

Is his news trending on Facebook? Complete with a color picture? Was it on the front page of Reddit? If it was so great, why didn't he call me?

"You obviously didn't hear."

Thrilled to be the one to pass on the latest news, my mom gushes, "He won a contest."

"Really?"

"First place."

"No kidding."

"You'll never guess what kind of contest it was."

What a smart lady my mom is. I was trying to do that very thing.

"It was a St. Paddy's Day limerick contest sponsored by the restaurant."

My mouth drops open. After I snap my choppers shut, I stammer, "You're kidding?"

"No dear. I'm not kidding." Her voice is dead serious. "You know what a funny boy he is."

Did I know that? "What did he get?"

"Fifty dollars!"

"Fifty dollars!" He won actual money? Not a cornbeefan cabbish dinner?

"Let me see if I can remember the poem."

I imagine my mother curling her mouth to the side and tapping her chin.

"There once was a pretty young model..."

Naturally she finishes up the whole thing, remembering each line accurately and delivering it perfectly. As must have been the case with young Frankie, her delivery isn't hindered by thin, green beer or erroneous visions of leprechauns.

Stinking kids and their stinking limericks.

"Yeah, that is a good one," I mumble when she gets to the end. "I'll have to call Frankie and tell him good job."

"You do that. Your Aunt Sandy tells me he has some others, but, well, she threatened to take his DS away if he told one of the really bad ones for the contest. Some of those limericks can be, well..." Her chattering fades for a few seconds then she breaks the silence buzzing between us with, "So, we'll see you on Saturday?"

I can't hold it all in. "Um, hey, Mom...?"

She hums into the phone, very mom-like.

"It's not going to be, I don't want..."

Again the pause, puff of breath then reply, "No one is going to say anything about...about...*it.*"

The way she puts emphasis on that single two-letter word tells me what I need to know. They—that means the whole country side of town—aren't over what happened last spring. That day I 'ruined everything for everyone'.

As we say our goodbyes, Tony slips out of Caroline's office and I wave him off as he goes out of the side door.

Chapter Eight

Fail-Proof Ways to Loosen His Lips and Get Him Talking

Later that same day, I'm getting ready for the much-anticipated night with Clifford the Big Red Dog, and Nick is angled on my couch, pulling handfuls of pork rinds out of the crackling bag balanced on his chest. He's watching ESPN. Him lying around on my couch for no reason is usually no big deal. But today he is…weird. He keeps looking at me like he's going to say something but then decides not to. Finally a question tumbles out, "What do you know about this guy anyway?"

I'm not about to admit the truth, that I know close to nothing, so I hedge with, "He's from Josie's dating thing."

"Does she do a background check on these guys?"

Here I can state the facts so I tip my head out to yell back at him, "She calls references, asks for their current place of employment and photocopies their driver's license."

I hear the crumble of the empty bag as he wads it up. "You didn't ask her that. Riana did," he calls, brandishing his bottled water.

"So what?" I wave my brow pencil at him. "I know he's safe."

"What else do you know?"

I duck back in to finish my eyes. "He plays football at Wayne. On scholarship."

A sputtering choking sound is followed by silence. When Nick speaks again, his voice sounds too tight. "What position?"

Typical guy question. Who cares? They all wear those pads, don't they? They all have helmets and run around smashing into each other.

I sigh when Nick asks again. "I don't know."

Did I hear him mutter 'of course not'? Or was he simply mumbling to himself?

I think about trying to provoke him by asking, *Is there a reason you want to know all this stuff?* But instead, I say, "I'll be sure to ask him."

"You do that."

Sarcasm?

I can do better than provoking him with a question. I dash across the hall and grab my black dress. Laying it across myself so Nick will be able to imagine what it'll look like, I ask, "This? Or jeans and a T-shirt?"

He eyes me skeptically, barely even looking at the dress. "Which T-shirt?"

"Power Puff Girls? Or that Abercrombie one you like."

A grimace settles over his mouth and his eyebrows drop. "Don't wear that one. And don't you think everyone stopped caring about the Power Puff Girls?"

In a huff, I spin on my heels and stomp back to my closet. "Fine, I'll wear the dress," I holler as I slip it off the hanger.

"Whatever."

Even more annoyed that he's going to sit there stewing on something but not do anything about it, I accidently forget I'm wearing only my panties and bra and march out and set my hands on my hips. "Thank you so much for coming over and helping me get ready."

His face gets a weird pained look as his gaze skims over me. He clicks off the TV, scrambles to his feet, not saying anything. Especially not, *'Sorry for being a rude shithead who put his hand on your leg and got you thinking things but did nothing about stopping you from going out with another guy'*. Then he steps toward me and for a crazy second I think he's going to grab me and kiss me but then that insanity passes. Funny thing, though, the second it passes I want it back. Without saying anything more, he spins around and stalks to the door, his wide shoulders shifting as he moves quickly. I shout to his blue and red flannelled back as he swings open the door, "Be sure to call me next time you're getting ready to go on a date. I'll come over and eat nasty food and act like an asshole."

He looks back and casts me a weak smile, one that almost makes me forgive him, and says, "Don't ask him what position he plays. Have fun."

The door closes with a solid click.

Back in my room, I wiggle into the black dress then slide into my knee-high boots.

I have no idea where The Dog plans on taking me but that'll be no problem. No thanks to Nick, I've made the right choice. I've got Basic Black. I can go anywhere and the tight-but-not-too-tight cling, well, it lets him know I mean business.

At six o'clock I drop onto the couch in the very spot Nick vacated. I take a deep breath and catch a whiff of his scent. Crabby thing that he was. I won't think about him. Must think about something else.

Urgh.

Although I have managed to avoid them for the past twelve hours, the jitters finally track me down and move in.

Guys don't have to go through all this.

Why did I agree to this? Nick is right. I know nothing about this guy except that he's good looking in a big-shouldered, lumbering kind of way. He might be a dull simpleton with no redeeming characteristics.

Except for those hands. I watched that disc enough times that I remember each wide, sturdy curve.

A shocking thought ripples across my brain.

He's arranged to go out with me without even knowing what I look like.

I check my phone. Four minutes.

I wonder if the guy pays before the date or after. What if he refuses to pay? How embarrassing.

Two flights down, the door slams shut. Heavy feet clamor up the steps. There's a pause.

Please don't let him—or any of his disgusting smells—be out in the hall.

The pounding resumes, and I hop to my feet. One last glance in the mirror. Bright eyes, subtle lips. Hair in place but not stiff. Good to go.

After he knocks, I wait a reasonable space of time then swing open the door.

Concentrating on not searching for those hands, I smile at his face and say, unoriginally I might add, "Hi."

Picking up on my conventional greeting style, he replies, "Hi." His green gaze skims over my dress and for some unfathomable reason, he actually frowns. "Are you ready?" he asks, after his eyes focus on mine.

Don't I look ready?

"Yeah," I stammer and wobble a bit. Should I ask what the problem is? He hates dresses? He thinks I'm a witch? "I have to grab my purse."

He nods so I turn away to snatch up my smaller, going-out-with-a-guy purse. Scotty—Hairdresser to the Stars—and I agreed that men are afraid of women who carry huge over-stuffed purses so I always stick to the 'smaller is better' approach.

The Dog and I shuffle around each other in the hall. I giggle stupidly, lock the door then start working my way down the steps in my high-heeled boots. It isn't easy and I'm already rethinking my footwear choice.

Also, me being in front of him is not at all right.

I twist sideways and force him to look at my face by saying, "Did you have any trouble finding this place?"

"Um. No." Then, perhaps because he realizes I can see him staring straight at my butt, his nicely squared chin jerks up. For no apparent reason a bright smile flashes across his face. By this time, we've reached the bottom of the steps so I take the opportunity to sweep the door open and hold it for him. He lumbers past and I get a whiff of his aftershave. Very clean. And manly.

Pretty good stuff actually.

His shoulders are robustly wide and much more substantial than any other guy I've ever been out with. Even the muscles of his back bend and flex as he walks.

My heart starts to pound with weird nervous energy.

Have I been overlooking an entire section of the male population? The big, muscular athletes? Honestly, I'd never even considered them before but I don't like basketball and never watched football, except with my dad. I don't have to care about the sport to like the man who comes off the field. And right now, I'm liking this particular man very much. His body, anyway.

Sure, there is more to a man than arms and legs, but I'm not thinking about living the rest of my life with this guy. I only want a night out. A chance to step out of that fog that has followed me from the country, live some, forget some.

What does he want?

"Pizza in Greektown okay with you, Hayley?"

Of course. He wants food. How could he not? He must need at least three thousand calories a day just to carry himself around.

He yanks open the passenger door of his red, four-door car, so I climb in. Once he's behind the wheel, I reply with what I hope is a cute smile that says — 'you like me already'. "Pizza is fine."

"Some girls don't like pizza. All that wheat and carbs."

Since when is wheat bad?

The car rumbles away from the battered curb and we weave through the potholed side streets of Detroit. Greektown is a weird slice of the city about seven blocks from the Detroit River and Hart Plaza. Hart Plaza is a cement park that runs alongside the murky river. All summer there are dozens of free concerts there.

Imagine the world's largest free outdoor country music festival right smack in the middle of Motown. Thousands of boot-wearing, hat-toting displaced hilljacks gargling Coors. The ferocity of their fun is fueled by their fat, factory paychecks from Ford.

Frightening? Yes. That's why it was moved and they started charging to get in. But not everything unsettling gets moved. How about the world's largest techno music festival? Hundreds of geeky German guys—yes, with real accents and bristly mustaches, and direct from Metro Airport—trying to pick up rich high-school girls from West Bloomfield. There's something really unsettling about pink-haired girls from the suburbs wearing those frayed, elephant leg pants and sucking on pacifiers. Those poor Germans. At least the candy necklaces are cheap.

Back to Greentown.

It's one street lined with Greek restaurants and bakeries. It looks pretty much the same as it has for years, except there's a casino there now. Courtesy of Dennis Archer, Former Mayor Extraordinaire.

I don't think the muscle men that guard the polished chrome and glass doors of the casino are Greek or even care about being Greek. They're there to look threatening and make the people who feed the slot machines feel either—one, safe or, two, daring and fearless for venturing to the wild and dangerous streets of downtown Detroit.

I glance over at Clifford and admire the great way his cheekbones are sculpted. Because he doesn't appear to notice me staring at him, I let my gaze linger.

Hmmmmm. Nice.

The last guy I went out with, Timothy, was small and brittle looking. Artistic. Sensitive and thoughtful.

The kind of guy who can watch endless episodes of Portlandia without laughing.

This wedge of beef doesn't have a delicate inch on him. And there are a lot of inches. Hard, thick, unyielding inches.

"You play football, right?"

His square chin bobs up and down as he scans the street for a place to park. "Ever since sixth grade."

"You like it a lot?"

"Uh-huh."

Nick never did say why I wasn't supposed to ask The Dog what position he played. "What position are you?"

"This year?"

Hoping to encourage him to put together more than four words, I nod and work to make my face as non-threatening as possible.

"This year I'm tight-end. It's a good position for me."

That doesn't tell me much since I know nothing about football. Luckily, by this time we're walking down the street and the need for conversation is diminished. After we stroll along the sidewalk for about two blocks, Clifford taps my shoulder and jerks his head toward one of the restaurant doors. "Okay?"

Because I haven't thought of anything dazzling to say to liven him up and get him talking, I nod.

Inside, three Greek men linger by the register. The oldest is stretched across the counter, the other two are standing side-by-side with their arms folded. The youngest is clutching a handful of plastic-coated menus.

The one holding the menus leads us to a table. As I slip into a chair, I spot Clifford staring at me. His face is pinched.

"Could you stand up a minute?"

After I rise, he places those big hands on the edges of the table and while he's still sitting down, lifts it straight up off the floor and sets it about a foot away from himself. Then he scoots his chair away from the wall and settles himself as well as he can.

Well! I've never been out with a guy who was too big to fit into a typical restaurant space.

"Does that happen often?" I ask, feeling very waiflike as I slide daintily into my chair.

"I guess so. After a while you get used to it."

When my face pales, he actually seems to notice. "Um, guys get used to it, I mean. Not you." He looks me over and leaves a trail of heat in the wake of his gaze. "You look great."

Chapter Nine

Good Girls Go for It Too

After dinner, we climb back into his car, he starts the engine up and off we go.

As his car hums along the street, I realize I don't know where we're going. Since we're heading north, away from my apartment, he isn't taking me home.

He's taking me to his place?

Sure, I could ask. But I don't.

By this time, I've figured out that the way to enjoy this big red dog is to sit back and admire the view. He made it plain that he likes what he sees when he looks at me, so hey, I'm just letting him know I feel the same.

He pulls into the huge parking lot of the Eight Mile Roller Rink. The neon sign blinks at me, mocking me and my dress.

"You like to skate?" he asks, parking his car.

Is he serious?

If he were a witty type, I'd assume he was joking and I'd laugh.

"It's what I had planned. Wednesday's the best night."

Has he not seen what I'm wearing?

"I guess. If that's what you want to do."

"It's what I had planned."

Stunned, I nod.

He stuffs his keys into his pocket and lunges out of the car. He opens the passenger door and offers his hand. I lift my own and position it neutrally. First, he clasps my fingertips while I swing my booted legs out of the car then he lifts our hands as I climb out of the seat. After he reaches around me to shut the door, he pulls my fingers into his palm. The light friction of his palm gliding across mine feels damn good.

Because our conversation so far has consisted of a series of my questions and his four word answers, I don't know what we have in common, but that doesn't stop me from wondering how he'd look without his shirt on. The heat from his hand is seeping through me so I move closer and smile up at him. "Do you go skating often?"

"Used to, when I was little. My dad brought us here all the time."

"You have brothers or sisters?"

A silly grin slants across his mouth. "Four brothers. I'm the baby."

"Five boys? No girls? Your poor mother."

He laughs and pulls open the door. "Yeah. She kept threatening to throw away the furniture and make us all sit on wooden crates. I guess we were pretty hard on things like chairs. And doors. And walls."

This is the most I've got out of him all night. So I ask him a couple more questions. By the time we have our skates, I've learned all the basic stuff.

Childhood dog named Axel. Two brothers married, one with kids. Two brothers single. After Clifford left for college, his parents moved to a house on Lake Michigan where they're spending their retired days fixing up an old sailboat.

"Need help with you skates?"

Clifford already has his skates on. Me? I'm on the carpet-covered bench, bent over and twisted sideways as I struggle to get the skates on without exposing my black lace VS panties. It's okay if Clifford gets a look but that forty-something dude wrestling with the wild toddler, he has to go home to his wife.

Without waiting for an answer to his inquiry, The Dog drops to his knees and takes my left foot in his hand. The sight of my instep curving into the palm of his huge mitt makes my mouth go dry. Even though there is no hint of seduction in his action, quivering lust warms me from toe to head.

By the time he grabs the right foot, my heart is pumping soundly and a giddy nervous laugh is threatening to tumble out. That will never do so I hold my lips together and stare at the short strands of his strawberry blond hair. Unfortunately, he chooses that exact second to look up. He finds me staring at him with my face pulled together like I've just downed a shot of tequila.

His gaze stays on my face long enough for me to smile. He hops to his feet. "Okay?" he asks, over the loud music and squeals of preteen girls.

I still can't believe I'm about to skate in a dress but I'll try anything once. Off we go.

It isn't as bad as I thought. We're moving along pretty well. In the corner, near the yellow lockers, a DJ is waving his arms and gyrating. Gorillaz *Feel Good Inc.* comes on, and all of a sudden I'm glad to be rolling around, dodging scruffy seven-year-olds. Clifford's hold on my hand is just right and I figure, hey, why not skate in a dress?

Clifford? He's a great skater. I can see why he wanted to come. The heads of single girls, and even a few with guys, tip his way and I glimpse their amazement that a big guy can be so graceful. It's working on them and it's working on me. I'm not thinking about Nick. Not one little bit.

We circle around about a dozen or so times and I'm enjoying the music and the hum of my wheels gliding over the polished wooden floors. Every few strides, Clifford's leg bumps into my hip and I'm liking that too.

About ten feet in front of us, a couple glides along with their hands stuffed in each other's back pockets. Seven feet to our left, there's a couple crisscrossing past each other as they whiz along.

Clifford and I must look pretty dull.

About the time a tiny, black-haired girl flies past, I'm starting to feel the need to fancy up my style. I watch her for a few minutes, then as we bend into the next corner, I place my right leg in front of my left, the way she does. Only when she does it, she zips around the corner.

Me?

Smack.

That's right, I fall flat on my face. Actually on my hands and knees with Clifford standing behind me.

His eyes spark with sexual interest. "I guess it's hard to skate in that dress," he says without breaking his gaze from my ass.

This is what I had to do?

My guy is rooted to the floor so tightly, it's almost funny. Except I don't laugh because the way his green eyes are getting darker by the second is making my throat tighten and my mind start thinking about his bare chest again. For a split second it looks like Clifford's going to drop down beside me but instead he rolls close enough to offer me his hand.

"Guess it's time to go."

I nod as I take his hand and curl my fingers around the solid muscles of his palm. After I stagger to my feet, he wraps his arm around my waist and pulls me against him. We mesh together like two pieces of the same fence.

Within minutes we're in his car and heading back downtown. He pulls to a stop at the curb in front of my apartment, turns off the engine then looks over at me. I lean forward to let him know a kiss isn't out of the question. He takes me up on the offer.

The kiss starts out slowly but by this time I've realized this big hunk of a guy makes me hot. There isn't a whole lot of emotional connection but he has an amazing body and let's face it, it's been a while for me. And, I know this might be lame, but I want to be sure I still have what it takes.

Clifford responds by putting his giant hand on my thigh. *Oh. That again.* Only this time there is no awkward question of friendship. The solid weight on my leg moves me from wanting this kiss to wanting a hell of a lot more.

He lifts his mouth and sits back. "Want me to come in?"

I nod.

He looks at me, considering. "I thought you and Josie were friends."

"We are," I say, trying to figure out what that has to do with this.

"She said I was supposed to take it easy with you because you're a nice girl."

I suppose that was kind of her to say but nice isn't what I'm after right now. I point to the alley behind my apartment building. "If you park back there you won't get a ticket as long as you move it by six."

Clifford smiles as he starts up the car then parks it right where I pointed.

And we get out.

Once we're in my apartment I ask him if he wants some wine.

"No thanks."

Because I can't think of anything else to do, I make a big deal out of setting my purse across the magazines scattered over the table. There is a half-full coffee cup and Nick's empty pork rind bag so I pick them up and take them out to the kitchen.

I switch off the overheard kitchen light and the room turns nearly black, except for the slice of yellow haze gliding in from the street lamps at the corner. As I cross to the couch, my eyes adjust and I can see well enough to know I won't miss anything. Careful not to position myself too far to the center or too close to the arm of the couch, I sit and cross my legs. After wiggling a bit, I get the hem of my skirt halfway up my thighs.

Clifford drops his big self down next to me.

After he stretches his arm behind my back and grabs my shoulder, he kisses me thoroughly. It's as though somewhere along the line he read that a guy shouldn't have sex with a girl without kissing her first because he does an incredibly complete job of arousing and relaxing me with just his mouth. There isn't a lot of romance in the kiss, he isn't holding my face or pausing to look into my eyes, but there is a lot of physical attraction.

About the time I'm nearly panting, he lifts his mouth from mine and runs his wet lips down my neck. The trail of his breath makes me aware of the slick wetness of my pussy. He scraps his teeth lightly over my skin and I shiver so hard my clit stiffens and, trying to get some needed friction, I rub my thighs together.

The rock-solid muscles beneath his shirt contract as he moves his free arm to slide his hand under my dress into my thong then cups me between my legs. I pull in a sharp breath when he flips his hand over and his knuckle brushes against my clit. Gradually he starts moving his mouth back up my neck. By the time his mouth finally connects with mine again, I've got my hands on his shoulders. The rough texture of his wide palm rasps across my thigh, and the sheer size of his fingers makes me feel petite and fragile. And so ready to fuck him. My sigh sounds more like a moan.

No wonder I have a thing for hands.

Really.

Now he's seriously kissing me and I'm returning his enthusiasm with plenty of my own. Each caress of his lips and sweep of his tongue makes me hotter and I can feel the pulse of my own blood as it zips through my veins. The kissing, the touching, it's awesome. But I'm not getting enough from his hand. I want more skin-on-skin contact. But when he starts to push me back against the couch and tug at my panties with his amazing hands, I stiffen and press my palms across his chest.

We are not going any further with his shirt on.

After I jerk the shirttails from his pants, I work down the buttons. As I reach the last one, he gets the picture and pulls at his sleeves then whips the shirt to the floor.

My hands connect with the smooth warm cotton of his undershirt. The swell of his chest. The solid, tight curves of his stomach.

Mmmmmmmmmm. If heaven is only about physical satisfaction, I'm there.

Again he tries to push me back but I'm determined to get what I want so I tug at the hem of his undershirt.

Apparently he's used to girls giving him signals to undress, because in the blink of an eye he reaches back, grabs the back of his shirt and slips it over his head.

Shit.

My wide-eyed stare catches his eye and he grins as he straightens and takes a deep breath that makes his chest swell. "Coach works us pretty hard."

For the first time that night, I'm the one with nothing to say.

All that rock-hard, heated muscle sitting right there on my couch. Waiting for me.

He kisses me again, this time without asking, and slides his hand back under my dress. Farther up this time, until his hand is curved around my ass. Not one to waste an opportunity, I gradually glide my hands across his thick back. Each time he moves his arms, the giant muscles shift under my fingers making me even dizzier with lust.

He tangles his fingers in the thin waistband of my black thong and I lift my hips. He mumbles something that is probably a comment of approval, because he works the scrap of lace down far enough to touch my clit. His pressure is light at first, but when I begin moving against his fingers he gradually applies more pressure.

This guy has experience making girls feel good.

Damn good.

While he works his magic, I fumble with the buckle of his belt. After two unsuccessful attempts, I get it undone then start on his fly. The task is hard to accomplish with waves of heated pleasure buzzing through me but I'm more determined than ever to see all of him so I keep at it.

The weak light from the street is enough for me to make out the striped pattern of his boxer briefs. Because of his erection, the fabric is pointed up like a tent. If I weren't so hot to get him naked, I would've taken a minute to laugh.

But I don't have a minute to waste so I tug at his pants and briefs. I'm all over him and the couch, bent around in a bunch of different positions as he shifts forward to push his clothes down and out of the way. Then his cock is standing there and it's huge and hard, just like the rest of him.

He's still caressing me with his thumb and I don't want him to stop. I figure the best way to keep him doing what he's doing is to make him feel good too so I bob down and put the tip of his shaft between my lips. The salty skin is tight and smooth, and I take my time licking every inch to get him good and wet before covering him completely with my mouth. I do my best to get one of my hands on his bare ass, squeezing and stroking all the solid muscles I can find.

After I've been at it long enough to taste the first drops of cum, he groans and thrusts forward, clenching his ass cheeks and shoving his big cock deeper into my mouth. A surge of sexual power rolls over me and I seize it, sucking on the long, firm shaft of his dick with new appreciation for my own skills.

He grunts and before I know what's happening, he grabs me and flips me upside down so my mouth has easier access to his dick and his mouth is between my legs. He spreads my legs and starts licking my clit with long, smooth motions while caressing the cheeks of my ass with those giant mitts. It's glorious and wild, so weirdly sexual I don't know what to do. I stiffen for a few seconds then catch a glimpse of his hard cock, glistening from my careful attention and cover it with my mouth. For a crazy second I think about how amazing I must look, with that incredible hunk of a man holding my ass and going after my pussy like that.

He moves his tongue across my stiff clit, over and over with featherlight licks that make me wiggle my hips to get the pressure I need. He holds my ass steady, as though he's determined to keep me in position long enough to finish sucking him off. I am happy to oblige. Even though my release is so fierce that I begin to tremble, I still manage to keep gliding my mouth up and down his dick until I swallow every last salty drop of his cum. While we thrash about on the couch until the very last of the explosions, he holds onto me so tightly that I don't fall onto the floor.

In the back of my mind I thank him for that.

And, well, the other.

* * * *

Forty-five minutes later, after my teeth are brushed and my phone is plugged in for the night, I slide into bed. I can't complain, I tell myself. I'd gotten what I was after.

So why do I feel so out of sorts? Like that wasn't what I'd wanted?

I smack my pillow, turn onto my side, then stare at my phone.

It would be kind of weird for me to send a text to Nick, telling him how the night went. No way would I offer all the details, but…

Nah. I won't text him. If Nick wanted to know how it went, he'd ask. He can, after all, text me.

Right?

I close my eyes, force my mind away from Clifford and that scene on the couch, but the images keep tumbling back to me. Finally I give up and let myself scrutinize each and every second until my mind gives in to the day and a welcome wave of sleepiness takes me over.

I'm standing at a door when it swings open. There's Clifford, wearing nothing but a bathrobe. I step forward and he takes my hand, pulls me in, shuts the door, then says, "Hey." Without another word, he shrugs out of the robe. He looks like some freakishly amazing garden statue. He is beautiful and powerfully elegant, except his dick is hard and sticking straight out. I'm pretty sure they don't design naked man statues like that — with erections, I mean.

After letting me take a good, long look, he leads me to a couch and pulls me onto his lap so I'm straddling his legs. My dress slides up my thighs, exposing my thong. I'm clutching his bare shoulders and trying to stay on his lap while he gently pulls my dress up higher and higher. I lift my arms so he can yank it off. He runs his fingertip down between my breasts, over the clasp of my bra, then continues until he reaches the waistband of my panties. He pinches the lace in his fingers and tugs up, forcing the lace between my pussy lips so it rubs against my clit. I wiggle my hips side to side and a zing of electricity zips up my spine.

He smiles, lets go, and now, he's moving his mouth to my shoulder, making a row of kisses as he pulls my bra strap down. Using the same sweet row-of-kisses technique, he moves to the other shoulder, and I feel my bra come loose. He uses his giant hands to undo the clasp. After I slide it off my arms then toss it over by my shirt, he cups one breast and begins sucking. He's taking his time, exploring the tight peak of my nipple with his mouth and feeling the fullness with his palms. It's then that I realize something about him has changed. He's so tender and attentive.

Maybe he doesn't understand I'm pretty much using him for sex. He's acting like this moment means something.

I put my hands on either side of his face and guide his head back so I can look into his eyes and maybe say something – even though I don't know what.

But when I push his head back I see that it isn't Clifford. It's Nick. And he's looking at me with a sexy sincerity that I've seen on his face before but right then his brown eyes are also dark with lust.

"Hayley."

I wait for him to say more, but instead of talking, he cups my other breast and begins licking the nipple. The flick of his tongue is so amazing that I arch my back, trying to shove more of my breast into his mouth. Each movement of his tongue make me hotter and wetter. He keeps at it until my pulse is fluttering. I'm panting when he lifts his mouth.

"I want – "

He doesn't have to finish. I know what he wants and I want the same thing.

Keeping my torso steady, I lean back and try to get my panties off. I wiggle them down as far as I can before having to break contact. I stand up and start sliding them down over my legs. I notice how carefully Nick is watching me, so I slow down and give him something worth watching. Inch by inch I bend down then I pivot to show off my ass. When I turn my back to him, he grabs me and puts me directly in front of him. Then, still holding onto me, he bends forward and places his mouth on mine. He runs his open mouth across my skin then licks and kisses my stomach. His hands are warm and his wet mouth is hot. That sweet tenderness is back, his attention so sweet its almost reverent. I've never been touched this way before, I realize. Then I realize I never want this to stop.

I run my fingers through his ruffled hair. He murmurs something I feel more than hear then he lowers his mouth to my pussy lips. When he slides the tip of his tongue across my clit I roll my hips forward and sigh. He licks me for what feels like forever but it's not enough. I'm aching for more.

He leans back and grabs my butt cheeks. "My Hayley has the sweetest pussy and the best ass."

I want to tell him how much he means to me but that heat coursing through my veins seems to have burned away my ability to speak. So instead of replying, I wiggle thanks with my hips then climb back onto his lap, putting one knee on each side of his thighs.

The skin-on-skin contact is glorious. I wrap my arms around his shoulders and press myself against him while he grabs my ass and caresses my cheeks. He nudges me back with his head and starts sucking on my nipple again. The tingles of electricity come back, fast and fierce and I'm more aware of his cock, pressing against my clit. I rock against him, taking advantage of the hard ridge of his dick.

My body is so prepped, my clit already stiff, that I pump up and down, hard and fast, shoving my breasts in his face as a turbulent orgasm takes control of me. For a few seconds my body is at the mercy of Nick's dick as the waves of pleasure tear through me.

Chapter Ten

Sex and Careers: Oh Yeah

"So how was it?" Josie wants to know first thing the next morning.

I have to remind myself that she's not asking about my too-naughty-for-words-sex-with-a-friend dream. "Hmmmm. It was good, I guess."

"Good. That's it? That's all I get?"

I force the very vivid dream from my mind and mentally flip through my evening with Clifford. "It wasn't what I expected."

Josie slides her coffee cup across Pastry Pete's chipped white counter. She pins me down with a steely blue-eyed stare. "You have to tell me more than that."

I glance at my watch and wonder why I agreed to meet Josie before work. Is she anxious because I'm her first match? Or because I'm her friend?

Either way, I'm not so keen on rehashing the whole went-roller-skating-in-a-dress and did-hot-but-weird-sex evening.

"Give me the play by play. What did you do first?"

"We went to Greektown for pizza."

With an exaggerated flip of her hand, she encourages me to continue. "And. How did that go?"

"Well..." I pick at the pastel sprinkles dotting the top of my chocolate frosted donut. "He ate a lot."

"Of course he ate a lot. Who cares? What did you do after you ate? Walk down Monroe and get a coffee? One of those boring pastries?"

I straighten defensively. "I like those tasteless Greek pastries."

She flicks her wrist again, only this time not so patiently. "Whatever."

I take a bite of my donut as a stalling tactic. After chewing as slowly as possible, I swallow and take a sip of coffee.

She's still staring at me. Where is Riana when I need her?

I sigh and wave the invisible, white flag of defeat. "We went roller-skating."

"I thought you wore that black dress?"

"I did."

Her eyebrows drop and her mouth rounds into an 'o'.

"Exactly."

An annoying chuckle ripples out of her.

"It's not funny," I mutter, staring at my frosting smeared plate.

"You roller-skating in that black dress is not funny?"

I set down what's left of my donut and cross my arms. "No. It's not." I cling to my defensiveness, because I know that it is funny. Only I'm not ready to laugh yet.

I sigh and roll my eyes. Maybe it is the only way.

She makes a face to let me know that she's done laughing at me. "Then what?"

"You mean after the skating debacle?"

"Oh, so now it's 'The Skating Debacle'? You can make a joke out of it but I can't?"

I lift my eyebrows and stare importantly down my nose at her. "Yes."

"Just tell me this. If he calls, are you going to go out with him again?"

I scramble for a reasonable answer that won't prompt more conversation. "We don't have much in common."

"Oh." She practically hops out of her seat. "That reminds me. My sister wants to interview you."

My mouth goes sour, completely ruining the aftertaste of my donut. "Interview me? What for?"

"To see how your night went."

"For her singles in Detroit article? You want me to help her with that? I don't think so."

She blows out a puff of air. "It might be fun."

"Yeah, right," I mutter as we get up to pay.

It's always the same with Josie and her sister. Eventually the article will be something they're doing together, then the reality that her sister is a selfish bitch will rear its ugly head once again.

Then Josie will be mad. Again. She'll cry. Again. Riana and I will draw faces on our chins and hang our heads off the bed so our mouths are upside down. We'll make the little faces say stupid stuff until Josie laughs. Then we'll eat too many Oreos and talk about how Josie will never ever help her sister with anything ever again.

Someday Josie will get a clue. Maybe her sister will get a clue. Until then, I have to play along.

Josie stuffs her sister's card into my coat pocket. I know I'll call the human sponge. I know I'll agree to get together with her. We'll talk. I'll hate it.

But I also know that I absolutely will not tell her the whole truth about the night with Clifford.

Instead, I'll paint a picture of a completely secure woman, one who has a challenging job she loves, goes out when she feels like it, and knows exactly where she's going in life. Not one that ran away from a scandal and now, apparently, is developing a wicked soul-consuming crush on one of her best friends. A crush that could ruin one of the few great things in this new city life. But also one that apparently can't be controlled.

After Josie and I shout goodbye, I head back to my car, wondering for the first time what it would be like to love my job. Give it my full attention like I should.

Lots of women do. Maybe I envy those well-heeled ladies in Ann Taylor slacks who set goals and achieve them. Not only do they understand what they're supposed to do at work, they get satisfaction from their successes and learn from their failures.

I slide into my car. Could I be like them?

Chapter Eleven

Life in the Fast Girl's Lane

Less than an hour later, I'm creeping past Bob Hastings who has his nose in the sports section. He tips the paper down long enough to say, "Only about two weeks until opening day, Hayley."

"Go Tigers!"

He grins, probably because he thinks I'm sharing his enthusiasm. I glide up the hill and park. Carrying my lunch in one hand and the possibility of appreciating my job in the other, I bust through the pretty French doors and march to my desk.

Yuck. Caroline has left me a message. Not one of the cute pink phone messages, one of her yellow you-have-to-do-this messages. But wait! I might be a new woman—one who is excited by the challenges of her workday—so after I put my lunch in the mini-fridge and manage to cram my purse into one of my desk drawers, I muster up a smile.

Oh. It isn't from Caroline after all.

It's from Mr. Neville.

Hayley,
Caroline says you're great with ideas so I'm passing this on to you. We need ideas for our big anniversary celebration — 15 Years of Luxurious Living at North Pointe Farms. Make a list of ideas and have them ready for me in a couple days.

Okay, I get it. He needs some ideas.

Ideas about what?

Hell if I know.

I tip sideways and spy Caroline at her desk. She's the picture of managerial perfection as she clicks away on her keyboard. I really don't want to go ask her what he's talking about. Every time I ask her anything, she looks at me with this pinched expression like I'm some kind of stupid asshole she's been saddled with.

Frantically I scan the top of my desk. Sadly, there is nothing else to do. Nothing work related anyway. So I either forget the notion that work challenges can be sources of growth or slink over to Caroline's office and ask her what exactly Mr. Neville is getting at. It's too soon to give up — even for me.

Caroline's toes are pointed forward and peeking out beneath her desk. That stiff smile spreads across her face after I say hi.

"I see you got Mr. Neville's memo."

My head bobs up and down as my gaze roams around her office. Her diploma from Michigan State is watching over her, daring anyone to question her abilities or professionalism. The frame that holds the photo of her and her boyfriend is a castle with long yellow banners flying across the top. Does she think it's cute or does she actually have a sense of humor and realize how stupid it is?

"Did you have a question or something?" she asks with her gaze trained on my knees.

Besides, 'why are you staring at my skirt like it has some secret message embedded in the fabric'? "These, um, ideas, he's talking about. What kind of things is he looking for?"

"*Ideas* to celebrate the anniversary. The whole Management Group will be invited so you want them to be really great."

Management Group? "You mean Tony and Bob?"

Her lip curls in a most unbecoming way and her gaze goes flat. "No, the Management Group from Regional."

Oh, right. Regional. I pretend smile back at her.

I've only been at North Pointe Farms for about six weeks, so honestly, I have no idea what the hell she's talking about. And the way she always assumes that I know what she's talking about really bugs the shit out of me. That's what I get for being a temp.

She pushes her keyboard away and leans toward me. "You'll need to make a flyer too."

Of course. A flyer for the *ideas*.

"But you probably don't have the best software for that. So draw a mock-up on some scrap sheets of paper then when you have something about ready to go you can use my computer to transfer the *ideas* into something we can print up and pass out to the residents."

Hmmmmmmmm.

I really wish she'd shut up because I have no clue what she's talking about. One thing is crystal clear. There's no point in asking any more questions, because if I do, I'm likely to get assigned yet another task, which I do not understand nor have the software for.

Tony is sitting on my desk when I get back to it. He's wearing at least three gold chains and they are flashing across his chest like...well, like something, but I don't know what.

"Mrs. Klonski is looking for you. She's out by the pool."

"Somebody trying to snatch Snickers again?"

"She didn't say."

Glad to have a reason to get some fresh air, I go out of the side door to hunt down Mrs. Klonski. She isn't there. Bob is. He's leaning on the iron fence that runs around the pool. I march over to him.

"What are you doing out of your booth?"

He frowns for a second then realizes I'm teasing him. "Tony said Mrs. Klonski was looking for me."

"That's weird. He told me the same thing."

He shoves his fists into his pockets and spins on his heels. "Don't see her anywhere around, do you?"

Just for fun, I spin on my heels. "Nope."

He shrugs and backs toward the driveway. "If you see her, tell her I'm in my booth."

I watch his square back sway a few times until he stops to add, "Big news about the anniversary celebration."

Mr. Hastings has been at North Pointe ever since the glorious day when they nailed together his booth so I'm not surprised that he's excited. "What have you heard about it?"

"Not all that much really. Mr. Neville says it's going to be like the one they had at East Pointe Farms last year."

"They?"

"The Management Group."

"Regional?"

"Yep. Regional was there. I sat right next to the Junior Vice President. He was in charge of publicity. Management Group did all the arrangements for that one but Mr. Neville says we're going to save a lot of money by having the celebration planned by regular staff."

Or the temp.

Oh! *Ideas!* From Mr. Hastings?

Sure, why not? He's got to have something better than my nothing.

All of a sudden I'm overcome by the urge to walk Bob Hastings back to his booth. So I do. He tells me about East Pointe's giant garage sale and how great it was. Then he tells me about how a bunch of the residents got together and planted a perennial flower garden.

Mr. Hastings slips back into his booth. "It's still there, Mr. Coleman tends it. He must be eighty-five if he's a day. Good gardener. Beautiful lilies..."

I wait a minute, wondering if he's going to say more but he doesn't. He doesn't even bother finishing that sentence before saying goodbye. I stroll back to the clubhouse—still no sign of Mrs. Klonski—wander to the kitchenette and start some coffee. Enjoying work is easier when awake.

* * * *

Later on, I'm at my desk, mulling over the stuff Mr. Hastings told me. Caroline has stepped out to check on the painting being done in one of the models and since she's not asked me to do anything in particular, I start digging through the East Pointe Farms web page, trying to get more *ideas*.

"Are you aware of the fact that Mrs. Klonski is wandering around the pool looking for you?"

Crap! Caroline is a sneaky bitch.

Very smoothly, I lean forward, leading her to believe that she has my full attention. "She's looking for me?"

"Yes. I told her you were inside. She has that damn dog with her so I made her wait out there. Would you please go see what she wants?" Upon making that gentle request, Caroline plants herself smack in the middle of the room and stares at me.

I smile at her, a bit stupidly, and ask her something I know she does not want to answer. "How's the painting going?"

"How do you think it's going? Those painting guys suck. You want to do something helpful? Find us some other painters." She snarls as she heads to her office. "Take care of Mrs. Klonski, will you please? Before she brings that obnoxious dog into the clubhouse."

I close the page and go outside to hunt down Mrs. Klonski. I walk around the pool. I even look behind the shrubs. Big surprise. She isn't there. I step back inside and drop myself behind my desk.

* * * *

Nick is waiting for me when I get home, sitting on the stoop of my apartment building. He sees me coming and rolls to his feet. "Hey," he says as he moves to stand beside me as I unlock the entrance door.

"Hi. Glad you could come." It sounds lame but it's true.

"Yeah. Me too."

We go in and start up the stairs. There's an odd tension in the air. Not bad. Intense. Like the snap in the air before a thunderstorm. I look over my shoulder to check if it's just me who feels it and see that Nick is staring at my ass. I keep going up and he keeps staring, totally unaware that I'm watching him watch me. When we reach the landing he finally looks up and I can tell he knows that I know he's been studying my ass.

After I smile, for a few seconds I wonder why I did but then I accept the truth. I like the way he was staring at me. He smiles back and my stomach does a little flip.

My hands shake as I slide the key in the lock and open the door.

Inside, I set my bag down, toss my keys to the floor then lock the door behind us. Neither of us says anything but that snap of electricity between us is so intense I can practically hear it humming.

Nick shrugs off his jacket. As it falls to the floor he grabs me. I wrap my arms around him and run my palms across his back.

The kiss isn't anything like Clifford's practiced seduction. He isn't lifting me, bending me, or swinging me upside down like a rag doll. He slides his hands slowly and gently around my waist and holds me. The kiss starts out soft but turns firm pretty quick. It's like he's afraid he won't be able to get enough of my mouth before I realize I'm making out with one of my best friends and pull back. I guess he doesn't know I don't want to pull back. About the time my heart is thumping in my chest and I really need a big gulp of air he lifts his mouth from mine and runs his lips down my neck. The warmth of his breath across my skin makes me tremble in the best possible way.

Still holding me, he backs me up to my couch and together we fall across it. He's on top of me, pinning me down with his weight as he starts kissing me again, moving his mouth across mine as though I belong to him, as though he's done it many times before. I settle in and give him what he wants and in turn get what I need. About the time my pussy is getting wet, he pushes his knees between my thighs and the hard ridge of his cock presses against my crotch. Even through the layers of clothes it's fantastic.

I twist to the side, trying to get my arm free. He rolls with me. In a tangle of arms and legs we drop to the floor. After the hard thump, we both start laughing.

I look over at him. "What are we doing?"

He pulls me on top of him so that my thighs are spread across his waist. "Kissing."

"Oh. Yeah." I wiggle lower on his body so that I can feel his hard cock beneath me then drop down to start kissing him again. He reaches up to cup my breasts. My nipples tighten and my whole body starts to feel hot and quivery and needy. I rock against him, rubbing my body across that bulge.

And that's when Nick lowers his hands. "We better stop."

It takes me a couple of seconds to figure out what he's saying. I don't want to quit but I know what he means. He gets to his feet and picks up his jacket. I'm so dizzy from all that kissing and grabbing and rolling around that I let him walk right out of my door.

* * * *

Twenty minutes later, I'm smacking my pillow and wondering if this is some new pattern in my life—me lying in bed, staring at my plugged-in phone and wondering about what I've just done with a guy. Or in this case, didn't do. Well, sort of did. I don't know.

I flip over and look at the cracks in the ceiling. Comparing Clifford to Nick doesn't really make sense. Nick is my friend. Friends aren't supposed to do that sort of thing. Are they? Maybe just once? A one-time casual, no-strings-attached make-out session must've been what I needed. It was obviously okay with Nick.

I flip around again and gaze at my phone.

If I do send Nick a text, what would I say?

With a sigh, I squeeze my eyes shut and wait for sleep.

* * * *

Nick's on his back and I'm straddling him, my bare ass pressing against his hard dick. My nipples, already stiff with lust, peak even tighter when he places his hands over my breasts. He squeezes them gently and I arch my back. His crooked smile is sinful, and seeing that look on his face makes me hotter and wetter but it also makes me want him to know I can be sweetly sinful too.

I wiggle backwards. Once I have myself settled between his thighs, I make a show of licking his cock. Giving him some slow, careful attention, I drag my tongue up his shaft over and over again. Once he gets totally hard, I slide his dick deep into my mouth and reach between his thighs to cup his balls and press my fingers ever so gently into his warm flesh.

He groans as he flexes his thighs to shove his tip further into my mouth. "Damn, you are so sexy."

But of course I can't reply because my mouth is full.

He rocks his hips up and down as I glide my mouth over him, making him wetter and to my amazement, even harder.

The first spurts of salty jizz drip onto my tongue and down the back of my throat. I can feel every motion of his body and I know I am the sole source of his attention. A sudden and consuming wave of power overcomes me, bringing my truly wicked side to the surface, and I lift my mouth up and look at his face. His eyes are closed but his mouth is open and he's moaning softly. Seeing him that way sends an intoxicating thrill of possession racing through me. "Do you want me to finish?" I ask.

He opens one eye and moans louder. "You know I do."

"Cause you need it?"

"Yeah. I need… I need you."

When I remain silent and stay still he opens both eyes and looks at me, pleading and needy. "Suck my cock, Hayley, please?"

I grin and turn my attention back to his dick. As I begin sucking, I feel the tension in his body ease then build again, his muscles tensing until his body is completely mine. Then I roll back onto my heels and grin evilly at him. "What if I don't finish?"

He grunts and lifts his head. "I'll throw you down on his bed and fuck you until you feel as desperate as I do."

I lift an eyebrow in question.

The next thing I know, I'm flipping through the air and landing flat on my back. Nick pins my shoulders to the bed and spreads my thighs with quick sweeps of his knees. This isn't the tender, gentle Nick who kissed my stomach and squeezed my ass. This Nick is dark and demanding and is making me quiver in ways I never knew I could. I'm helpless with lust and need and so ready to have his cock inside me I'm whimpering.

He lowers his hips until the tip of his cock brushes my thigh. "Want me to finish?"

"God yes."

"*But I haven't even started?*"

I shove one of his arms away and grab his leg, pulling him on top of me. He grunts and adjusts his body so his cock begins to enter my wet pussy. He enters me quickly, filling me completely. Slow, easy thrusts give way to quick hard ones. Within seconds I'm grinding against him, clawing at his back and gasping for air.

My body tightens, stiffening as the fierce climax takes hold. He's pumping faster and faster, working himself, and me, into lusty dizziness. From there, my thoughts disappear as the explosion of pleasure squeezes the last of my control and I let Nick possess me until we are both spent and gasping to catch our breaths.

C h a p t e r   T w e l v e

M&Ms, Pop Rocks, and Other Cool Kid Candies

We're at Fairlane Fabulous where Scotty is showing Josie a new highlighting process he learned at a hair show in Atlanta. Riana is the guinea pig/client. I'm holding a Diet Coke with one hand and flipping through *InStyle* with the other.

Riana looks so completely crazy that I know her hair is either going to look—

a) Fantastic

Or b) Like hell.

Knowing Scotty, it'll be fantastic. But at the moment it is a mess of plastic pipes and foil.

"This," Scotty is saying as he points to the crazy bits of foil crisscrossing the top of Riana's head, "is the main thing you have to watch out for. The foil pieces must not overlap more than a quarter inch." He looks at Josie's face. "Don't give me any of your 'I'm math challenged' bullshit. Even you can tell how much a quarter inch is. See?" He points down with his pinky. "That. That's a quarter inch. Got it?"

Josie nods.

"Now we wait," he says, reaching for the timer. "Seventeen minutes. I'll be back. After my smoke." He stops to yell over his shoulder, "Keep your hands off the foil, Josie!"

Josie drops her arms as she rolls her eyes and steps away from Riana's ferocious fountain of hair. She falls into a chair and fixes me with an unsympathetic gaze. "Back to your interview with my sister."

I glance over at Riana for help, but she's busy talking on her cell. I can tell by the look on her face that she's talking to Peter, the stupid boyfriend.

Josie is still on my case. "You don't have to tell her anything personal. Just talk about your experience with the program so far."

I toss the *InStyle* onto the counter behind me. "So now it's a program?"

"You said you'd talk to her. She'll pay for dinner. Free food! What do you have to lose? You don't have a date tonight or anything. Right?"

I have nothing. "Do I get to pick the restaurant?"

"I don't see what difference it makes. Text her. Tell her where and when to meet and she'll be there."

I hold in a sigh—I so know where this whole deal is going and as usual I am helpless to do anything but go along for the bumpy and twisted ride. At least I know how it will all end.

"Fine but you owe me."

"Don't be like that. It'll be cool."

She's your sister, you go talk to her. No, I won't say that. It will be a free meal. If the bitch shows up.

* * * *

Two hours later, after deciding that beers with Josie's sister would be easier to handle than food, I'm sitting at Anthony's on Elizabeth, a few blocks away from Greektown. While I'm staring at the row of ancient metal lunch boxes running across the back bar, I wonder what the deal is with the guy who owns the place. No way did he grow up in Detroit. His accent is so thick that not even the knife of mundane conversation can cut through it. Maybe that's why he's trying so hard to capture the ultimate American experience.

Included in the dozens of boxes are The Love Boat, Sabrina the Teenage Witch—from the Archie comics, not the show. And my personal favorite—CHiPs. Who can resist hot cops on motorcycles? Even if their legs are so short they barely reach the ground. With those leather gloves, who cares? Too bad they never had an episode where Ponch and John went undercover at a roller rink. I'd love to see them gliding around in their brown uniforms.

Oh, that wouldn't be undercover would it? Put them in blue jeans instead. With a dark-haired girl in a body-conscious black dress.

I pause and consider.

Nope. I'm still not ready to laugh that off. Yet.

I haul my backpack onto the bench I'm sitting on and dig for the professional looking notebook I've brought. If Josie's sister shows up to find me carefully outlining my *ideas* for the Big Anniversary Celebration at North Pointe Farms, she'll believe all the garbage I'm going to feed her about loving the challenge my work brings.

Surprise, surprise. I even have a couple of things written down.

"Hey, Hayley." Josie's sister slides onto the opposite bench. I'll bet it took her at least twenty minutes to get her blonde hair to look like she just crawled out of bed. A *Motor City Times* tee that is so tight it could be a tattoo instead of a shirt is stretched across her chest.

My return smile is as fake as it is wide. It doesn't matter though, because Josie's sister isn't looking at me.

Her arm snakes across the table and her hand bites my wrist. She moves close and says, "Oh, my, God, is that Kid Rock?"

Just as I am about to turn around to look, she whispers, "Don't turn around! He'll see us."

I shrug. Whatever. Does anyone care about Kid Rock? I thought... Well, it doesn't matter what I thought, because Josie's sister obviously cares. She's leaning against the wooden back of the booth and the wording of her shirt is more prominent than it was a minute ago.

"Why don't you go ask him?" *Maybe he'll want to do an interview.*

Her big eyes narrow and her gaze slides back over my shoulder. "I do have experience, you know. I've interviewed some local names."

"Local names?" I sputter. *Who could that possibly be?* I imagine her scooting in to get all the Detroit gossip from Scotty while the two of them get drunk on Coors in the bathroom.

She scowls as she climbs out of the booth then heads to the bar.

With her gone, I'm free to spin around and gawk, which I do. There's a ratty looking guy hunched over, gripping a long neck beer with one hand and a pack of Marlboro Reds in the other. He's wearing a black Aerosmith T-shirt. But no hat.

"Stop staring."

It's okay for her? I spin back around and pick up the pen I'd dropped across my professional looking note pad. "So. What are your questions?"

"Oh yeah, that." She peels her attention off Kid Rock, takes a ladylike sip of her can of Bud, a feat in itself, then wiggles further into the booth. "Tell me about your date."

"Don't you want to know about how Josie got it—the program—all set up?"

She points to my scribbled notes. "Did you put something down for me? Because, well"—she frowns and her mouth puckers like it has a bad taste loitering within—"I do my own writing."

I straighten and try to look important, successful and intelligent. "These are some *ideas* I'm working on for a promotion I'm in charge of at work."

"Oh. Okay."

Did I need her permission?

Out loud she reviews what she knows about Josie's dating service, and I nod while she talks because she actually has all the details straight. She even gets the part about why girls don't have to pay. "Why should they?" she finishes with a smile then snorts. "I wouldn't."

I have to know. "Have you watched any of the videos?"

Her perfectly waxed and penciled eyebrows lift. "I never considered it."

The unsaid thing—that not only did I consider it, I did it—goes unsaid and her gaze wanders over my shoulder to watch Kid Rock. She mumbles something about whether or not it's actually him or just some guy who drinks so much that he looks like an old rock star.

I can't believe it—I'd rather be talking about Clifford than speculating over celebrities. I've never been into that whole making it to the big time thing. Maybe that's why I spend my days temping at a stupid apartment complex instead of staring out of the window of a RenCen office. "Um...by the way...what did you want to ask me?"

She pulls herself back to our table. "Why you did it, for starters."

Nothing like diving right in. *'In the video he looked like a hottie?'* No, not going to say that. *'He had big hands?'* No, not that either. "Are you going to use my name?"

"You don't want me to?"

Why is she making me feel so stupid? No wonder Josie has such a hard time dealing with this girl.

"No, I don't. I don't think it would be good for Josie's business."

"I hadn't thought of that."

No surprise there.

"Okay." She traces the top of her beer can with her bright pink nails. "I'll keep your name out of it."

"And Clifford's?"

"That was his name? Your video date?" She jots something down in teeny tiny letters then looks up. "No real names."

I'm not sure if I can trust her. What does it matter since I'm not going to tell her the truth anyway? "I did it because Josie asked me to and I thought it might be fun."

"Where did you go? What did you do?"

I answer and provide a brief sketch of what we did, omitting the facts that he ate an entire pizza and that when we went skating I was wearing a dress. As I chatter along she asks a few questions but overall she stuns me by being a good listener.

After a while, I forget that she is writing stuff down.

But I never forget that she is an evil sponge woman waiting for me to slip up and hand her something she can use against either Josie or me — or even better, both of us.

A low rumble of laughter comes from the Kid Rock table. This time I look around without thinking about it. There are two more guys. The guys aren't much to look at. But what can you expect in a place that smells like stale beer and has collectible lunch boxes circling the bar?

Josie's sister is downing her beer. "I'm going to go over there and talk to them."

I'm not sure I want to stick around to see this. "You going to ask him for an interview?"

She sets down the empty can and pulls her pink lipstick out of her purse. "I'll start by telling him how much I loved that thing he did on the MTV awards show way back. To show him what a long-time fan I am. You know that performance, right? It's on YouTube, ya know? That song about the kid who stuffed his pregnant girlfriend into the trunk of his car then drove off a cliff? That song, well it really was the beginning...um...new things...in music."

I resist the urge to rub my ears. "*Stan*?"

"Is that what it's called?"

"Yeah, that's the name of that song." But as someone who made a careful study of all things Detroit before moving here, I know she has one very key fact wrong.

"What a powerful performance."

Is this a test? Or is she really that out of it? "Do you pay much attention to the Detroit rock scene?"

She rolls her eyes.

For the first time that night a real smile moves onto my face. If she actually goes over there and tells Kid

Rock how much she liked his performance of *Stan* she's really going to make an ass of herself. And I could be there to see it. "You should do it. Really, as a writer you have to be willing to take chances." I set aside my half-empty beer bottle, showing her I'm willing to go over there with her.

"You think so?"

Is that insecurity? Thinking of all the times Josie called me in tears, I slide out of the booth. "Come on."

What do I care if we make fools of ourselves? It can't be any worse than being booed off the stage by a bunch of drunks.

Josie's sister slips out and brushes past me. Wearing a new attitude, she glides over to the table and tucks her little self in next to a weasely looking guy wearing a Sponge Bob Square Pants T-shirt.

She smiles at him. I'm standing stupidly by the corner of the table wondering if this whole 'embarrass your friend's sister' plan is such a good idea.

Josie's sister is smiling at Sponge Bob and I'm seeing for the first time why she always gets what she wants when she wants it. He's already shouting to the bartender for more beer and she's laughing and tossing her hair around.

Me?

That's right, I'm holding onto the side of the table.

Realizing I have two options. One — stand there like the dull chick who never wants to have fun. Or, two — play along. I grab a chair from another table and pop into the group like they were expecting me.

"What are you girls up to tonight?"

Josie's sister points at me. "I've been asking Hayley here about a date she went on last night."

One of the guys, not Sponge Bob and not Kid Rock, a long-haired guy wearing a biker leather chuckles.

"Well," he says, stretching the word out like a flavorless piece of gum. "Tell us the good parts."

All eyes on me. How did this happen? I came over here to watch Josie's sister make a fool of herself.

My choices —

a) Dash for the door.

b) Pretend I don't speak English — *Hablar Espanol?*

c) Chat with the rock dudes.

What the hell. "We went roller-skating. You guys been lately?"

Sitting there watching the old rock dudes talk to Josie's sister gets old fast. They say some stuff. She says some stuff. After I get really bored, I try to look cool and busy by messing with my phone. But who am I kidding? Facebook is dead, Twitter is dull and I am not going to Instagram a picture of me sitting at Anthony's with Kid Rock and his ancient friends. It'd be so desperate.

I have to get out of there but after this evening I don't want to be by myself. The whole conversation with Josie's sister has me feeling lonely and lost.

So I text Nick. Asking him if he wants to meet at my place.

"Who're you texting?" All of a sudden Josie's sister is interested in me. "Another video date?"

That gets a round of laughter from the old men. The one in the leather starts to cough and gag then excuses himself to go outside for a smoke. The remaining two stare at me, actually expecting me to respond. Which, unfortunately, I do.

"Nah. Just this guy."

"A friend with bennies?" Sponge Bob laughs at his own crudeness. "Your fuck buddy?"

Good God I hate everyone over thirty. Really. They should know better than to go out in public. My phone buzzes and to my complete surprise Josie's sister snatches it out of my hand and reads Nick's response aloud.

"'Be there in thirty.' Guess you better hurry, Hayley," she says in an annoying sing-song voice.

I snatch the phone back and try to laugh it off, like I don't care that she's such a rude bitch. I wave goodbye and dash out.

* * * *

"It should just be about the sex," I say to Nick. This way, I justify, I don't have to tell him about Waylon.

We're lying side by side, facing each other. I'm wearing yoga pants with no panties and a tank top. I can tell by the way he keeps looking at my nipples that he's noticed there's nothing underneath that either. He's wearing jeans and a Wayne State T-shirt. His boots are by the doorway. One of his socks is in the middle floor. The other is next to the bed.

"What about the friendship?" he wants to know.

It's a reasonable question, seeing as we've been friends long enough to know our friendship matters to both of us.

"I can't imagine not being friends, so the friendship stays. I was thinking that would be...you know...something on the side."

"Gee. Thanks." He rolls onto his back and the edge of his T-shirt twists up so I can see the pale skin of his stomach and the fine line of hair leading to his dick. He shoves his hand behind his neck and looks upward. "When you put it that way it sounds so..."

"Well thought out?"

He glances at me from the corner of his eye. His long lashes sweep down when he looks away again. "Not exactly what I was going to say."

I look at his lips and remember the way he made me feel, just by putting his mouth on mine. Then I remember the Nick of my dreams and wonder which one is closer to reality—the tender one of the fierce one. Hopefully it's both. "I've been thinking, you know, ever since the kiss. It's obvious we both liked it. We both wanted to do something about it. So we might as well."

He keeps staring at the ceiling, not saying anything.

"We can't go back and pretend it never happened," I add, to clarify. He's quiet for so long that my heart begins to pound.

"Since you've been so thoughtful about this, let me ask you a question."

It's my turn to stare and say nothing, waiting with my heart thumping

He opens his mouth, and I wait for words to come out but none do. Instead of talking, he rolls onto his side and reaches for me with the hand that had just been behind his neck. His fingers are warm and my skin tingles. The tingle ignites a skitter of electricity that surges up my spine as quickly as it flows down through my stomach and into my pussy. The heat makes me wet and I forget that Nick wanted to say something important about us but changed his mind.

He glides his hand up my stomach then he cups my breast, flicking his thumb across my nipple. I arch my back, let out a soft sigh, wonder when he's going to kiss me again, then realize I could go ahead and kiss him. I grab his shoulders, pull him on top of me and find his mouth with mine. The weight of his body pushes me into my bed and he uses his thighs to spread mine apart. He doesn't waste any time, grinding his dick between my legs and kissing me back, pressing his lips to mine and forcing my mouth open. The heat of his tongue is nothing compared to the heat burning inside me.

The kiss is more intense than the other and not just because he's on top of me. It's like every smile, every touch, and every accidental moment of flirting have come together in a frenzied explosion of grabbing and kissing. And this real life Nick is an impossible combination of forcefulness and gentleness. His breath is on my face, his arms under my shoulders and his weight holding me down. I move my hands over his back, running my fingers across his muscles. He moans, the sound a mixture of yearning and satisfaction. Each place I put my hands, his body quivers in response. I recognize the quiver because my body is doing the same, nearly shivering with want, excitement and nervous anxiety. He moves his mouth to my neck, down my throat and works his way to my collarbone. He's kissing me softly, as though he's afraid I'll disappear.

When I grab the hem of his shirt, he moves back to give me space enough to pull it up and run my palms across his chest. His ribs expand quickly as he sucks in air. I reach down and wriggle out of my yoga pants, kicking my legs with quick snaps to get them off. He braces himself with one hand and uses the other to unhook his belt and unzip his jeans. Together, we pull his pants down. His briefs go down next then off onto the floor near that single sock.

For a split second our gazes connect, acknowledging the reality that we are about to have sex. I wonder if he's having second thoughts but he's grabbing for the condom box, tearing it open like a madman. I admire his hard dick and his lean, solid body as he gets out a condom and covers his cock. Once he's done, he whips off his T-shirt. I take off my tank.

After he climbs back on top of me, he holds my face in his hands and stares into my eyes. His body is still but I can feel his heart thumping and see the quickness of his breath in the way his chest moves. I can practically feel my pussy dripping. Does he possibly expect me to change my mind? *Hurry up and fuck me*, I want to say.

But I say, "Yes," instead.

"Good." He strokes my mouth with one thumb. The trace of a smile curves his lips right before he presses them to mine, caressing my mouth with soft determination. He takes his time, kissing each corner of my mouth. But my body is nearly shaking with lust. I don't want him to take his time. I want him thrusting inside me, driving his dick into my slick core. I lift my hips, rubbing a thigh against his cock, urging him to put himself inside me.

He gets the idea.

His hot breath crosses over my ear as he shifts his legs so that his tip is pressing against my wet pussy lips. He eases his thick shaft into me, slowly. My body adjusts to his size as he gradually enters me, filling me so perfectly I can't believe we have never done this before. The familiar scent of his aftershave drifts into my nose then it clicks.

This is Nick I'm doing it with.

Not some hot, random, but-already-checked-out guy. Not a fantasy Nick my mind conjured up, but the real Nick. My friend who I've apparently been lusting about for longer than I knew. The realization is a mixture of too many things, intense things I can't possibly sort out. I turn my head, tell myself to stop thinking about the emotional part and enjoy the size of his dick and the way he's sliding in and out of me, picking up speed and grunting into my ear each time he drives all the way in. It takes only seconds before all rational thoughts scatter from my mind.

The power of his arms surrounds me and I gulp in deep breaths of air, savoring his heat and scent. I wrap my legs around him and angle my hips so that he goes even deeper with each thrust.

His cock glides in and out of me, working me into a frenzy. I squeeze my ass cheeks and move my legs even higher up his back. The move does the trick and within seconds flecks of color flash in my closed eyes. A soul-stealing explosion tears through my body, and I whimper when it lingers so long that it nearly hurts. Nearly but not quite. The near pain melts into hot liquid pleasure that pours over me, softening every inch of the crazed tension that was holding my muscles so tightly.

Nick is right there with me. Grunting, panting, tense. Then melting and moaning.

Too soon, it's over. He kisses me on the cheek, rolls off, then very politely excuses himself to take care of what needs to be taken care of.

I'm settled into the pillow, the cover pulled over me when he returns. He climbs into bed, slips his arm behind my neck and pulls me to him. My heart has settled down enough that I could probably talk normally but my throat is dry and I have no idea what to say. I was expecting a hot time, something like I'd had with Clifford. What did I get instead? An explosive experience that blew my mind.

He kisses the top of my head and pulls me closer to his naked body.

I want to say something... *Thanks? I liked it...* But how lame is that?

"Friends?" he asks softly. "We're still friends, right?"

All of a sudden the word doesn't sound right but I don't have another to replace it. I swallow hard and nod.

He lets out a sigh and we lie like that until I fall asleep.

Chapter Thirteen

Positively Powerful: The Workout for Your Life

"It's been a week since you and my sister went to Anthony's and she wants to know what you did to Kid Rock that made him not call her."

I rub my eyes then stare at the ceiling, tracing the path of the crack above me. The same crack I look at every morning as I think about Nick. Of course we're still texting and talking but neither of us has said anything about the 'friends who do it' thing. Why? After a week? Maybe that idea of mine wasn't such a good one. It sure seemed like it at the time. Didn't it? I'm still clicking through my questions when Josie repeats herself.

"Is this a serious question," I ask, "or do you have an ulterior motive? Because" — I bend my neck to look at the clock — "it's eight a.m."

"Did you guys actually meet him?"

While I try to wake up, I hear the ladies at Josie's salon chatter and wonder how they can bear sitting upright this early in the morning, then I wonder what they're talking about.

It is Friday. At least a couple of them should have somewhere to go. All I have penciled into my non-existence planner is going home on Saturday to help my dad with his birds then trying to ignore all the stares and gossip at the April Fool's Dance. All of that will be accomplished while alternately thinking about Nick and trying to not think about Nick.

Josie is still waiting for my answer and I have to get up eventually so I push myself into a semi-sitting position. "I guess we met him, if that's what you want to call it and I didn't *do* anything to him. I didn't even talk to him. I ended up talking to Sponge Bob."

"Sponge Bob?"

"Never mind." I throw the quilt off my legs and stand up. "I kind of doubt Kid Rock is going to call your sister for an interview. Seriously."

"She sounded so sure he would." After she mumbles something to somebody else, she switches gears and asks, "What are you doing tonight?"

Watching videos on YouTube so if I meet a rock star I won't get his songs mixed up with somebody else's.

"Nothing?" she cuts into my mental sarcasm. "Good, because one of my clients gave me two tickets to a one-night seminar on the power of positive thinking."

What does that have to do with me?

"I know you want to go. Be at my apartment at seven. It starts at seven-thirty. I'll drive."

Inwardly, I bristle. "No, I think I have a date. With my couch."

And my fantasies. And insecurities.

"That's stupid. You're going because I know you want to go. You're just being stubborn."

Me, stubborn?

I'm not being stubborn, given my current mindset I just don't know if positive thinking is for me. It sounds so time consuming...and would probably require effort on my part. It may also require me to be completely honest with myself and others. A seminar...it's...so public. It's one thing to strive for self-improvement in the privacy of your own home, but going public like that...it's a statement. Worse than that...it's a commitment.

"If you don't come with me, I'm going to tell Nick the stuff about Clifford that you didn't tell him yourself."

"All right." I give in with a groan. She doesn't know the half of it, does she? Thank goodness, because as long as Nick and I keep pretending that night didn't happen, I don't know what's going on either. "I'll go but we're going out afterward."

She agrees and we hang up.

* * * *

Twelve hours later, Josie and I are at Wayne State and one of us is geeked. The other one isn't.

A screen hanging at the front of the auditorium reads, 'The Power of Positive Thinking'. All around Josie and me, thirty-something ladies wearing expensive casual wear are chatting and digging through their purses.

Already, I realize I am out of it. I left my purse in Josie's car and my Old Navy jeans cost twelve dollars fifty.

How do I get myself into these things?

I cast a sideways glance at Josie. She's talking self-improvementese to a short-haired, pixie woman seated in the row in front of us.

Effectiveness seminars, past life regressions, twelve-step organizational plans.

Josie doesn't belong here. Could anybody be more positive thinking?

She works endless hours a week and still has the energy and desire to start her own business. A weird business, sure, but from what she says it's actually making money.

The question, why are we here, drifts hopelessly around my mouth like a tiny hot air balloon looking for a place to land in a swamp.

Josie leans over and says, softly, "You said you wanted to get yourself together and work harder at North Pointe."

How did she know that? Did I say that? I need to shut up.

I start to defend my stupidity by saying I've just been reading too many magazines but she shushes me. "Here she comes!"

Music swells out of the walls and the lights dim. The platoon of thirty-somethings sit up. Even I sit up.

A noise too loud to be a real human voice erupts from the walls. "You do not need to be defeated by anything. You do not need to be a whiner who struggles aimlessly through life, weighed down by resentment and anger.

"Tomorrow and every day after for the rest of your life you will be full of satisfaction."

All the refugees applaud and Josie nudges me enthusiastically. The noise of it all makes my skull vibrate.

I scan the stage. Where did that huge voice come from? The only person on the stage is a tiny lady in a pink suit with a gray, chin-length bob.

It's her yelling like that? How can one tiny person make so much noise?

"Welcome to the power to be positive!" Her words boom out again. "This one night will change the rest of your life!"

The pixie mom in front of us claps so hard that her little shoulders shake up and down. The music builds again and lavender strobe lights roll across the stage until they stop on the loud lady. She raises her hands to the crowd and smiles the huge grin of a lady making big bucks to yell at people she can't see.

I smirk and lean back in my padded chair but I still listen. How could I not with her voice booming into every nook and cranny?

Josie has her iPad resting on her knee and she taps in key points as the phrases flash onto the screen. A whirlwind of encouragement whips around the auditorium and spins us all into a frenzy of affirmation. One by one, the loud lady's commandments roll up and Josie writes them down.

1. *Believe that you are entitled to what you want!*
2. *Surround yourself with positive people and situations!*
3. *Break through your worries and personal problems!*
4. *Keep track of your successes and keep pressing forward!*

That's all good stuff and I think I've read it before. Probably in Oprah's magazine. And in Caroline's copies of *Redbook*. If I've read it, it's a sure thing that these ladies have read it too, because they look to be the got-it-going-on together types. So why did we all have to come here to hear it again?

I glance at my watch. And why has it taken two and a half hours to get it said?

No point in asking, because the whole thing is over and all the ladies are on their feet and pounding through a round of applause that would make Kid Rock jealous.

Well...probably not since most of these women are too old and too sober, still, these are some powerfully positive people.

"She is so right," Josie gushes as we weave through the crowd to the parking lot. "Why waste time with whiners and losers? They only bring you down."

For some reason I don't want to uncover, all the excitement is really depressing me. Why can't I be energized and thrilled about the positive possibilities for my life?

The horror. Am I one of the whining losers?

Maybe I should I ask. I glance over at Josie's shining face. Maybe I shouldn't.

* * * *

About thirty minutes later, Josie and I are at The Fitzgerald, a cigar bar near the Renaissance Center. It's the sort of swanky place where successful business types go after work to smoke overpriced cigars while they admire each other and network.

Josie is still basking in the afterglow of the loud lady's pep talk, and I'm still reeling with confusion that feels a little too much like regret. Regret as in, why did I ever think self-improvement was a good idea? Why did I have to open this whole can of worms? What compelled me to search for my inner self? Why does life have to have meaning? Maybe I don't care if I'm a messed-up whining loser and my life goes nowhere. Maybe I want to hide from everyone back in the country and the truth about why I left home.

Maybe I do. Maybe I don't.

"And then she came back two days later and asked me to cut it again. The picture she brought in wasn't anything like what she had with her the first time. Some people have no idea what they want."

No kidding.

Josie taps her cigarillo into the ashtray and scans the crowd. "Check out that guy staring at you."

I spin around and lock eyes with Todd Winslow.

Impossible. But true.

He grins like the sturdy farm boy he is and waves. Unfortunately, his arms are so big that he nearly knocks out some blue-suited, gray-haired guy who is trying to get the attention of a blonde in a red dress. I ignore him, looking past his giant body. It does no good. He waves again. A weak smile wrinkles my mouth. I know what will happen next as surely as I know I am helpless to prevent it. He's blundering through the bar, turning more than a few heads as he goes. Who could miss a bear-sized guy in pressed flannel and Carhartts?

"Do you know him?" Josie asks, astonishment trimming her voice.

I nod but she's staring at me, wanting more than just the obvious answer. "He, um, does some stuff with my dad." It's actually *for* my dad, like help burn brush piles, sell scrap metal, and trim flight feathers on the chickens. And, well, he is the best friend of Waylon Walker, my high-school sweetheart, the guy I was engaged to, planned a wedding with, and bought a dress for.

There is that little, teeny, tiny thing.

As Todd moves toward us, easily maneuvering through the after work crowd, I'm sure my face is becoming a mixture of horror and despair. Each step that brings him closer is another step that pulls my two worlds together.

He plants his oversized county self right in front of us and grins. Then he looks me square in the face and says, "Hey, Hayley. Whatcha doin'?"

Hoping to look casual, I place my hand on the bar to steady myself as I set my other hand on his shoulder and give him a painfully fake I'm-totally-cool-with-seeing-you-here hug and manage to speak, "Hi, Todd."

He holds out his hand and Josie takes it. After he jerks her arm up and down a couple of times, he lets go and stands awkwardly. There's an uncomfortable bubble of silence, which I know should be filled by me, introducing Josie and Todd or by me saying something friendly to my hometown friend, like the lie, 'It's great to see you', but my mouth is dry and my eyes can't believe what I'm seeing.

"So whatcha doin'?" he asks me again, plowing through my shock, dread and what must look like rudeness.

Gripping the edge of the bar, I tip my head at our drinks. "Having some Diet Cokes." I finally get myself together enough to introduce them.

"Cool." He holds up his glass in salute to Josie. "I'm havin' a Vernors." His square head moves slowly as he looks around then comes back to me. "I can't believe I ran into you. I'm staying overnight at the Pontchartrain down the street. My dad was supposed to come but our hired man got sick." He turns a proud smile to Josie and says, "We're dairy farmers." Then gets back to both of us, "Dad bid on a PBS auction and got the night at the hotel and dinner at The Greektown Casino. Geez, what a place. All those lights and all that money. Bet you guys go there all the time." He looks right at me "That's the sort of stuff you came here for, right, Hayley?"

I glance over at Josie, to see if she is horrified that I know this guy but, to her credit, she's ignoring the odd way he's looking at me. Like he's trying to see into my brain and figure out what I'm thinking. I recognize the expression because I saw it often in the weeks before I packed up and moved. "Are you having a good time?" she asks him.

"Sure. I wish my dad could've come too. He would've loved that casino. All those lights and stuff." Todd's mouth shifts to the side. "It wasn't as much like the movies about Las Vegas as I thought it was going to be. There seemed to be less...um... I mean, more..."

Josie jumps in with, "Less hotties and more old people?"

His head bobs up and down and a boyish smile slants across his mouth. He's forgotten about me and I'm glad. "Yeah."

Josie laughs and he laughs too. For a few minutes after that, he and Josie chuckle about the casino, the ridiculous monorail that nobody uses and everyone calls the Mugger Mover and the crazy escalators in the RenCen. The next thing I know, Josie is telling Todd about the seminar and all the great advice the loud lady had. He's nodding and looking totally convinced.

While they go on from there to talk about movies then somehow get on the subject of spring break horror stories before finally landing on jobs. Josie puffs on her cigar and tells him about her dating discs business. Through it all I take sips of my drink, nod occasionally and pretend that I'm right there with them. But I'm not with them at all. I'm in my own world of shock. Unfortunately, their conversation ultimately loops around to include me as a topic.

"You seein' anybody, Hayley?" Todd asks.

I blurt out the answer, "No."

Todd leans away from my outburst.

"What about Nick?" Josie says with a soft smile.

For a brief second I actually think I'm going to pass out. Then I get myself together but still sound bewildered when I reply, "Nick and I aren't going out. We're *friends*."

There is a pause, then Todd and Josie laugh. Together. At me. I did sound kind of crazy for a second there, but I get sick of people giving me shit about Nick. I have enough of my own confusion to deal with. And the tension crawling up my spine is screaming for a way out.

Once Todd stops chuckling, he looks away from Josie long enough to ask me, "What about you? How're you doin'?"

That's quite a loaded question, isn't it Todd? "Great. Fine. Good. Okay." But of course he really wants to know if I'm over *it*.

"Waylon's great," he says, probably hoping I'll take the bait and ask for more.

When I don't, he continues, "He started a new company doing painting, carpentry, that kind of stuff."

My face gets hot and my throat closes up. I look away from both of them.

Todd keeps talking, "Guess he didn't want to be a farmer either. Want to know where he moved to?"

Again the one word tumbles out, "No." No to that and no to all of this. This conversation. This whole night. That whole part of my life.

He smiles and toasts me with his Vernors. "Sure. Yeah. All on your own. Just how you wanted it, then. Huh?" Then he turns to Josie. "You guys must have met here, in the city, huh?"

Josie looks from Todd to me then back and forth. Finally she rescues me by talking, "Yep. I saved her hair from a bad color job."

It wasn't bad color, it was a horrible, disgusting, embarrassment of bright orange streaks. Something I tried to get away from myself.

While I'm standing there, dumbstruck, Josie talks for both of us. "I figured that anybody who had hair like that needed a friend. After I saved her hair, she took me to the mall to look at clothes and then she bought us lattes at Starbucks. A couple of weeks later she brought her friend Riana in to get her hair done. The three of us have been hanging out together ever since."

"Cool. Girl stuff."

I sit there a while, listening to Josie and Todd chit-chat about nothing. Finally, Josie runs out of steam. Todd fumbles around with his hands until deciding to give us both hugs. She seems fine with it but for me it's really awkward because the last time I hugged him was after he'd agreed to be the best man at my wedding that never happened. Finally he lumbers his way out, the brown of his jacket disappearing behind all the tweed suits.

"Was that kind of tense or what?" she asks.

Leave it to Josie to be direct. "Yeah. But it's no big deal."

She picks up the cigar she'd set aside and relights it. After a few puffs she slides a look at me and lifts an eyebrow. "Have any more to add 'cause it seems like I'm missing something. Who's Waylon?"

"Guy from back home."

"Yeah. I guessed that part." She taps her cigar. "And?"

"And we broke up."

"Don't want to talk about it?"

I shake my head, trying to look casual like it's no big deal that humiliation and shame follow me around like twin ghosts, passing on the judgment and gossip of a whole town.

She takes another puff and I think she's going to press me for more but she doesn't.

I know now it's only a matter of time before I have to come to terms with what happened at home and go back and undo the one lie I left behind.

Chapter Fourteen

Don't be a Fool This April

Saturday March 31st – Short-term Goals for today –
1. Throw away trash covering countertop
2. Throw away rotting fruit in fridge
3. Throw away the unopened bank statements
4. Avoid thinking about Waylon
5. Avoid acknowledging that dark cloud of judgment floating around me
6.
7.

Okay. I admit it.

Some of the seminar did rub off on me. And that kick in the ass from running into Todd, yeah, that stirred me up for sure.

When I'd arrived in Detroit I'd been full of determination. I'd gotten an apartment and a job, signed up for school, even had gone to class that whole semester. Where did that motivation go? What the hell happened? Never mind. I don't have to answer those questions. I am upright and dressed before ten o'clock on this rainy weekend morning. If it weren't for the rain, I'd be able to open the window and get rid of some of the smell drifting up from downstairs. Whatever he is cooking down there smells like old man feet.

I pull my scented candle closer.

Josie made me buy the loud lady's *Optional Handout Packet*. So I've read that and even started filling in some of the worksheets. I like lists, I excel at short-term planning, and I always like to do the easiest thing first, so here I am. If only I could think of some more essential tasks to add to my list of short-term goals. Perhaps something more elevated than throwing away trash. I let my mind wander and it lands on the second part of last night. Josie and Todd. Talking.

The two worlds of my life have crashed together and I am not happy about it. I wanted them to stay separate. That way, when I am here, at home in the city where I belong, I can pretend the other place — the place I left — does not exist.

My gaze goes to the corners of the three bank statements sticking out from under the magazines. The oldest one has a coffee mug stain from when Nick and I stayed up all night watching *The Walking Dead*. One I used as a bookmark until I realized what it was. The third one is from last week. If I had the nerve to open them, they would show that I hadn't touched that account since the day I made the one deposit. I take a fortifying breath, grab them all with one tight pitch of my thumb and forefinger then carry them to the trash can by the sink.

There.

Gone.

I look back at the list. Must write something down.

My phone hums and saves me from the impending sense of failure threatening to turn me into a complete losing whiner.

"Oh, honey. I'm afraid I'm going to disappoint you today."

"Hi, Mom." I stare at the screaming white space on my goal sheet. I'm afraid I'm already disappointed.

"They had to change the date for the April Fool's Dance. Now it's April twenty-first."

"Hello? Mom? April twenty-first? Doesn't that seem kind of strange, even for out there, having an April Fool's Dance on April twenty-first?"

As usual she ignores my sarcasm. "There was a mix-up with the hall schedule."

"That's a pretty big mix-up."

"Are you real disappointed?"

Oh! This means I don't have to spend my Saturday night sitting with the farm ladies talking about who's doing what for their 4-H projects and the price of pigs at last year's county fair. I won't have to answer questions about where I buy my clothes and whether or not it's true that everyone in the city gets mugged. Best of all, I won't have to pretend not to notice when people stare. I won't have to hear those notes of assumption when they ask, '*How are you, really*?'. "I'll get over the disappointment, Mom. Really, don't worry about it."

"You'll still come for dinner?"

Won the battle but lost the war. "It won't be chicken will it?"

"No, they had problems at the processor. Machines broke down last week."

Lucky me. Lucky birds. "What time?"

After we work out the details, I hang up and examine my short-term goals. Maybe I need to think bigger.

Saturday March 31st – Long-term Goals
1.
2.
3.
4.
5.
6.
7.

It always comes back to this, doesn't it? Why do we have to know where we want to go? Why can't we just go along for the ride and wait to see where life takes us?

I like waiting. It's peaceful. Relaxing.

What's the rush?

The loud lady's words spin around my head, *'If you don't know where you want to go, you won't know when you get there.'*

I guess that's true.

If you get on a bus, but don't know which stop you want to get off at, you'll end up sitting next to some sweaty kid playing his DS for hours. Maybe even days. You'll end up panicked and desperate. Biting your nails and watching everyone out there living their lives and going places. Streets and stores will zip by – out of your reach.

Desperation doesn't go over well in Detroit. They can see it in your eyes. It's how they know you failed. I will not be desperate in Detroit. I will not go back home a failure.

So there it is. My biggest fear.

It isn't like I haven't thought about this stuff in the past. So why is it bothering me now? Even worse than before. My gaze settles on the *Optional Handout Packet*.

I look up. I see Todd's face but think about Waylon. He isn't a bad guy, just not my guy or my life.

What about Nick? Is he my guy?

No, I remind myself. I'm the one who made a point out of staying 'friends'. But what choice do I have? I'm not ready for a relationship? Look at the mess I made of the last one.

I'd like to get my hands on that annoyingly thought-provoking, bestselling author and award-winning speaker. That loud little lady may have ruined my life. Why couldn't she be friendly and encouraging and write a fun book like Helen's *Sex and the Single Girl*?

I poke my pen through one of the holes in the page and spin it around. I lean back and stare out of the rain splattered window until my phone hums again.

"Hi, is this Hayley?"

Yeah, it's me, but I have no idea who is asking.

"It's me, Caroline."

Caroline?

That name is horrifying familiar yet at the same time terrifyingly out of place. Caroline.

"From North Pointe."

The palpable touch of irritation in her tone kicks me in the shins. "Right, of course. Hi."

There is a long, clumsy pause, then she says, "Yesterday Mr. Neville told me he talked to you about the anniversary celebration we're planning."

I slide the empty sheet off my pen and smack it onto the table. "We talked a little bit. I told him a couple things."

"Like what?"

"Like some *ideas* I came up with."

"What kind of *ideas*?"

Good ones? Bad ones? How the hell should I know? "He's supposed to come back on Monday so he and I can talk some more. I didn't tell him everything I came up with."

"I think you better tell me what you're considering. So you don't make a fool of yourself by saying something really stupid."

I try to shove away the invisible insecurity blanket I have been carrying ever since I woke up and did not feel positively powerful and in control of my life. Unfortunately, it clings to me like a bad smell. So instead of keeping my mouth shut in a confident and powerful way, I sing like the caged bird I have become.

Chapter Fifteen

Birds of a Feather

"Dinner was fun last night. Like old times. Don't you think, Hayley? I'm glad you stayed overnight, honey. Your mom misses you. Ever since you moved to the city things haven't been the same. Your Aunt Sandy comes over a lot though. Takes Mom's mind off things. The house bein' so empty and all. They still worry about— Oh, right, I guess we aren't supposed to talk about you not getting married."

I take another sip of coffee from my Harold's Feed 'n Seed travel mug and try to think of something to say to my dad. Nothing comes to mind.

He nods but doesn't say anything as he turns left onto a gravel road. The brown fields, the low slant of the early morning sunshine blinking off the hood of the truck and the constant, dissatisfied clucks of the chickens crammed into the cages piled in the bed— these things remind me of my childhood.

My dad stares straight ahead and I wonder what he thinks about his life. Did he get off at the right bus stop?

Or is he still sitting on a sticky seat wondering why he never learned to read a route schedule? Does he wonder about my life?

He slows the truck when we reach the narrow, flat building and turns into a rutted driveway. "They're only open today 'cause they had to close down for a couple weeks after that problem Tom had a while back. With the machinery. I know he hates working on Sunday. Anyway, he called and said to bring the broilers in at least. Those turkeys can wait a couple days, these ones though"—he jerks his thumb over his shoulder—"well you know. Any bigger and their legs'll snap. All that meat wasted. They got everything taken care of now, the machines, so we'll have some good eating in the freezer for a couple months at least. Except I have to give Kale Ferguson seven because he knocked down our corner field last fall. That's what your mom says anyway."

Good God. Has he always been like this?

The truck crawls to a stop. He tosses the keys onto the dashboard and hops out.

I don't think my dad got off at the right bus stop, I don't think he's still on the bus. I think he's hailing a taxi in a cornfield and wondering why it's passing him by.

Have I been standing there with him? Is this sort of inability to get a grip on life genetic?

Not willing to be the girl sitting in the truck because she can't bear the sight of helpless birds being taken to their death, I swing open my door and stroll past a brown-suited man leaning against the side of the pole barn that holds whatever machinery is used to kill the birds, tear out their feathers then slip what's left of them into neat and tidy plastic bags.

While I wait beside my dad for the chipper, red-haired lady to ask the usual questions, a guy limps out of a narrow door at the end of the building and slinks over to the brown-suited man. The limper smacks a pack of cigarettes against his palm, slips one out then lights up. Both of them stare straight at me — unblinking and unbothered by the obvious fact that they are being very rude.

I roll my eyes and turn away.

My dad and I are in a line of sorts. The lady in front of us has cut three jagged holes into the lid of the cardboard box she has stuffed her ducks into then wrapped with silver duct tape. A Peking has poked its head out one of the holes and is quacking with fierce determination — *What the hell is going on here? This is fucking ridiculous. Whose bullshit idea is this, anyway?*

The portly, gray geese in the wooden crate next to the outraged duck are more dignified about being led to their deaths. They hold their chins high, refusing to squawk or honk or do whatever it is that geese do. They stare straight ahead, watching the fat man with the gut-smeared, blue plastic apron stuff shit-coated cardboard boxes into a dumpster.

"How many you got today, Carl?" the redhead asks.

My dad bends down to look into the three shallow cages he's unloaded from his Chevy. "Twenty-three. Keep 'em all whole. She hates messing with all those pieces."

For some reason the chipper woman always thinks my dad is funny. Either that or she is looking for humor in the deathly chaos she calls work.

While she and my dad are arranging a pick up time, the blue plastic apron man lumbers over and flips open the latch of the first crate. His dusty hair flops forward to stick to his forehead.

"How many?" he asks, not looking at me but staring in at the awkward broilers who are so fat that they can barely stand.

"Twenty-three."

He grabs a bird by its feet. It squawks goodbye to life as it flies upside down to land in a wire cage, this one marked with a tag showing our name.

The redhead moves past us to say, "How many?" to a couple of teenagers who, to my well-trained eye, look hung-over.

My dad and I watch as our birds get tossed from one cage to the other. All in all they had a good life. The bird pen at home is huge and they got to be outside instead of living in a one-foot square like in the big commercial places.

But is that enough?

Should they have wanted more from life?

Should they have got it?

At least they didn't have to worry about short-term and long-term goals.

Small consolation, I bet.

Avoiding the sections smeared with chicken shit, I grab one of the cages and toss it into the bed of the Chevy. My dad puts in the other two then slams the tailgate.

He props one elbow on the side of the truck. "Ready?"

In spite of the grim fog following me around ever since that positively powerful little lady teamed up with Todd to enlighten me to the glaring fact that I need to try harder if I want a better life, I lean on the opposite side of the truck and grin back at my dad. "No, I thought we could hang around here for a while." I sweep my arm in a big circle, taking in all the cages, boxes, and crates crammed with poultry awaiting their death.

My dad twists his mouth as he scans the whole scene before coming back to me with, "A Texas Chainsaw Massacre meets Deliverance sort of thing, huh. Don't have this kind of thing in the city, do ya?"

There's a new glimmer in his eyes, something I've never seen before.

I smile and he smiles back.

Chapter Sixteen

Bitchy Bosses: What Not to Do

The first Monday of the month is crappy because I have to call the deadbeats who ignored the 'nice' pay-rent-or-else reminders I sent them two weeks ago. I don't want to hear about cars that break down, bosses who don't pay—does that really happen?—or sick kids.

Why do they have to go on and on with explanations? They have to know I'll be calling them and they must know I can't do anything about crap that happens. Why don't they screen their calls so I don't have to listen to their endless excuses? Like I can do anything other than send another notice, one that is not so 'nice'.

Thankfully, I only have two deadbeats to call. I grab the phone. Instead of dialing I stare at Caroline's office door. She and Mr. Neville went in there forty minutes ago.

Please don't let them be having sex. I don't think I could hold down the coffee I drank for lunch if Ollie comes out smirking and adjusting his tie.

What else could they be doing in there with the door closed? Who closed the door anyway? Was it him or her?

Unfortunately, I forgot my list of *ideas* at home. But I do remember it. Telling them to Mr. Neville in person will be a nice touch. Right?

No time to decide, because Mr. Neville has just pushed the door open. He's smiling. It's not an I-just-had-sex-with-an-employee-who-could-end-up-suing-me smile. Thank God.

He stops in front of my desk so I set the phone down and give him my full attention, ready to tell him the great stuff I came up with.

"Two things, Hayley. You need to talk your *ideas* over with Caroline. She's on the right track with what she has come up with so far. And I need you to help her with the raffle ticket thing she came up with. Giving residents one ticket for each year they've been at North Pointe is a fantastic *idea*. And prizes. People love prizes."

My stomach bottoms out and flips over as I remember actually trusting Caroline during her surprise phone call. "Raffle thing?"

His square chin tips down while his aristocratic gaze stays fixed on my face. "It is exactly the sort of thing I was hoping you'd come up with."

I am sure my eyes are glazing over. Is it anger? Shock? I'm speechless. He isn't.

"Because Caroline is so busy, managing things, I need you to call around to the local businesses and get donations for prizes. As she pointed out, they'll be glad to donate prizes because it'll be great advertising." I shrink back as he leans over my desk to ask, "Think you can do that?"

Caroline comes bustling out. "Getting everything settled here?"

It'll be a while before everything is settled. I don't say that. I don't say anything because the only words that will come willingly out of my mouth are — *You fucking bitch you stole my idea*. But I don't think that is the helpful sort of attitude the big boss is looking for.

After throwing a smile at Caroline, Mr. Neville straightens. While he is setting his palm on her rounded shoulder and saying, "Hayley's going to help you get donations and prizes," I spot Tony slip through the side door by Caroline's office. After a quick glance at their backs, he sneaks into her sanctuary and gently pushes the door until it's almost closed.

Mr. Neville steps toward the French doors. "Caroline, let me know if you need anything else. Be a team player, Hayley, and help her out."

After the door whooshes shut, Caroline steps away, heading back to her office. The anger that started fermenting inside me a minute ago is getting smellier by the second. "Um, Caroline?"

She spins on the heel of her Payless pumps and sets her hands on her JC Penny hips. Her head tilts but as usual her over-sprayed hair remains motionless. "Yeah?"

"Did it occur to you that the raffle *idea* was mine?"

She smacks her mouth in an ugly way. "Yeah, it did. But you're only a temp. Who cares if you come up with any good *ideas*?"

The answer surprises me but it's the truth. "I do."

"Why? Really, Hayley, don't be so naïve. Think teamwork. You should be glad I told Mr. Neville

137

about the raffle. If I look good, you look good—because you work for me."

"I don't work for you, Caroline. I work for North Pointe Farms."

She scoffs. "You work for the temp agency. If you want to keep being stubborn about it, look at it this way—you do what I tell you, right?" After an annoying know-it-all silence, she adds, "See? So you do work for me." She laughs, the first time I've ever heard her laugh really loud, then says, "So start working by calling around and coming up with some prizes." She turns away, chuckling.

Oh. My. God. What. A. Bitch.

Caroline reaches for her door handle but the door flies open and smacks her forehead. The thud and her swearing are music to my ears.

"Oh, sorry, Caroline," Tony says as he curves around the door. "I didn't know you were about to open the door."

"What were you doing in my office, Tony?"

He glances over at me. "Um, hi, Hayley."

I can't decide which might be funnier, if I were inclined to find something funny which at the moment I am not, the strained look on Caroline's face or the slippery way Tony's features keep readjusting themselves.

"What were you doing in my office?"

His face settles into an all-purpose blank expression. "Looking for you?"

She puts her hands back on her hips. "I wasn't in there. How long did it take you to figure that out?"

"Not long."

"What did you want?"

"Uh…it's about that one unit."

"Which one unit?" Caroline eyes him skeptically. "You know what" — she struts past him — "I don't have time for this. Get a unit information slip from Hayley, fill it out, and put it in the maintenance memo box. I'll look it over later."

With that departing order, she slithers around her door and shuts it.

Glad to have something to take my attention off The Horrible Bitch Event, I get out of my chair and prop myself on the edge of my desk. "So what were you really doing in there?" I ask softly.

"I forgot something."

I lean forward and lift an eyebrow. "You left something in Caroline's office?"

"I got it back though."

"What did you leave in there?"

He moves away from the desk and scans the walls of the office. He stares at the cheap oil painting of Belle Isle hanging by the door. "What was Mr. Neville here for?"

"That anniversary thing."

He looks from the discount art to me. "How's that going?"

I get it. You quit asking me, I'll quit asking you. To finish the circle of let's pretend, I dig out a unit information form from my desk drawer. "You want one of these?"

"Yeah, I guess I better."

Chapter Seventeen

Keeping the Friend in Friendship

Five days later, it's Saturday morning and Nick and I are staring at Pastry Pete donuts.

"You taste these three and tell me which is best." Abdul points at Nick. "You too. I need someone to taste them, tell me which is best."

I look over the three donuts, each on its own plate. One has blue frosting with white and red sprinkles, one is a red donut with white frosting that's striped with blue glaze and one looks like some little kid made it. I point to the third one. "What's the deal with that one?"

"My niece, she made it. Cute, huh?"

"Would you want to eat it?"

He throws one hand in the air and waves at the plates with the other. "Who cares what I want to eat?"

"You know what I want to know," Nick says, sitting up and leaning toward Abdul.

"What? What you want to know, big man?"

"Why you call this place Pastry Pete's when your name's Abdul?"

This time Abdul waves both his hands. "You want to go to Pastry Abdul's?"

Nick nods and his gaze shifts back to the row of donuts. "Okay. I get it. Eat one, Hayley."

Abdul's little brother steps up to refill my coffee cup then stares at me. *What is this, the Pillsbury Bake-Off?*

I tap the plate holding the one with the multi-layered frosting and mounds of sprinkles. "Are you serious about that one?"

"You don't think so?" Abdul frowns. "You don't think I am serious with that one?"

"With that one?" I shake my head. "No, I don't think so."

"Okay, no. I'm not serious about that one." When Abdul's little brother grabs it and takes a bite, Abdul says, "There. Now you try the others. They are good, you'll see. But which is best?"

I take a bite of the red one first, rinse my palate with coffee then try the other. Poor Abdul. "They taste the same."

"Okay, the food coloring for the red one, it makes no difference. But you tell me, which looks better? More American?"

Nick rubs his chin, his hand grazing over his sexy weekend stubble. "Go with the red one. That you won't see anywhere else."

"Yes! We go with that one. It's the best, yeah?"

Abdul reaches out to scoop up the plates, but I stop him by swooping them aside. "We'll finish eating and let you know for sure."

The brothers laugh as they head back to the counter.

I push the red donut toward Nick with a smile. "You like it, you eat it."

"Haven't really talked to you in a while. You haven't even posted anything on Facebook. It's like you're in exile." He takes a bite then talks around it, "How was the dance? Have a good time with the hometown fellas?"

Does he care if I danced with other guys? Or is he simply teasing me, trying to give me a hard time for fun? I stare at him for a minute but can't tell which it is. There's nothing there except that same steady brown-eyed gaze. When he brushes some crumbs from his lower lip, I look at his fingers and mouth and a thick flicker of lust curls through me. I look away as I answer, "The dance was postponed. Rescheduled for April twenty-first. Mix-up with the VFW hall scheduling."

He kicks my foot under the table and keeps at it until I look at him. "They rescheduled an April Fool's Day Dance?" He drinks his coffee with mock thoughtfulness. "You going to take Clifford to the non-April Fool's Dance?"

"What?" Honestly, it takes me a minute to even remember who that guy is. "Oh, no."

He kicks me under the table again. "Clifford's busy?"

My face feels so hot, I know I'm blushing like an idiot. "I have no idea what he's doing," I say, trying to sound casual but not pulling it off. That lust is melting my mind.

When Nick keeps staring at me, the images of those dirty dreams drifting through my mind get so vivid I swear he knows what I'm thinking.

I look longingly at the door. This would be a good time for Riana to show up. This thing Nick and I are doing, pretending that nothing ever happened, is getting more and more difficult because I keep looking at his hands and his mouth and getting all hot in the face.

When I don't add anything more about Clifford, he smugly pops the last of his red donut into his mouth. We eat in silence until both our donuts are gone and the only evidence of the All-American Taste-Off are the empty plates dotted with crumbs. Silence hangs over the table, unwelcome and uncomfortable. I try to chase it away. "How's work?"

He shrugs then shoves his plate toward the edge of the table.

I cast a sideways glance at him, thinking maybe I ought to come right out and say something about that night, and all the awkwardness that's followed, but Riana walks through the door.

Or is she limping?

"Hey there," she says, sliding in next to me.

I point at her sweaty self. "I thought we were going to ride bikes together."

She frowns and nods at Abdul's little brother when he asks if she wants coffee. "We are but I wanted to do two laps at Kensington first." She pulls a sheet of crumpled paper out of her pocket, smoothes it out then puts it on the table.

I pick it up and read the training schedule outlined in neat columns. "You get it off the race site?"

Her mouth flattens and she shakes her head. "Peter sent it to me. I think he might be trying to make me quit."

"You're kidding," I reply, letting more disgust sound in my voice than I meant to.

Riana doesn't say anything, she fiddles with the salt and pepper shakers.

I try to fold the sheet up but it's too rumpled so I slide it over to Nick.

"Why would he want to make you quit?" he asks.

Riana scowls. "It turns out he was training for a bike rally a couple years ago. It wasn't a charity thing like mine. It was the same distance and he, um, didn't finish."

"What does that have to do with you?"

Riana grabs the paper, wads it up then stuffs it into the pocket of her fleece vest. "He doesn't think I'm in good enough shape. He says I'm going to end up making a fool of myself because I won't be able to make it to the end."

Nick cocks his head. "That's crap."

"He's wrong," I say softly.

After a pause, Nick shakes his head. "Sorry to be so blunt— What's his problem?"

Riana pushes her coffee cup around. "He's just trying to help."

I offer an explanation to Nick, "Peter is competitive."

He nods and says, "Maybe if you explained again why you're doing it, he'd get it and support you."

I'm pretty sure that it wouldn't make any difference to a guy like Peter but I don't see the point in going on with it. He's a part of Riana's life and she has to deal with him in her own way.

"Speaking of competitive people." Nick looks at me. "You take care of Caroline yet?"

Riana picks up the thread. "Yeah, what's up with that? That girl could use a good square smack in the face."

They're both right but I don't say that. Instead I say, "I got some good prizes for the raffle. Tanning packages, a free dinner at that French restaurant over by the Fox Theatre."

"She's still going to get credit for your *idea*."

"I'll come up with something else. Besides, it isn't such a big deal."

Even after the words are out in the open I'm still not buying them. I've been trying to sell them to myself all week—it's not working. Nick looks right at me and smiles. Not a smug or a cocky one, but a sweet one. It takes some of the sting out of Caroline's horribleness.

I smile back then toss money on the table to pay for our coffee. "You ready to go?"

"I guess." Riana slides out and wobbles toward the door. "You coming, Nick?"

"No. I gotta go help my mom paint her garage."

"I'd rather do that," she says.

"No, you'd rather pedal yourself into even better shape so you can beat all those other bikers' asses."

"I just want to finish," Riana replies a little too quickly.

I quirk my eyebrow at her.

"I only want to do the ride to raise money for kids. And for the challenge." She pushes against the door.

Nick steps over to assure Abdul that the red one is the best then catches up with us at the door. "Riana, has it ever occurred to you that you don't have to prove anything to anybody?"

Nick's right. Unable to keep my mouth shut, I cut in with, "Peter is *important*. He's worried about his *reputation*. If his girlfriend looks stupid, then he looks stupid."

Riana defends him, as usual. "He's not really like that. You don't know him like I do."

Something I am really glad about.

"When is the ride again?" Nick asks.

"May twenty-sixth and twenty-seventh."

"Let me know where the finish line is because I want to be there to see you streak across it."

"What if I don't?" she moans.

"You will," he says firmly.

A pleased smile lifts Riana's mouth. "Thanks, Nick."

Nick lingers by the door. "See ya, Hayley."

I feel all goofy and girly and for a second it's normal between us. "Bye, Nick."

Electricity skitters through me as I grab Riana's sleeve. "Come on."

* * * *

Three hours later, Riana and I are flopped on our backs gazing at a cloudless sky. Expansive stretches of blue are damn unusual in Michigan, so even though it hurts our eyes to keep looking up, we do. It's a Michigan thing. Londoners would understand.

"You can do it, Riana. You could win that race on determination alone."

"I don't care if I win! It isn't supposed to be a race," she grumbles.

"I know that and you know that but he doesn't know that."

"Let's not talk about it anymore."

After a while, Riana breaks our quiet. "Do you think if I wasn't with Peter—not that I'm not going to be with him—but, do you think that if I wasn't, Josie would set me up with her dating thing?"

Interesting line of thinking.

Even though I could take a guess at the answer to her question, I sidestep my hunch with, "Did you ask her?"

"No." She weakens and drops her arm across her face to block out the eye-piercing rays. "I didn't want to put her on the spot."

"You're too nice."

"Even if I were, which I'm not, what would that have to do with anything?"

"Nothing, I guess." I give in and fold my arm across my face.

She smacks my shoulder. "If you're so un-nice why don't you expose Caroline? Tell that Mr. Neville she stole your *idea*."

Even though it's a lie, I say, "It doesn't matter."

"If it were me, it would matter."

"You're driven. Me, I don't care about that stuff." Either I don't care or I'm not woman enough to stand up for myself.

Chapter Eighteen

Give Him What He Wants, Maybe

Saturday night, I'm at my place, on the couch with Nick and I'm so tense I could snap.

"Really, Nick, you do not want to go. It's an April Fool's Day Dance on April twenty-first. What does that tell you?" I wave my hands. "That you don't want to go."

Nick nudges me with his foot. "I want to meet your parents. I want to see all the people you're always complaining about."

I groan and put my hands on my head. Why doesn't he let this whole thing go and grab me the way he did the other night? What is keeping him from kissing me? Didn't he like it? Doesn't he know that I did?

"Are you taking another video guy?"

My nervousness spills out as a laugh then I fall silent when I see the way he's looking at me with his eyes all dark and serious.

"Shall I take that as a no?" he asks, crossing one leg over the other and still staring at me.

"Definitely. No way."

"I'm glad he's a no. What should I wear?"

"Nothing."

"Okay but I would've thought you'd want me to blend in."

The image of his hard dick is followed by one of his bare chest. Before I make a fool of myself by jumping on him, I banish it. He starts rubbing my shoulders and I lean back into the circular motion of his warm, strong hands. Yes, he makes me feel good in ways I never have. But I can't take chances. "You aren't going," I say.

"Give me a good reason."

With no convincing lies handy, I offer part of the truth. "I'm afraid if you go, you won't want to be my friend anymore. It'll be like peeking behind the curtain and realizing that I'm all bells and whistles."

"Are you trying to tell me you're a short, bald man wearing a bright green suit and top hat?"

No. I am, like every girl looking to find herself, Dorothy. And until I do get myself together there is no way I can take Nick anywhere near my hometown.

He sighs and pushes himself upright. "Really, Hayley. What's the big deal?"

Before I can come up with a reply to that, my phone vibrates. I tumble off the couch to get it. There is a ruckus in the background. When my mom finally gets to me, she's laughing and having a grand time—on a Saturday night no less.

"Hey, Mom."

"I just wanted to tell you, before you even ask," my mom is saying, "*he* won't be at the dance on Saturday."

I glance at Nick and he's smiling. My heart does a hard flip as I try to tell if he can hear what she's saying. I lean back, hoping to put more distance between my mom's words and Nick's ears.

"None of the Walkers will be there. I checked. I figured you'd want to know. So it's all settled."

Oh no, it isn't. It hasn't been settled now, even after almost a year, and it isn't ever going to be settled unless I take care of that one last thing. Make that visit I never made.

There's a shuffling sound then she asks, "Do you want to talk to your cousin? He has another one of those silly poems you like."

I open my mouth to say sure why not, but I don't have to bother because Frankie is already saying, "Hello." Then asking, "Ready to hear my new limerick?"

"I heard you won some money with that other one."

"Yeah, fifty dollars."

Someday, when he is older and can appreciate the potential growth experience that comes from making a total ass of oneself on St. Patrick's Day, I'll tell him how I fared with his funny poem.

Nick is staring at me and mouthing something. I can't tell what it is. When he hops up to raise his arms and spin around with an invisible girl, I'm pretty sure it has something to do with the dance. Stubborn guy. I shift so I can't see him.

"So, you want to hear the new one now or wait until you come for the dance? I don't get to go to the dance but I'm sure I'll see you. Right?"

"Why don't you tell me now. I can't handle suspense."

"I gotta do it fast. Before they get back inside. Ready?"

"Yep."

Same as last time, he giggles then clears his throat.

"There once was a man from Nantucket – "

"Frankie," I cut him off, "are you gonna get yourself in trouble?"

He chuckles softly. "I only promised not to say the one about Bart. I made this one up last night so she hasn't had a chance to tell me not to say it yet."

I sigh. Who can argue with kid logic? "Go ahead."

"There once was a man from Nantucket.
Who ate all the clams in his bucket.
He went to the shore,
To look for some more,
But then said aw hell, fuckit."

He laughs at his cleverness and, I suspect, the way he managed to get fuck into a limerick that's not about sex. I chuckle with him until he says, "The one about Bart is even better."

"You can tell me sometime when we're alone."

"You're cool, Hayley."

"Thanks, Frankie. You're cool too."

After I assure him I don't want to talk to my mom again, we say goodbye and hang up. As soon as I set the phone down Nick pokes me with his foot. "Everything okay at home?"

"Oh sure. My cousin just wanted to tell me his new limerick."

Nick's mouth curves into the wicked smile that always makes me goofy. "You worried I'm going to try and make you remember it? Is that why you look so nervous?"

Despite my dread, I laugh. "Never again."

"You know you're going to take me. Who else is going to keep you out of trouble?"

I smirk to hide my apprehension. "Keep me out? It was you who got me into that mess."

"I know. I need to redeem myself." The cocky smile fades and for a split second he looks as vulnerable as I feel. "And...you know it'll be more fun if I'm there."

Fun? *Will spending an entire night being afraid the world will unravel be fun?*

Chapter Nineteen

Stand and Deliver

Tuesday afternoon, Mr. Neville, my lunch companion, tosses some money next to the restaurant bill then stands up. "Walk with me, Hayley," he says, then strides through the restaurant, assuming that I'll scramble out of my chair and follow.

I do. I stare at his pinstriped back and wonder for the twenty-seventh time why he invited me to lunch.

He pauses at the door long enough for me to catch up. "You like working with us?"

He's serious?

Does 'us' include Caroline?

Hmmmmmm.

Riana, Josie and I do have a shit load of fun laughing about her.

Mr. Neville is staring at me, his hazel eyes unblinking. Answer time.

"Yes, of course I like working with...you...and everybody else...and Caroline."

His aristocratic chin dips down. "Good. Good."

Why do I feel like I'm talking to somebody's nervous father?

"Let's walk."

We stroll down Kerchival and it's a typical mid-April day in Gross Pointe, Michigan. There is only enough sunlight creeping through the clouds to assure me that the sun does exist and that somewhere on the planet earth somebody might even be getting enough of it to really enjoy it.

We stroll along, side by side, him saying nothing and me wondering what the hell is going on. Mr. Neville never paid much attention to me before. I preferred it that way, because then I could create a personality for him. One that I am realizing more and more by the minute is much more sophisticated and worldly than the one he's got. Because in actuality, he is a small-time businessman who buys his suits at The Men's Wearhouse and probably waits until twilight to golf. I bet he's divorced. His wife took the kids and now he spends his nights at the bar for old guys crying into his cheap mixed drinks.

No. He's not that bad. I'm being nasty.

Still walking, we pass by a dry cleaners then turn a corner.

"You've been with us for a while now," he says.

I nod but the uncomfortableness of the situation keeps me silent. I'm hating myself for being too much of a lame ass to tell Mr. Neville that Caroline stole my raffle ticket *idea* and resenting him for not knowing what a bitch she is.

"You in college, Hayley? What are your long-term goals? Where do you see yourself in five years?"

Him too? What is it with goals? It's like a cult or something.

Visions of empty lists dance in my head. Did that loud lady put him up to this? More importantly, why does Ollie care what my goals are?

We pass by an outdoor café, where a few ridiculous people are sitting at iron tables and pretending it's nice outside. Ollie's staring at me out of the corner of his eye, waiting. Lists? Goals? College? I don't even know where to start. "I-I was going to Wayne County."

"Full-time?"

"I was full-time, but, um, it gets expensive and, well…" I grit my teeth. I'm lame. Boring. Weak.

"No need to explain, I understand. I have a couple kids in school and those bills…" He lets the rest float off into space and chuckles like we're two chums relating to each other.

If the peculiar, unnerving reaction in my stomach weren't so strong, I might ask him about those kids but this whole situation is just too damn awkward.

I stare at the bricked sidewalk. I'm pretty sure something notable is coming. What though? What am I missing here?

About this time, we've reached his light brown Oldsmobile so we climb in. He drives without talking. It's a quick trip back to North Pointe, which should be a good thing except I can't get past the feeling that some great opportunity is passing me by.

"I'm glad we had this time together, Hayley," he says, after we wave at Mr. Hastings. "I think I have a good feel for where you're headed."

Mind telling me? "Thanks for lunch, Mr. Neville."

"Sure thing, Hayley." He gets out then comes around to open my door. "I'm glad we had a chance to talk."

Something inside me snaps and words tumble out, "I have an *idea*, Mr. Neville."

He blinks with surprise. "An *idea*?"

"Yeah. I mean, yes, I do." I chatter on about how after seeing the route map for Riana's bike rally I realized that those crazy people would be pedaling right past Bob Hastings' charming security booth right about the time we'd be doing the raffle drawing. "And I think we should find a way to tie the two things together."

Seconds creep along until he responds, "Excellent, Hayley. Write it up. Email me a memo. See you later."

Email Mr. Neville? He wants a memo from me? Well! Isn't that something?

Light on my feet, I wave goodbye then scurry past the fading daffodils. Up by the door some tulips are getting ready to bloom. Will they be red? I hope so. I love red tulips.

Who's whistling? Oh, it's me.

With a wide, sweeping gesture, I swing the door open yet stop short.

Crap.

Caroline is sitting at my desk. Her stupid smile keeps me rooted by the door.

"Did you have a nice lunch with Mr. Neville?" she asks.

Is this a test question? "I had salmon. He had some kind of sandwich."

She leans back in my chair and scans my desk. "I told Mr. Neville that we've been busy working on The Celebration. That's coming up, you know."

How could I forget? I'd been on the phone for hours digging up prizes for the raffle.

Anger propels me into the room. "Neat thing how you got credit for my *idea*."

"Your *idea*?" she scoffs, dropping forward.

The nerve of that bitch. "The raffle?"

"Oh. We already went over that. I'm the manager, Hayley." When I keep glaring at her, she adds, "It's about teamwork and what's best for the company."

Best for the company? What is this, Russia? Even they don't really believe in communism anymore.

"You should be thanking me for telling Mr. Neville how helpful you've been. You really have got us some great giveaways. Good work." She slides out of my chair and rests her ample hip on the corner of my mostly bare desk.

"I told him about this other *idea* I came up with and he wants me to get started on it right away."

"Oh. Well. Good for you." She picks up one of my pens and points it at me. "Have you been using my computer to go online?"

Nasty thing that she is, she isn't even going to ask what my *idea* is. "No." *But Tony has.*

She tosses the pen down. "You sure?"

"Yep."

"Who else has access to my computer?"

Everybody. I'm not a rat so I shrug. "Ask Mr. Neville about getting a password. I have one."

"You do?" After she sizes me up with a cunning once-over, her mouth flattens and she sweeps herself toward her door.

Was that an earth tremor? Or a slight shift in our employee-boss relationship?

Chapter Twenty

Cyber Secrets: Stay Safe

Thursday afternoon, Josie, Riana and I are shopping. I'm trying to find something to wear to what I'm now thinking of as The Fool's Fools Dance. We're scouting around one of the second-hand shops in Royal Oak, and Josie keeps laughing at the retro dresses.

Josie hangs up a floral number she thinks is especially funny and Riana is saying it looks like it came from one of *Justified's* wardrobe trailers. While they're laughing hysterically, I'm thinking the dresses look like the ones my neighbors wore to school.

After a while, we're at the counter. The salesgirl, who's sporting a pink wig with yellow ducky barrettes clipped across the bangs, rings up my shirt — a glittery T-shirt that says *Charlie's Angels* across the front.

I drag them into a Starbucks, we get grande lattes — with whole milk thank you very much — then squeeze into one of the tiny tables on the sidewalk. Riana sits down more slowly than Josie and me.

"My sister's article comes out next week," Josie is saying. "They're trying to tie it in with some other pieces on singles in the city."

As I listen to Josie talk about her sister's article, the hairs on the back of my neck stand up. Something isn't right, there has to be a catch somewhere. Josie has been burned by her sister one too many times. "Have you read it? The article?" I ask.

"No, she told me what it's about."

Josie is too unconcerned. Riana and I exchange glances. She's worried about the fall out too.

"She won't use my name, right?"

"Of course not."

I sip my latte, doubtful. Using my name really wouldn't add anything to the piece — unless she's out to get me because in her deluded brain she thinks I messed things up with The Kid.

The possibility is too much to ignore. "Did she ever get in touch with Kid Rock?"

Josie sips her coffee then shakes her head. "If she did, she didn't mention it. I guess she stopped caring about it."

Doubtful.

We fall silent. Me stewing alternately between my job hellishness and Josie's sister. Riana is probably stewing over Peter's stupid competitiveness. Josie? Who knows what's going on inside her head.

"Get any more clients?" I ask.

"Didn't have time to call people back last week. We've been really busy at work. With Easter coming…everybody wants to look, oh I don't know, Easterish." She pokes at the lid of her coffee. We sip our coffees and watch the Royal Oak people stroll by.

Royal Oak used to be a humdrum kind of place. Now it's a suburban hot spot. Goth kids slump on benches and overpriced restaurants fill the sidewalks of Main Street with quaint outdoor tables.

Riana and Josie start commenting on the alarming number of hipsters and how it's impossible to tell if they're serious with the work boots they're wearing or not. Did they buy them distressed or did they actually do enough work to earn the scratches and tears? While I'm listening to them, my phone buzzes.

What time do you want me to pick you up?

Nick is so stubborn.

I didn't say yes.

If I was being truthful with myself, I'd admit I bought that glittery shirt because I knew Nick would like it. He loves *Charlie's Angels*. But me and honesty haven't been on good terms in a while.

His response is immediate.

I'm saying yes for both of us.

A hot wave of panic rushes through me.

"What's up, Hayley?"

I look up and find both Josie and Riana staring at me. Their eyebrows are pulled in and the smiles from earlier are totally gone.

"Oh, nothing. Just, um, just nothing."

"You sure?" Riana asks.

"Yep. It's just me being PMS-y. Everything is a big deal when it isn't." I laugh it off, but inside I'm a tattered mess. I turn off my phone, toss it into my purse and go back to listening to Riana and Josie's blow-by-blow fashion commentary.

* * * *

Friday morning at work, Tony slinks in and scans the empty space around my desk. "Caroline around?"

I'm tempted to tell him she's hiding under my desk, then I remember my promise not to be so hard on Tony. Still, he's up to something, I can tell.

"No, she's at some meeting or something. I don't know, lately she just leaves and doesn't say where she's going."

He inches toward her office.

"She knows somebody has been messing with her computer, Tony. What gives?"

His gaze darts to her door, skims across the floor to his feet then creeps up to my face. "Promise you won't tell?"

"I already didn't tell. She asked me if I was using it. I told her I wasn't and that I didn't know who was. So the way I see it, you already owe me an explanation."

Deciding whether or not to trust me, he rocks back on his heels. As I am already an accomplice, he is a little late I think.

"I live with someone."

I stare expectantly, silently telling him I want the whole story.

"And I'm sort of seeing somebody else."

Oh, this is good. More silence from me.

"The somebody I've been, well…kind of seeing, is working on a website. It should be live any day now. And the thing is, I'm afraid to use the computer at home. I don't want the person I live with to know I was on the website."

The way he enunciates website really gets my attention. "What kind of website?"

"I submitted some pictures for it." He steps toward Caroline's office. "That's what I do, take pictures."

"You're a photographer?"

He bobs his head several times. "That's right, I'm a photographer. And I just want to see if the pictures I submitted got used." With that, he dodges through Caroline's doorway.

I know there is more to this story but I'll have to dig out the next installment later. Because I was actually in the middle of doing something before Tony rolled in.

The whole goal writing business has stayed with me so I'm working on the list of things I need to accomplish for the day. A couple of them are left over tasks from an underproductive Thursday. According to the pages in the Optional Handout Packet—now clipped neatly in a binder—it is okay to have incomplete tasks as long as they stay on the list.

Here's my latest.

Friday, April 20th

1. Return call from Ms. Kulpa — the woman who is organizing the bike race.

2. Decide which prizes will be the top prizes for the raffle and number the others — I wish I could screw that up somehow so Caroline would end up looking like the loser she is. Alas, it is too late.

3. Find a new company to do the end of lease cleaning and repair on the units — Thanks Caroline for dumping that one on me.

4. Call Riana at lunch — She can complain to me about her training.

5. Call Josie after lunch.

5. Avoid thinking about how stressed I'll be 34 hours from now — Gave in and agreed to let Nick come to the Fool's Fools Dance.

Only three of the tasks are work related but that's a big improvement for somebody who didn't even plan for the next five minutes a couple of weeks ago. Writing things down does make me feel like I'm more in control of my life. The tidy lines and careful printing look so orderly. Feeling encouraged, I try some long-term goals again.

I grab the pen and dig out a fresh sheet of paper.

Five Year Plan –
1.
2.
3.

The blank page giggles at me. Not a nice, friendly giggle. An evil one. I need to try a different approach. I draw some curlicues across the top of the page and some neat little graphics across the bottom.

Better, but not quite there. It needs something else.

So I add some swirly things around the edges and curvy things around the numbers. It looks pretty good.

Creative and full of energy.

Ha. Ha! Who's giggling now?

I look again at what I drew and realize the page is winning again.

Because apparently for the next five years I will be under the attack of a fleet of evil snails. After the deranged snakes get done with me.

I wad it up then toss it out.

And regroup, rethink and try again.

Things I will Get Done in the Next Six Months –
1.

2.

3.

Should I move from mostly self-help magazine articles to mostly self-help books? Go to another seminar? No. I don't think so... Find another guy to hook up with?

Several long minutes march through time while I'm thinking, or rather trying to think, about the direction of my life. New idea!

Things I will NOT Get Done in the Next Six Months –

1. I will not let Caroline take advantage of me again – Yep. That's right.

2. I will not be shamed by my family and/or the country people back home – Are embarrassment and shame the same thing?

3. I will not give up trying to figure out who I am and what it is I want to do with my life.

Where did that come from? Crap.

That seems awfully serious. I glance over my shoulder to see if someone snuck in and wrote that – someone who isn't me.

Nobody there – and I'm the one holding the pen.

I sigh and ease back in my chair.

Chapter Twenty-One

Cool Looks for Hot Farm Girls

Saturday evening, warm, moist, spring air ruffles my hair while I wait in Nick's truck, staring at the corner store like an anxious hunting dog. He thought I was kidding about stopping to get a little nip before going to face the crowd at the Fool's Fools Dance, then when I grabbed the steering wheel and nearly made him drive into a ditch, he got the idea.

About the time I hope he may have ducked out on the whole belated April Fool's Day Dance and snuck out of the back door, he shuffles out dragging his heels across the parking lot and gripping a brown paper package in his left hand. His right hand is stuffed into his pocket.

I lean toward him and shout, "Are you practicing to be a good ole boy?"

That makes him laugh. "Yessim."

I stretch across the seat to open his door. "Shut up and get in."

He climbs in with that goofy smile still on his face. "I didn't see Bo and Luke in there. They must be out chasin' Boss Hog."

I grab the bottle and yank it out of his grasp. "Bo and Luke?"

"*The Dukes of Hazzard.*"

"Oh. My. God. Shut up."

He's staring at the bag. I peel the paper off.

The all too familiar red and orange label with the glowing flames. "Hot Damn!?"

"Yessim." He bobs his head then goes on using the stupidest country accent I have ever heard. "The girl behind the counter told me it's what chicks in this neck of the woods like best."

In spite of the cloak of shame resting on my shoulders, I laugh. "I bet she did. Did she get your phone number too?"

"No, ma'am."

I swivel off the cap. "Cut that ma'am shit out. Right now."

"Oh"—he leers at me—"you're tougher than the country girls I grew up with."

I stop glaring at him long enough to take a healthy swig.

"Geez, Hayley. You could have at least waited until we got out of the parking lot."

I cast him another sidelong glance, this one laced with vulnerability, down another shot then wipe my mouth with the back of my hand. The inexplicable expression that spreads across his face catches me so completely off guard I have to look away and pretend I didn't notice. And that sudden heat? Must be the alcohol.

He starts driving. I hold onto the bottle and gaze out of the window until he pulls off on a side road. He creeps along until he parks in the shadow of some trees about a half mile from the VFW hall.

"Give me some of that before you drink it all," he says, snatching for the bottle. Our hands get tangled and a weird zip shoots up my arm. I relinquish the bottle as Kid Rock's *Cowboy* comes on the radio.

"It's your boy, Hayley." Nick flashes me a grin then takes a long drink. After he swallows, he lowers the bottle to his lap and howls louder than the music. "Hot damn, that's some good shit."

He looks so crazy, I laugh hard enough to shake off some of the dread I'd been holding tightly to all week. "Pass it on over, let's put that bad boy to bed."

About a minute later, we pull into the VFW lot, and Nick glides around looking for a place to park. He finds a space behind a red F-150 pickup truck that has a white window decal of a woman's silhouette on the driver's side. She's flexing her biceps and grinning from beneath wind-blown hair. It reads—'Fear This City Boy'. Nick stares at it then at the one on the passenger side that reads—'Redneck Girl'. He points and laughs. "I feel right at home."

I should but I don't. I can already feel the weight of the stares and hear the whispers of rumors. I turn away from Nick as I cringe, feeling like maybe I should tell him about Waylon. It'd be better if he heard it from me but my stomach turns sour just thinking about saying the words aloud. My own stupidity and shame swirl in my heart and make my chest hot.

I'm just not ready. Yet.

We pay at the door then zip straight in. All of a sudden it's like we don't know each other. We stand there, looking around, not saying anything.

The band is setting up on the low stage in the center of the hall and some country song I don't recognize is wailing from the tall, high-tech, black speakers sitting like 2001 Space Odyssey monoliths on the battered dance floor.

Out of the corner of my eye, I watch Nick scan the crowd—clusters of narrow-shouldered, old men wearing plaid dress shirts and pressed blue jeans, ladies with feathered bangs and ponytails. I guess I don't have to worry about anyone else showing up in a glittery *Charlie's Angels* T-shirt.

Then again, maybe I do.

"So where's Mom and Dad?" Nick nudges me. "When do I get to say hi to the 'rents?"

"They usually hide in the back, so the only way to find them is to actually go looking for them."

He sets his hand at the base of my spine as we start walking.

For a second that electricity comes back but then I spot my dad in a back corner with his arm draped around my mom's shoulders. In a couple of seconds he'll say something to make all the other couples laugh—there, he just did—then he'll shake my mom's shoulders—he just did—because she's laughing with everyone else.

When I nudge Nick in their direction, Duane Sod half rises out of his chair, points his fat finger at me and hollers, "Here she is, Carl. And look there, she's brought a date."

For some inane reason, everyone thinks that's the most hilarious thing they've heard in ages, because they're all guffawing and chortling while they give Nick the once-over. Explaining that he's a friend would just be asking for more speculation so I let the misunderstanding go.

The men get done looking him over and go back to their Buds and Bud Lites. The womenfolk let their gazes linger.

"Hi, everybody," I offer lamely. "This is Nick."

"Hey there, Nick," says Duane, as he reaches across the table to stick out his pudgy mitt.

"Hey there, everybody." Nick waves to the mob with one hand while he shakes Duane's hand with the other.

"Nick lives in the city too," my mom says to the crowd. Then she goes on to explain he's from a country town as well, as though that alone makes him okay.

Duane stares at Nick and asks, "You play ball in high school?"

Everyone except a short, dark-haired man I don't recognize, leans forward and listens for the reply. They're all measuring him up against Waylon, football captain and son of the wealthiest farmer on our side of town, the man who would've been my husband if I hadn't jilted him at the altar. "Football?" Nick shakes his head. "No, sir."

"Basketball?"

"No."

Duane is determined. "Wrestle?"

Nick glances at me. "Nope. I'm an engineering student at Wayne," he says.

They all give him a blank stare. Then, once those dissipate, they smile and nod.

The short, dark-haired man slips out of his seat to pull a couple of chairs over to the table. "Have a seat, you two." He grins at me, and I try to place his accent.

Nick and I say thanks at the same time then we bump into each other when we reach for the same chair — the one farthest away from everybody else.

A dim-witted, nervous laugh bubbles out of me as I grab a chair and sit down.

"So, honey," my mom is saying to me but looking from my face to Nick's, "what have you two been doing?"

Drinking schnapps on the side of the road.

My dad and all his friends are staring at me. "Um...we—"

"We just got here." Nick sits then turns to my mom and smiles.

I nod idiotically. "Yeah and we, Nick and I, just got here. And, um, here we are."

My mom giggles, and Duane Sod smacks his legs.

Parents are supposed to be standing in the kitchen yelling or seated behind the steering wheel. They are not supposed to be sitting around with their friends getting, well, tipsy.

It's not natural.

Nick isn't bothered by the disequilibria that has me off balance. He's talking to my dad and the short man who's holding his palms about four feet off the ground. Nick is shaking his head and laughing. "No way," he says, between laughs.

I shift closer.

"I don't believe it," Nick's saying.

I can't help myself. "What? Don't believe what?"

My dad tips his head toward the short, dark-haired man. "Emilio here is a rancher. And a promoter. He's up from Cisco, Texas. Do you know where that is? Probably not. It's a real small town"—he glances over at Emilio—"on the western side of the state?" After Emilio nods, he rambles on some more and I pretty much tune him out to stare at the people milling around.

In my mind, I'm rolling one hand over the other, wishing he would get to the point. *Hello! Dad. Come back on around to the land of people who make sense when they talk.*

I check Emilio out. He has a mustache and is wearing a new-looking Tigers baseball cap. Texas explains the accent, I guess. What could this little man, who comes from a place called Cisco — in Texas! — be promoting that is so unbelievable?

"...to meet with the county fair commission. He's been talking to people all around the Detroit area, him and some of the riders — your cousin, Rodney, went to college with one of them, you know — about his show and he wants to bring it, his show, up here for fair week and — "

I notice Nick staring at me. The corner of his mouth is curved up like he's sharing a little secret with — himself? Holy shit, this place is making me paranoid already. My dad is grinning and Emilio is sitting up straighter with a proud tilt to his head.

"What?" I hear myself say.

"They ride the bulls," my dad says, as though that explains everything.

He still isn't making sense. "Who ride the bulls?"

"The midgets."

The music must be too loud. "Midgets?"

Everyone, including Nick, nods. "From Mexico."

"Mexican midgets?" *Are these people fucking crazy?*

"Honestly, Hayley. I explained it all to you. Didn't you listen to anything I said?"

When I speak again, my voice comes out very small, "Mexican midgets ride the bulls."

Nick leans close and his elbow bumps mine. "Miniature bulls."

Everyone is nodding and smiling, as though this conversation is acceptable, reasonable even. I swallow against the utter disbelief tightening my throat and speak again, frantically hoping I've got it all wrong. "Mexican midgets riding miniature bulls."

"Yes, of course. That's the show he's promoting. That's why he's here to talk to the fair commission. To see if they want to include the show as part of the Bullmania rodeo we have every Tuesday during fair week. We all think it's a great idea."

Emilio raises his palm so it is about four feet off the floor. "The bulls are quito. You know, miniature."

I nod and try not to let my face show that I think they are all fucking insane. "Excuse me." I whisper to Nick, "I have to go to the bathroom."

I offer a weak smile to everybody who's looking and whimper away from the table.

Nick turns back to my dad and Emilio to say something I can't hear. Good thing, because I probably couldn't handle any more.

The band hasn't started playing yet but the crowd isn't waiting for them. The dance floor is already so full I have to zigzag along the edges to reach the bathroom door.

Once there, I lean against the lime green cement block wall and listen to the moms report on their kids and the younger women gossip about each other.

"OhmiGod! Hayley!"

The smile of the girl grabbing me is so frighteningly huge it takes me a minute to remember who she is. "Hey, Misty. What's new?" I say lamely.

"What's new! OhmiGod! I didn't know you were coming! Your parents didn't mention it!"

I unsuccessfully try to merge with the wall because the moms and their younger counterparts are all staring at Misty and me. To avoid their speculative gazes, I keep my eyes focused on Misty's cheerful round face. "You still working at the fabric store?"

"Yeah. They've got me scheduled part time right now. I bet soon I'll be back to full time. You know — with May and June right around the corner! Prom dresses, bridesmaids dresses" — she wiggles her thin eyebrows — "wedding dresses!"

Subtle isn't a word that describes Misty. "Anything I should know?"

"You guessed it, girlfriend!" She holds out her hand so I can see the modest engagement ring sitting on her finger. Two of the non-moms lean over, warily checking out the rock. The moms smile at each other.

The glow in Misty's eyes is pretty amazing. "That's great," I say. "When's the big day?"

"June sixteenth!"

She grins at me for so long that I wish I could think of something else to say. *'Have you heard about the Mexican midgets?'* No. I need something nice. Pleasant. At least appropriate.

I eye her carefully. She's happy and excited about her future. Confident. I bet she has long- and short-term goals.

"So" — she's not put off by my silence — "are you seeing anybody seriously, Hayley?"

"Seriously?" I parrot back.

"Yeah, you know, anybody special? Anybody who might pop the question!"

She sees my face fall and slides into a rambling apology until I cut her off. "No, I'm not."

She props her hand on her hip. "Well! What about the guy you're here with? He's a hunk."

"His name is Nick and we're just friends."

"Really?"

"Yeah, we're just friends."

Why is she looking so doubtful? Maybe because I am.

Her grin splits even wider. "You won't care if Karen asks him to dance then?"

"No, um, of course not," I lie. "He'd probably — um — be glad to, um."

She doesn't even wait to hear the rest. She's out of the door and zipping through the crowd.

By the time I get out of the bathroom, Nick is on the dance floor with Karen's arms wrapped snugly around his neck. A disgusted scowl pulls on my mouth. It doesn't seem right that any adult human would be able to arch her back like that. I don't know which is worse, the way her breasts are shoved in his face or the fact that her crotch is flat against his.

I wipe all emotion from my face and peruse the hall. How many other single women are stalking my friend, waiting for their chance to paw him? How annoying. But he doesn't look very annoyed. He's got his hands resting easily on her waist and is laughing.

Grrrr.

"Hiya, Hayley."

It's Todd. He's wearing a crisp, white shirt and a pasteurized smile. "Your new boyfriend looks like he's having a really good time."

"Like I said before, Nick isn't my boyfriend."

"Bet you're glad Waylon isn't here."

I shrug.

"Don't you want to know where he is?"

I shake my head.

It's his turn to shrug. Then he tells me there's free beer over by the men's room. I decide against the free beer then go out into the entranceway to get a Diet Coke from the machine. I stand there for a while, looking through the smudgy glass door, watching trucks roll around the parking lot and wondering about Nick.

Eventually, I get fed up with my own sulking and go sit with my parents. We talk about work, of all things, until finally, about the time my mom and dad head to the dance floor, the hometown girls give Nick a rest.

He spots me, grins like he did when he handed over that Hot Damn!, stuffs his hands into his pockets then swaggers toward me.

He smirks at my scowl and says, "Havin' fun with the 'rents?"

I press my lips together and stare at him.

He points to the back wall where a fat man is still guarding the kegs and now some middle-school kids are leaning on the popcorn machine. "Popcorn? Hot dog?"

"Food sounds good."

He strolls off, smiling at people along the way.

I watch him chat with the food dudes. They're laughing like good ole boys. Nick hands me a bag of popcorn and says, "Check the label."

I read the bright red print on the bag, "Hot 'N Fresh."

He winks. "Yeah, just like you."

"Shut the hell up."

He laughs and hands me a hotdog with a neat swipe of mustard, then pulls up a chair, which he places right next to mine. "Whatcha been doing?"

I think of Misty and Todd. "Catching up with friends." The emphasis I put on friends gets lost in a burst of someone else's laughter.

He leans back in the chair, watches the action on the dance floor, and grins like he owns the place. The popcorn churns in my stomach.

"How long are you going to sit there like that? With that look on your face?"

I spin my head and glare at him. "As long as I want."

"I don't think so." He pops to his feet and reaches for my arm. "Come on."

I cross my arms, letting him know I'm not going anywhere with him.

He ignores my gesture and moves around to stand beside me. He wraps his arm behind my back and kind of shoves, kind of guides me to my feet. Next thing I know I'm heading outside.

"Where are we going?" I ask. I know I'm being petulant and petty and even a bit ugly.

"You're better than this, Hayley."

"I know. That's why I moved."

He leads me to his truck. "You're better than this attitude thing you've got going."

He swings open the passenger door then gestures to the seat. I climb in. He slams the door, goes around then gets in and settles himself. That fun, teasing mood we shared earlier in the cab is totally gone and has been replaced by some kind of weird tension. His bossiness and the way he dragged me out to his truck, it's really not like him.

"What's going on with you?" I ask.

"Me? Nothing." But he sits there, his eyes fixed on my face as he watches me watch him.

I shift on the seat.

He watches that too.

He's making me so nervous, staring at me like that, that I press my lips together then twist them. My heart starts to thump and my chest tightens and when he starts to lean toward me, I lean toward him. He kisses me, I kiss him back.

Then, just as he's easing my mouth open with his lips, I realize how quickly he makes my body hum, how much I want him to make my body hum and it scares the shit out of me. I feel my spine stiffen and I guess he does too because he slows up and gradually lifts his mouth from mine.

"I'm not going to apologize," he whispers into my ear, still holding me. "Because I'm not sorry. About this. Or that night."

I know I should say something but I don't. I look out of the window, skimming my gaze across the mud-coated trucks and beat up mini-vans filling the lot. Over in the far corner, I spot Todd, talking on his phone.

Nick bumps his shoulder against mine. "You're one of them but it's okay."

He's wrong. I turn to tell him so but he holds up his hands, smiles, then kisses me on the cheek. I turn my head and press my mouth against him and he kisses me back. It's only a matter of seconds before we're right back where we were, him pressed against me so tightly I can feel his heart thumping. I want to relax but the truth crawls its way up my spine and chills my heart. I push him away. "I—I—"

He leans in, ready to kiss me some more. "You don't have to explain."

Yes, I do. But the truth stays stuck in my throat and I can tell by the expression on his face that he knows something is hiding inside me. "Want to go back in and say goodbye to your parents?"

If I go back in there, I'll start crying for sure. I pull out my phone. "I'll just text my mom."

"You ready, then?"

After I nod, he slides his keys into the ignition.

Chapter Twenty-Two

When Opportunity Doesn't Knock

Tuesday at lunchtime, Josie, who's visiting me at work, is howling as she crosses to my desk. "Those assholes canceled my sister's piece!" Her fitted T-shirt with a huge picture of Wonder Woman across it is screaming too. It's blaring—*look at me!*

I push aside the 'nice' reminders I was supposed to send out last week but was just finishing up. "The one I was supposed to be in?"

She stops in front of my desk, her gaze is zigzagging around the room. "It was about how people are hooking up these days."

Second try. "The one about your videos?"

Now she's looking at me. "Yes. I can't believe it. What fucking assholes."

I don't want to ask the obvious questions—'Why the ax?' and, 'Who was the weakest link?'—because the answer may be, well...me. Maybe I was such a bore that I killed the whole thing.

"That stinks." A truly generic comment.

"Stinks? It's fucking absurd." She's pacing now, scowling at the tastefully neutral décor of the clubhouse. "They obviously don't understand what's going on these days. The editor is probably some loser who goes to 80s dance nights to pick up bleach blondes, stuffs them into his Saturn Sky, then takes them to his condo so they can have sex in his hot tub."

"What did your sister say?"

"Oh, you know her," Josie says, smoothing out her short, red skirt. "Always a professional."

Since when?

Contradicting Josie on anything regarding her sister can be dangerous—and pointless—territory so I shut up while she goes on about what assholes they are.

The article getting shelved is probably a good thing. Whatever Josie's sister wrote, somehow she would've claimed the digital dating concept as her own and Josie would have ended up hurt. Again.

"Can you believe they said that? How stupid is that?"

I really need to get myself together and remember to listen to people when they talk to me. "Said what?"

"That my sister is out of touch with what's going on? That she isn't current?"

"How... What?"

Josie steps back and throws her hands in the air. "Some bullshit about Kid Rock, I don't know."

Ohhhhh.

"They're going to have her cover topics aimed at a different demographic. Old people or the environment, some shit like that."

No way am I going to offer the little info I have, that her sister is so out of it that she doesn't know the difference between hometown boys Kid Rock and Eminem. "Maybe she'll like the change."

Josie frowns, so I half-heartedly tidy up my desk and change the subject, "Ready for lunch?"

She says she is then adds, "What's up with that guy in the security booth?"

I grab my purse from my desk drawer and go over to pull open the French door. "That's Bob Hastings, he's okay."

"He looked at me weird."

"Maybe he was admiring your shirt."

She glances down at the thin layer of fabric skimming over her breasts. "Ya think?"

"Yeah, I think." We head to my car. "Is Riana meeting us?"

"She didn't know if she could make it, some court thing."

After we get in the car, Josie asks, "So how was your weekend? Did you go home?"

As we roll past Mr. Hastings, he leans lower than usual to wave back.

"See you in an hour," I call as we zoom out onto Grand River Avenue and head east.

"You know, one of these days you're going have to have tell me about your family and friends back home and that guy Waylon and all the whatever." She looks at my tight expression and laughs. "Your shit can't be any crazier than mine."

"It's not that they're all that crazy…"

She lets me get away with not finishing and we drive in silence for a while.

After I parallel park, Riana taps on the window.

We climb out and I notice Riana's walking like a zombie. After saying hi, I add, "Only four weeks and four days to go! You ready?"

"I guess so. Peter keeps asking me about my training schedule. He says my bike is too old." She sighs and stops walking so she can look at Josie and me. "I don't want to talk about it anymore. Okay?"

Josie and I know when to back off so when we start walking again we talk about Josie's thing, which still needs an official name, then move on to a general conversation about work. Naturally, I lead off with my most recent complaints about Caroline.

After I'm done, Riana tries to top me, "That's nothing. At least she's reasonably sane. Get this — because I'm the low girl on the totem pole, I have to talk to all the certified loonies. I had this lady today who called up and started shrieking about how she's going to grieve the lawyers because they let the state send her kids to live with their paternal grandparents. She said, 'I was found incompetent to stand trial so how can the state just come and take my kids away? I didn't have a trial!'

"Try and explain that one." Riana droops in her chair. "To a crazy woman."

Riana does look wiped out. Still, I envy her passion. Whatever she decides to do, she goes for it. All out.

Maybe someday she'll realize what a go-getter she is. Wouldn't that be something?

I peer at Josie. She works so damn hard, always setting goals — and achieving them no less — like she's got something to prove. I guess in her eyes she'll never match up to the huge success her sister is.

Josie and Riana keep talking about the crazy people Riana has to call, while the server pours our coffees. As I listen to them, and think about how proud I am of them, an unfortunate thought takes root in the back of my mind. I spray mental Round Up on it, figuring it's a weed but it doesn't wilt. Instead, it fights back and grows so big that I have to acknowledge it.

They're both moving ahead and I'm not.

Me? Where will I be in five years? Two years? Still temping and thinking about going back to college? The questions roll through my brain like loose pennies looking for a place to plop down.

Stalling, although it has always been my MO, is not working and it's not going to work. Self-help books and programs will not rush to my rescue. If I want my life to have any kind of meaning at all, I need to do something. Anything. And that one thing.

It's time to step off the curb, Hayley. Stop waiting for some magic bus to rumble up, swing open its glittering doors and take you to the most perfect life ever.

Unaware of my personal crisis, Josie and Riana chatter on, laughing, swapping news and charging ahead with their lives.

The waitress brings my salad. Not even the thick slices of cheese and ham spread across the top cheer me up. I listen to Josie and Riana, occasionally chuckling along with them. For once my heart isn't in it. I'm too busy feeling like I don't know who or what I am, and stewing on the mess my life has become.

I start thinking about Nick. I think about how he and I are unsuccessfully trying to pretend it didn't happen. But it did happen and I'm glad it did. Maybe this is one area of my life where I can take action.

Instead of just waiting around to see what's going to happen next, I can take the first step—act instead of react. That way, I'll be in control of what happens. What a great *idea*. I'm not sure if being proactive is something I read, something the loud lady told us, or something I made up myself. But in this case it actually doesn't matter where the *idea* came from.

While Riana is telling Josie about some new tires she might get for her bike, I send Nick a text and ask him if he wants me to stop by.

He texts back— *Sure.*

The second I read that single word, I start to have second thoughts but shove them aside.

* * * *

Before I push the buzzer beside Nick's apartment door, it swings open.

"Hey." Nick steps back and waves me in. He pulls me through his doorway and into his front room. He turns back to lock the door then leads me to the couch.

"So, what's up?"

On my way over, the plan was so clear in my mind. But now, the words I rehearsed stick in my throat. I look away from him. There's a basket of laundry in the La-Z-Boy chair and stacks of books all around the shag carpet.

I turn back to him and my gaze wanders across his shoulders. He's stretched one arm across the back and if I leaned back, in a matter of seconds I'd be nestled in his arms. I don't lean back. "Just thought I'd stop by."

He looks at my breasts, outlined by my snug sweater. "Yeah?"

I stare at his mouth. This isn't going as I planned at all. What happened to my plan? My idea that I'd be in control? "Yeah."

"You mean like before?" he asks, touching my chin with his thumb.

"Yeah," is all I can manage again.

He moves his other hand onto my shoulder and pulls me back. I stop caring about who's in control as he lifts my face upward so he can kiss me. His lips are warm and his breath smells like mint. For a split second the fact that he already knew this was why I came over goes through my mind. Then he deepens the kiss and the thought vanishes.

Using the hand on my shoulder he pushes me onto his lap. I'm sideways, while he's facing forward. The angle makes it easy for him to slip one hand under my sweater and caress my skin. His gentle strokes make me both nervous and excited. I arch back and he moves his hand up and over my breasts. Even with my bra on, I feel the heat of his palm and my nipples tighten. After I moan from the sudden need, he moves his hands across the silky fabric several times then between my breasts.

"I do like the clasp in the front," he says. "Convenient."

One little twist and the fabric falls away, and my breasts are exposed. I don't have time to be concerned about what he thinks because I can already see the approval in his dark eyes.

"Even better than I remembered," he says, then starts lifting my sweater. My breasts bounce as I twist, lifting my arms overhead so he can get it off. Once it's gone, he guides me back and covers one nipple with his mouth. It peaks, and he tugs lightly, making a streak of lust shoot straight to my clit. Once that nipple is thoroughly wet and totally tight he moves to the other, licking and sucking with the same careful attention. I give in to the delicious sensations.

Nick slides his hand under my skirt and tugs on the waistband of my tights. They come down easily and soon are bunched between my knees. He cups my pussy, putting some pressure on my clit with the palm of his hand. I start to reach for him and try to sit up, but he pushes me back again.

"Lie still."

When I reach for him again, he adds, "Put your hands above your head."

My back arches even more, and I feel sexy as hell all stretched out for him with my nipples tight and my pussy wet from his attention.

He speaks again, and this time his voice is nearly a growl, "I've been wanting to do this ever since that night you came over." He starts to shift away from me, moving down the couch then settling himself between my thighs. He takes one of my legs and drapes it over his back then lowers his mouth to lick my clit.

He glides his tongue up and down as he slips his hands under my ass to grasp my butt cheeks. The brush of his warm tongue over my wet clit is amazing, and already my body is tensing with desperation. Needing more pressure, I rock my hips, raising myself off the couch and nearer to his mouth.

A spiral of intense pleasure whips around me, squeezing me tighter and tighter until it's a struggle to breathe. I can't move. My entire body is taut, anticipating each flick of his tongue. Stroke by stroke he brings me closer to the edge until finally, just when I think I can't take it any longer, the first rings of my release circle around me. The orgasm whips through me, stealing the last of my precious control and making me cry out. The cry ends in a whimper.

He lifts his mouth from my clit and works his way upward so that he's lying alongside me. When he kisses me, his lips taste like my pussy. "You better get going," he says, scooting away from me.

"Don't you want me—"

I stop because he's handing me my sweater. That's a pretty clear message he doesn't want a return-the-favor blow job. It's hard for me to stand, but I manage.

Once I'm on my feet, Nick kisses me. "Talk to you tomorrow?"

A couple of minutes later, he's watching me walk to my car and I'm wondering what the hell just happened.

Chapter Twenty-Three

Racy Red Respect

Two days later, I'm pacing in front of the pretty clubhouse doors waiting for Caroline to arrive so she can unlock them. Five minutes pass and still there is no sign of Caroline.

Ten minutes more. Dare I hope a tornado has actually found her and sucked her up? And I missed it? Talk about unfair.

While I'm daydreaming about Caroline sitting atop an ugly, black bicycle as she spins through the air, Mr. Neville pulls up in his Olds. I'm sure the official name of the color is not brown, it's probably toffee or café tan, but no marketing savvy can mask the boringness of the color.

"Morning, Hayley."

No—'Why are you standing out here?' Or—'Are you waiting outside while Caroline hangs up her cape and puts away her broom?' Instead, he gets out of his car and smoothes his navy blue tie, which is dotted with tiny, gold anchors.

"I have something for you," he says, swinging up the walk.

Did he read my mind back when I thought he was handsome? Instinctively, I inch backward only to bump into a post.

He pauses long enough to smile and point at the door. "Let's go in. I know you're going to be excited."

I don't want to be excited. I'd rather be annoyed by Caroline than led along by Mr. Wanna-Be Continental. "It's locked," I say when he reaches for the handle. But before his hand connects with the brass knob, Tony's head pops out.

"Oh, um...hi." He steps out, leaving the door slightly ajar and crams his hands into the pockets of his brown pants. "Looking for Caroline, Mr. Neville? She's, um, not here."

"She's at a power breakfast with Management," Mr. Neville says to Tony as he sweeps the door open and ushers me in. "Well," he asks me, "what do you think of *it*?"

I'm on a life-size page of Where's Waldo, only instead of looking for a jaunty fellow I'm looking for *it*. God help me, I have no idea what the man is talking about. "I don't know what to say, Mr. Neville, really I—"

"Hayley," Tony, cuts in, "it's gorgeous. That velvety, red fabric, ohhh, just sitting in it will be a dream. You lucky girl."

Two thoughts pop into my head at the same time.

a) Mr. Neville has presented me with a posh crimson chair.

b) Macho Tony has not only noticed a change in office furnishings but described said change as a dream.

Mr. Neville nudges me. "Go on, have a seat. See how you like it."

I glance at Tony who is practically drooling and slide over to place myself upon the plush, red padding.

Ohhh.

It is a dream. The honest smile that spreads across my face catches my boss's eye.

"I want you to know how much I appreciate your hard work here at North Pointe Farms and I thought this chair would make you more comfortable" — he chuckles — "and even more productive."

I've been productive? Seriously? When I start to feel like a low budget model in an office supply catalog, I hop out and wave at Tony. "You try, it's great."

As though realizing that he has somehow exposed a better kept quiet part of himself, Tony stiffens until I point demandingly at the chair, causing him to step over and plop into it. He nods, spins in a circle then lumbers out. "Yeah."

For several minutes, we stare at the pretty chair, as though it has some special meaning. I suppose, for each of us, it does.

We're still standing like that when Caroline strolls in, fresh from her power breakfast. "Hello, Mr. Neville," she starts off in her 'I'm such a big important deal' voice. Her confidence fades with each of the next few words, "Did you stop…by…to…?"

Her poor face drops and her shoulders slump until they congeal, and a grimace pulls on her mouth.

"It's a beauty, isn't it?" Clueless Mr. Neville pivots and gestures to the chair sitting proudly behind my desk. "I'm sure you agree, Caroline, that Hayley is doing a wonderful job here and we want her to know how much we appreciate her."

When Caroline remains silent, he prods her. "Don't you agree?"

"Yes, of course." She turns her shoulder to Ollie and a phony smile to me. "We all want you to know how we feel about having you out here. In the reception area. Where you belong."

Basking in the joy of getting under Caroline's skin, I amble over to the chair and ease myself into it, bit by bit. "Ahhhhh. Like a dream. Really. Do you want to try it, Caroline?"

Her face sours even more, then she pulls herself together to spin away from me to Ollie. "Come in, umm...please." She waves him to her sanctuary. "I'll tell you what we discussed at the breakfast."

As she's closing the door I hear some of Ollie's words, "Exciting...developments..."

Tony rests his hip on the corner of my desk. "What gives, Hayley?" he asks quietly. "You doing some special projects for Mr. Neville? Providing some extra services?"

"No," I whisper back.

The tables are turned and for once he's the harasser. He lifts an eyebrow and stares down at me.

"We're even now. Thanks."

When his face stays blank, I pat the armrests and add, "For noticing the chair. I really had no idea what he was trying to show me."

After a pause, Tony says, "I noticed it because, I, um, sat in it. I was looking for a pencil in your desk, and well, that's how I noticed."

Did he find it? The pencil? In my desk? "I don't care how or why, I'm just glad you did because otherwise I would've been standing there like some idiot, trying to figure out what the hell had him so excited."

The word excited brings a sparkle to Tony's eye. I point to Caroline's door. "You checking the net again?"

Tony hops off my desk and backs toward the French doors, almost stepping into one of the potted fig trees. "Yeah, nothing there. I'm working on…a new project. I think it's better than…" He lets that tidbit of information go, then smacks his hands together. "Stay out of trouble." He then whips around to add, "Later."

Something is definitely going on with that guy.

After he's gone, I take the opportunity to spin around as fast as possible. *Sweet!* The chair doesn't make a sound but is it getting higher or are my legs shrinking?

I swirl the other way and my feet touch the floor again.

I go up and down until my stomach feels sufficiently queasy. How cool is this? I have a lovely crimson chair that could probably make me throw up.

On impulse I grab my phone and hit 'Nick'.

He answers on the third ring. After he says "Hi" I fill him in on the whole chair thing. He tells me to start spinning, so we can see how long I can keep talking while going in circles. I make it about six times around before I get too dizzy to make sense. It feels good to laugh about something so stupid. For a few seconds it puts us back where we were before we got naked and fucked.

But then he asks me if I'm okay and I know what he means.

"I'm fine," I say.

"Fine with the way things are?" he asks. "The *friends* thing?"

I know I should say something I actually mean, but instead I say, "Yes. Fine with the way things are."

Chapter Twenty-Four

When it's His Way or the Highway

Sunday night, after spending the day with my family, I push open the door to my apartment to find Nick has popped in to get the details of my visit home. He's stretched out on my couch with a John Grisham paperback. He glances up and grins. Glad to see him, I grin back.

"Good time?" he asks, tossing me the keys I leave hidden under one of the cement blocks that line the parking lot of my building.

I set my purse on the surprisingly empty table that usually houses my newly arrived magazines and unopened envelopes. "Yeah. We ate at my aunt's house. Pot roast and chocolate cake."

"You're a happy girl."

He knows those are my favorite foods.

"Yeah." I fiddle with my keys, remembering the last time I sat on the couch with him.

"Come on over and tell me about it," he says, hefting himself upright and smacking the cushion next to him.

I drop down at the opposite end of the couch.

When I don't answer his question, he angles back. "You mad at me?"

"No. That's stupid. Why would you think that?"

He pokes my arm. "Text much? Check your voicemail?"

I avoid the truth, that I don't know how to handle the way he makes me feel and go with the modern woman's stand-by. Work. "The whole thing at North Pointe, you know."

He's staring at me with a blank face. "Nothing else?"

I shake my head and scramble for something to talk about. "Something's wrong with Caroline. She's going crazy right before my eyes."

"Crazy with excitement?" He laughs.

"I don't know... Ever since Mr. Neville put her in charge of the pool party that's going to be happening before the raffle drawing, which I've pretty much taken over, she's hardly been around and she's been acting really weird."

"Is she going to be there, at the celebration thing?"

"You better believe it."

He sets his book onto the coffee table. "Why are you still doing all her work?"

"I'm not. Like I said, she's doing the pool party."

We're too quiet for too long, probably because he's trying to figure out if the real Hayley has been abducted by aliens and replaced by one who actually cares about her job.

"I think I better check my messages." I hit speaker then play.

"Hey, sweetie, it's Mom, I can't believe I forgot to tell you. Rodney's wedding has been moved up because his fiancé got a job offer in California and they have to move over the Memorial Day weekend. So, the wedding is on

Saturday. This Saturday. The nineteenth. You'll be able to make it. Right? Bring Nick. Everyone loves him."

Nick's laughing. "Hot damn," he howls. "A weddin'. We'll have us a fine time."

A cloud of awkwardness forms above me, and I slouch into the cushions. Drops of mortification fall on my head and render me speechless until I come up with, "You don't have to go."

He looks smug. "Yes, I do. Everyone loves me. I don't want to disappoint my people."

"Really, Nick. You don't want to go. It'll be boring. All that sitting around being happy for other people. Really, what's so fun about that?"

"Ahh, that's my Hayley. Always the romantic."

Chapter Twenty-Five

De Nile, Spring's Hot Travel Spot

Even though it's Wednesday and I'm at work, I'm in a good mood. You see, I've found a way to set aside sorting out my real feelings for Nick and the notion that I need long-term goals and plans by focusing on my short-term successes and doing important things like organizing my desk. Who would've ever guessed the joys of tidy drawers? Also, in this way, I avoid all the tiresome thinking that comes with questions that lead to real personal growth and change by keeping busy making calls and filing stuff.

I've put away all my self-help materials — books, the Optional Handout Packet, and magazines. Whatever I've learned from them will have to be enough for now. I am alone, yes, yet full of words and ideas that sound great as they play through the soundtrack of my mind.

Who says task avoidance is a bad thing? It's working for me. Things are going my way.

For one thing, Caroline has become a truly rare bird. Instead of flitting around my desk, pecking around for the magazines I used to have hidden under papers and in file folders, she stays in her sanctuary. Or leaves for hours on end.

In the past, that might've caused me to spend more time wasting time but I've been too busy dealing with the whole celebration. And it is actually coming along well, if I do say so myself.

Sure, I still think the whole thing is kind of stupid — really, who cares about the fifteen years of luxurious living? Not me. And not many other people. But any reason for a party is a good reason. That's what I've been telling myself and it's starting to make a difference.

I have enthusiasm. I even have a bit of team spirit. As long as I conveniently forget that Caroline is part of the team.

I used some review sites to find a new paint and repair company to take over for the crappy, unreliable one we've been using. They've done a couple of the units and Mr. Hastings says he's never seen better work. Mr. Neville is ecstatic.

Here's another thing. The woman in charge of organizing The Willing Wheels Ride loves the idea of coordinating the finish line activities with the raffle drawing. We've even expanded our raffle ticket distribution to include all the people who have sponsored the riders. So Josie, Riana and Nick will each get a ticket! That means more publicity for both North Pointe Farms and The Association for Diabetic Children.

Riana is thrilled.

Mr. Neville and Management are thrilled.

Even Regional is thrilled.

Caroline is not thrilled.

I couldn't be happier.

So happy, that even sending out the 'nice' mid-month reminders isn't so bad. I'm slipping them into envelopes when one of the French doors open and Mrs. Klonski pokes her head in. She's beaming.

"Come out here, Hayley dear. I know you'll want to see this."

Before I can respond, she ducks back out and disappears. Probably all that's waiting outside for me is an empty sidewalk. Maybe, 'You'll want to see this' is old lady code for let's play hide and seek.

I have things to do but who can resist an old Polish lady? *Oh! Maybe she has cookies!* I tumble out of my chair then go outside.

To the left is the empty parking lot so I head to the right. Three steps later, I hear Mrs. Klonski chattering softly to someone…something. It's Snickers.

No cookies are in sight, just poor, abused Snickers.

"Who's the cutest littlest patriot?" she asks.

Oddly enough the dog doesn't reply. Not one to be put off by an unresponsive pet, she answers herself, "Sweetie Snickers is!"

Mrs. Klonski glances up from where she's kneeling on the grass and waves me over. "We're getting ready for the big day. Isn't he a darling?"

I don't know which is crazier, the red, white and blue sweater she apparently knitted for the dog or the miniature star-spangled cowboy hat she has somehow gotten to stay on top of its head.

Snickers stares at me with eyes that say, 'Tell any of my friends and I'll sneak inside your apartment and chew holes in all your favorite underwear'.

"Did that sweater take you long to make?"

"No time at all." She tugs on the hem and smoothes it out. "Bob says Snickers will be the best-dressed dog here."

Chalk one up for Mr. Hastings. "He's absolutely right."

She smiles at me. "Do you need any help organizing the raffle tickets?"

Here we are at the real reason for this get-together. Mrs. Klonski has uncovered the unsecret secret way I'll be dividing up the raffle tickets. She knows that she's going to be getting more tickets than anyone else and she wants to be sure I know it too. "No, I can manage everything myself. Thanks, though."

She scoops up her little pooch and tucks him under one arm. "I'd be happy to help. It'd be no trouble."

"Really. Thanks for the offer but Mr. Neville said –" *Here comes lie number one but I'm sure he'd say this if he were here.* "I have to be the only person who handles the tickets."

She looks as though she's trying to come up with another angle so I add lie number two, "If anyone else touches them, the drawing will be declared illegal and nobody will win any of the prizes."

"Oh dear." She steps back. "I had no idea."

Lie number three – "It's serious business, raffle drawing. I bet there will even be an undercover policeman here."

As though he may already be here, picking out the perfect hiding spot, Mrs. Klonski scans the empty pool and the corners of the clubhouse.

Three fibs in a row is my limit so I change the subject. "Do you know anyone who'll be in the rally?"

"That bicycle thing?"

I nod as I walk backward. From experience I know that if I don't end this soon, I'll be jotting down recipes or bargain websites.

"No. I don't think I do know anybody. I bought my grandson a tricycle for his last birthday, though."

"That's wonderful. I'm sure he was thrilled."

"His mom wasn't so happy. Now she has to take him to the park every day or he cries."

Mrs. Klonski is following me back to the door, but I'm ready when we reach it. I frown. "Sorry, no dogs in the clubhouse."

She frowns back and tries to cover the dog's ears. The hat gets in the way. "Lil Snickers isn't a dog," she says quietly.

I'm dying to ask—*then what is he?*—except the answer might force me to accept that Mrs. Klonski is not sane. "Bye, Mrs. Klonski."

"Bye, Hayley dear."

I wave and slip back inside. My phone hums as the door is drifting shut. It's Josie.

"My sister wants to meet us at Anthony's tonight. Nine o'clock. Okay with you or do you have plans?"

What's up? Why us? Why me? I hedge with, "Um, I don't know."

"I think it's got something to do with the piece that was canceled. I think she's trying to rewrite it or something."

I remind myself of two important things—

1) Josie is my friend.

2) Josie's relationship with her sister runs only two ways. Hot and cold. Right now things are hot so they're like two ducks in a mud puddle. If one turns on me, they'll both turn on me.

"Let's invite Riana, too."

There is only the silence of chatter in the background. I offer up a reason. "She might have something to add. To the article."

"You think so?"

"Of course. Before Peter, she even went out with successful guys, real man types with careers."

"I guess. Go ahead and call her. I don't think she'll mind."

"She, Riana, or she, your sister."

"Either of them. Gotta go, my two forty-five is here."

With that she hangs up and I text Riana, trying to make some beers at Anthony's with Josie and her sister sound fun. Tricky business that.

But, I don't stress too much about whether or not she'll show because, like I said, things have been going my way lately and there is no reason to think that'll change.

I have things under control.

No problems here.

Not now, not ever.

I reach for my coffee, lean back in my posh chair, then set the heels of my black boots on my desk.

Yessiree, things are fiiinnnneeeeee.

Chapter Twenty-Six

The Dark Side of Business

That night at nine-thirty I park behind Anthony's then swing out of my car. I'm expecting the usual collection of bums selling produce they dug out of dumpsters and early bar hoppers anxious to get some cheap drinks. What I get is a horde of goths. They're leaning out of their cars, they're loitering by the curb, and they're milling around the parking lot. It's Purple Heart's cheap secondhand stuff meets Hot Topic's overpriced poser wear in a seriously bad way.

Five of them are slumped against the wall next to the back entrance. A girl with at least four bolts in her mouth snarls at me while the boy next to her mumbles to himself and sways side to side.

The other three? I don't even look.

No trouble. I won't stick out too bad in my short, khaki skirt and white T-shirt. If I cared, I'd go roll in the trash to get rid of my just-showered scent. Since I don't care, I push my way between the depressing and depressed until I spot Josie's bright hair shining like a beacon through the haze. After my eyes adjust to the sea of black hair—long, short, flat and spiked—and black clothes—stuff stolen from the Salvation Army donation bin and designer duds from the Somerset Collection in fancy smancy Troy—I spot Josie's sister and Riana.

They look a little out of place.

Kid Rock is nowhere in sight and I actually wish he were around somewhere, brightening the place with his non-all-black clothes. Josie's sister is probably glad though.

Drinks are in order. "Who needs what?" I ask from the end of their wobbly table.

Riana—"Beer."

Josie—"Beer."

Josie's sister—"Banana vodka on ice."

Yeah. Right.

As if I'm going to order that with a straight face. Here. Right now.

Anthony's wife is smiling at me from behind the bar. I must be a welcome sight with my laundered clothes and twenty-dollar bill. "Four beers."

She shouts at me, "You come to see Dying Virgin?"

Hell no. "What time are they going on?"

"Eleven-thirty."

Two hours to vacate the premises.

Using my best *barfrau* imitation, I fist the mugs and haul them over to the girls.

Things don't look good. Josie is sitting there looking goofy, Riana is talking and Josie's sister is writing. Beer sloshes over my wrists when I set the mugs down and slip into the only empty chair—next to Josie's sister.

I lean over and try to see what she's writing but she slides it away.

"So. What's up?" I ask after a swallow of beer.

Riana gestures to Josie's sister with one of the beers, "She's going to cover The Willing Wheels Ride."

I smell a rat. "You are? Why?"

"Human interest," she answers as though I should've already known.

Josie pulls one of the beers over to her. "It's better than the singles stuff. More real."

More real than being single. Is that possible?

Whatever.

"I'll even be doing mini-interviews, you know, before and after the event. Looking for an angle."

An angle?

Riana straightens. "What about watching me race through the finish line?" she asks loudly enough to turn several heads.

I salute Riana with my mug. Maybe she's found a way to shut Peter up.

But too soon, her smile falters. We all watch her poke at her mug handle until she looks up again. "It seems like the whole celebration thing is coming together really well, Hayley. I bet your boss'll be thrilled. I'll bet he's already impressed."

Josie breaks in. "Tell my sister about the chair."

How could I resist? Why would I?

I retell the whole tale, taking extra care with the details of Caroline's face. I'm so funny! We all laugh.

"The race, the raffle, what's your boss got to say about all that?" Josie's sister asks.

"She's been planning the pool party but she hasn't been around much lately. I hardly see her at all." I grin with satisfaction.

"That's kind of weird," Riana says. "You'd think you'd see her more."

I shrug and watch a pair of extra small goths slouch by. They're so short their heads only come up to my shoulder and I'm sitting down.

Riana asks, "Aren't you worried?"

I tear my eyes away from the tiny bits of darkness. "Worried?" Me worry? Why should I worry?

"She's got to be planning something," Riana says.

Josie nods. "Plotting against you."

I'm glad to have friends who look out for me, but really. "You guys are more paranoid than I am."

Riana shakes her head. "I don't think so. Think about it."

"Yeah, but—"

"But nothing," Josie adds, "You better watch your back."

I wave them off. "You guys are overreacting." I take a gulp of beer. "Besides, she already got all the credit for the raffle *idea* thing."

Riana leans forward and stares at me. "Who did all the work on that?"

"I did."

She goes on with, "Who's going to be there when it all happens? She will."

"So will I. She's going to be busy with her own stuff, the pool party, thank God."

I'm seriously wondering what the big deal is when someone beside me asks, "Does this Caroline write your evaluations?"

Drat. Why did she have to talk? I'd practically forgotten Josie's sister was there. Josie saves me from having to answer by filling in the blanks.

After a while, the therapeutic value of letting it all out makes itself apparent so I fill in the spots Josie misses, adding in as much humor as possible. Riana joins in too. Anthony's wife serves us a couple more rounds. We all laugh at Caroline's petty stupidity.

"To Caroline," I cry, raising my mug. "The ultimate bitchy boss."

We all laugh, even Josie's sister. Things go on that way for quite a while, because we all have work-related things to complain about and because we're all having a great time. When the band comes on, we stand on our chairs and cause such a scene that even Anthony's wife gets annoyed.

After midnight, we say goodbye to the goths, laugh our way to the street, and because Josie's sister only had that one beer, she drives us all home.

Chapter Twenty-Seven

Lost and Found

"Is she sure she lost it here?"

Scotty is not happy about spending his Friday evening crawling around the salon on his hands and knees, looking for a diamond tennis bracelet.

"Yes," Josie insists from her position under the shampoo bowls. "She got it cleaned right before she came in."

I can see that today I am the lucky one. My post is the reception area which is wide open. All I have to do is sit on my butt and spin around. I look under the chairs and tables again. No bling.

"How can she be sure?" Scotty is complaining again, as he scoots around under the manicure tables. "Did you ask her if she looked in her car?"

Josie shoots to her feet and eyes him. "Keep looking. She's one of my best clients and if she says she lost it here, she lost it here."

"If it's so important why isn't she here looking for it?"

"Hello!" Josie's voice is muffled because she's on her stomach and running her hand along the baseboards.

Yuck. I bet the floor back there is covered with hair.

"She came in today because her husband is getting a huge promotion and she had to go to a dinner."

"If he's so rich, why doesn't he get him to buy her another one?"

"Good God, Scotty. Stop being such an ass!"

"I knew I shouldn't have stayed after closing," he grumbles as he hunkers down and rubs his palms across the tiles under the chairs. "I should've told you to do your own hair."

I look across the room to where Riana is carefully scanning the shelves that hold the hair products. "How you doing, Riana? See anything?"

Her only answer is to shake her head.

I think I'm the only one who's noticed that she is unusually quiet tonight. Josie is freaked out about finding the bracelet so that Scotty can do her hair. Scotty, well, he's too into the drama of having to get down and dirty to do good. Whether he wants to or not.

Since meeting me in the parking lot fifteen minutes ago, Riana hasn't spoken a word apart from saying hi to everyone.

Something is up and I'm waiting for the right time to ask.

"Okay. Okay." Scotty is on his feet. "Let's be smart about this. Josie, you be her. Go to the door and do everything she did."

Josie is not moving fast enough to suit him. He's pulling her up and shouting, "Go. Get up."

"All right," she says, tugging at his hands.

Riana steps away from her post and comes to sit next to me in the waiting area. For the next few minutes, we watch as Josie reenacts the whole appointment. Manicure, shampoo, quick trim and blow out. Last step. The pay off.

"Fuck me!" Josie screams as she holds up the goods. The huge stones nearly light up the whole room. "I gotta text." With that, she snatches up the phone and takes care of business.

Scotty zips off to get his station ready.

I lean over to get Riana's attention. "What's up?"

"Peter and I are done."

I was expecting 'I have cramps' or 'the lawyers at work are control freaks'. Not this. "Done like over?"

She gets up and walks to the wide glass window that runs across the front of the shop. "Yeah."

I'm not shocked, only caught off guard. It's no secret that I'm not a fan of Peter but I hate seeing my friend look so sad. "You guys broke up?"

"Yep," she replies, looking at my reflection in the window.

"Oh. Okay."

Josie hangs up the phone and spins around. "Did I hear that right? You're done with Peter?"

Riana is still gazing out of the window. "Want to know why?"

We both nod. Of course we do. Even Scotty, who has come over to listen in, wants to know.

Riana's mouth pulls tight and she sucks in a soft breath before replying so quietly that we all have to lean forward to listen, "He's going to do The Willing Wheels Ride."

"Your rally?" Josie asks. "He thinks it's stupid."

Riana turns around and comes back to the reception area. "At first he said he was going to sign up to do it to help me with my training, then after I told him I didn't want his help, he got all mad and started saying that stuff about how I'll never make it to the finish line."

Scotty folds his arms across his chest and mutters something about guys being competitive assholes when its least appropriate.

I urge Riana to tell us the rest with, "And then?"

One side of her mouth lifts up. "I don't really remember what I said after that. I was pretty mad. I think he was surprised.

"I guess I told him I didn't need somebody to compete with. We're supposed to be friends, you know. Not just a couple, but friends that support each other. He called me stupid." She drops into a chair. "And that really did it. I walked out." She's quiet for a minute, then asks, "Do you guys think I'm stupid?"

Josie and I rush over to sit beside her. I tease her about her ridiculously awesome job that she is actually good at, and Josie teases her about how she always makes us look like idiots when we watch *Jeopardy*.

Scotty shakes his head and points out, "Riana you are the least stupid person I have ever met."

Riana doesn't look convinced but she's smiling. Sort of. She laughs, then says, "I called him an asshole. He's going to do the rally just to show me up."

I can't think of anything to say to make it better. I know how she feels but now isn't the time to explain why. Josie isn't saying anything either. The three of us sit in the chairs with our arms intertwined, hunched over and sad.

"It's a done deal." Scotty is all business, grabbing Josie and pulling her to his chair, while saying to Riana, "You did the right thing. Nobody needs a man like that. Especially you. You're better off now."

I want to hug Scotty right then for saying the exact right thing. If someone had said that very thing to me when I walked away from what everyone else said was going to be the perfect life, it would've been a lot easier. In the end I gave up trying to explain why I didn't want to stay in the country, be a farmer's wife weeks after graduating from high school and start having babies at eighteen.

Scotty being who he is, he's already over the crisis. "Come on over," he says to Riana and me. "Watch me make your friend into a princess."

Chapter Twenty-Eight

Bridal and Beautiful

Saturday. Wedding day.

Family. Friends. Togetherness.

Humiliation. Bad memories. Unfinished business. There's no way of getting around it. I have to call Nick so we can work out what time we're leaving and all that sort of stuff.

I'm staring at the phone when it vibrates.

I click it on and say hi to Riana.

"What're you going to wear?" she asks.

"You're thinking about that? Why aren't you searching for voodoo dolls online?"

I hear her half-hearted chuckle. "You think I need to? I could break its legs."

"He's got to be so out of shape. All those hours hunched over boring ass legal books? You'll streak past him."

Stressed silence is followed by, "He works out every morning."

The dislike I've felt for the guy for so long has finally found an outlet and I can't shut myself up. "So what? You've been training on your bike, Riana. You know what you're doing."

More silence so I add, "You're a lot stronger than you think. Okay?"

"So tell me what you're going to wear." She still doesn't sound convinced but I can hear more confidence in her voice so I let my mind wander over to my own problem.

I list my top three choices — pants and top, pants and jacket, and a floral dress — and she insists that I wear the most girlish one. The thing I least want to wear. It's sweet and I'm sour. At least on this event.

"It's a wedding!" She's annoyed with me. "You can't wear pants to a wedding."

She's right but the dress she's talking about, well…it's romantic. Pretty.

Due to the circumstances, I'd been leaning toward the beige suit I'd rescued from the clearance rack last spring at Macy's. It's been hanging in my closet waiting patiently for its debut.

But if I wear that, I'll look totally boring. Besides, doesn't the mother of the bride wear beige? What if the bride wears beige?

Beige is out.

"Hayley," Riana is nearly shouting, "are you listening to me?"

"Sure, yeah, of course."

Still, if I wear beige I might blend into the walls and nobody will even notice me. It'll be like camouflage. Think of all the conversations I could eavesdrop on. Too bad I wouldn't care what they were talking about.

"…and who knows, you might even have fun."

"Sure, yeah, of course."

"Hayley..."

I can tell she's getting impatient with me but because I haven't been listening I don't know why.

"It's a wedding, it'll be fun! Your mom and dad and brother will be there, right? And you'll see a bunch of people you haven't seen in a while, right? So stop being stupid."

She has no idea.

"Yeah. I guess." And I do. In theory going to a hometown wedding is fun. But in my case, it just serves as a reminder of things I want to forget. Like how everyone was excited about the future of my life until I walked away at the very last minute and ruined everything for everyone.

"What's Nick wearing?"

Nick. My plan is to follow him around everywhere. I'll glare at anyone who looks as though they may be thinking about saying anything about Waylon and the wedding that wasn't. "I don't know," I mumble, realizing that plan isn't viable.

Riana's exasperated sigh whistles through the phone. "What's wrong with you? Put the stupid dress on, call Nick and make sure he's wearing something that will look okay with the dress, then go have a good time."

I'd expect this sort of attitude from Josie. Apparently, Riana is more than a bit stressed.

"Call me tomorrow with all the details," she says. "Okay?"

"Yeah. Of course."

* * * *

Later, Nick and I are sitting in the parking lot of the church. It's warm for mid-May and we've got the

213

windows of his truck rolled down. Little snippets of conversations come from the window when people walk by. These bits of sound break up the unusually awkward silence that is hovering between us.

He glances over at me to ask, "Want to go in yet?"

I check my watch and shake my head. "Let's wait a couple more minutes."

"You want to end up in the back row?"

How did he guess? I grin and lift one shoulder. "We'll get out faster that way."

One corner of his mouth curves up then he turns away from me to watch twin girls spin in circles, making their dresses flare out. I stare at his profile.

He turns back to me so quickly he catches me staring at him. "You ever do that?" He points to the girls. "Spin around like that and make your dress fly out?"

"Everybody does."

As always, he doesn't put up with my attitude. He grins. "I don't."

I shift away from him. "We better go in. I don't want it to look like we got here late. My mom will notice and give me a hard time."

Without saying anything more, we get out and climb up the steps. There is a mob out front so we get stuck by the second set of doors where the relatives are chattering.

Nick offers me a quiet smile of encouragement.

"Hayley! Where's your brother?" It's my mom with Aunt Sandy, who is clinging so closely to her side that they could be Siamese twins. They're both wearing pearls and hugely floral dresses and they're staring at me. "Where have you been?"

"Outside," I say. But what I'm thinking is that I am—like they are—wearing a floral dress. We're a bigenerational set of country triplets and it is the worst thing ever.

Aunt Sandy is incredulous but not about the dresses. "The ceremony is going to start in twenty minutes. What were you doing out there?"

Avoiding you two and all my other relatives.

While I'm trying to come up with an appropriate answer, Nick rushes in with a convenient lie, "I was finishing up a call. About work."

"Oh, well. That explains it." My mom smiles and steps over to set her hand on Nick's arm. "I know how busy you must be. I understand. But I'm so glad you were able to take the day off and come."

I am thoroughly embarrassed by the way my mom is gushing over Nick. Telling him all about our family and friends who come to town for the day. When she starts to describe my high school graduation open house, I know exactly which other event is on her mind.

"Um, Mom," I cut in and pull Nick away. "We better go sit down."

Her eyes widen. "Of course. Sit on the groom's side." She actually giggles and smiles at Nick. "Of course. You knew that already."

I let one of the ushers take my arm and escort me down the aisle. Nick scoots in next to me.

"Your mom is pretty excited."

"Oh yeah," I reply, looking around us to make sure we aren't sitting near anyone who might try to talk to me. "I bet she's taking notes to make sure my wedding is better. Just a bit of friendly competition, you know."

Crap. Where did that comment come from?

Nick bumps my leg with his. "You're getting married?"

My face flashes hot. Apparently I'm the one who needs to keep their mouth shut.

"Nobody waiting in the wings?" he asks.

I give him a look.

He shifts around and gets comfortable. "I'll take that as a no."

Chapter Twenty-Nine

Surprises: Bigger isn't Better

The appearance of a lady wearing a midnight blue dress and seating herself at a piano that has been wheeled to the front of the sanctuary marks the beginning of my cousin's wedding. I know the piano has been wheeled in, because it's crammed into a corner no self-respecting volunteer would allow herself to be stuffed into every Sunday morning. Those steady women who play every Sunday must expect better working conditions. As the woman in the midnight blue dress begins playing, I consider this — if the piano has been wheeled in where does the usual accompanist sit? Has the usual organ been replaced by this fancy black piece? Where have they hidden it? The usual organ. Maybe I'm wrong and the volunteers are crammed into the corner like that every Sunday. If I were them, I'd complain. It isn't right to treat people that way and this is a church after all so people should be especially nice and considerate to each other. They can — I'm not sure I could. Sunday mornings don't usually work for me. About sixty-five percent of the time I'm not feeling so well. And there's that whole thing about not liking to get up early. Catholics have Saturday night services. I guess I could be a Catholic. But if I were a Catholic, I think I'd have to have a lot of children. If I had a lot of children, I'd have to get up early. Either that or marry someone who makes a lot of money so we could hire a live-in nanny who would feed, clean and dress the little darlings then bring them into me all fresh and ready for the day. I'd pat their sweet heads and kiss them then she'd take them off to play. So I could… What do good Catholic women do all day? Volunteer work. At the church. Where they would probably want to cram me into a corner.

"Hayley, stand up!"

Why is Nick hissing at me?

He grabs my arm and hauls me to my feet. *Oh!* The bride is coming down the aisle. White satin is swirling all around her and white lace is cascading down the back of her head. She looks beautiful, no doubt about that.

As she passes by, I take a slow, deep breath and wait to see if any of my disgrace or dishonor is going to rise to the surface. Am I overcome with pettiness, with the sudden rush to find something wrong with her dress? Or her flowers?

I am stunned to realize that the bridesmaids have already gone by in their tea-length sea-foam attire, and I haven't even wrinkled my lip at them. I have to admit that last summer, during the annual string of post-graduation weddings, I did on more than one occasion say an unkind thing or two about the dresses, tuxes, flowers, cakes, invitations, food, music, reception locations, reception decorations, rings, drunkenness of the mother of the bride, lack of alcoholic beverages, general stupidity of guests and annoying children relatives dancing.

Oddly, today, I feel no nastiness. I'm actually happy for my cousin that he has found the woman of his dreams and is starting a new life.

Is that sincere happiness for someone else I'm feeling? No petty jealousy? No skepticism?

What has changed? Certainly not my maturity level. As if.

After a while, I give up paying attention to what's going on up front. It isn't as if we're all watching a movie. We all know how this bit of business is going to end. Mr. and Mrs. will smile their way down the aisle and the rest of us will get one step closer to the food and I'll get to see what, if any, decent beverages are going to be made available. A few glasses of something will be in order if I'm going to make it through this night.

As they exchange rings, Nick grins at me. What's he got to smile about? I quirk my eyebrow at him, he keeps smiling.

Maybe he's thinking— *Thank God this is almost over and they better have something good to eat because I'm starving.* I want to tell him that he is sure to be disappointed because I don't think they'll be serving pork rinds, then I think better of it. Talking at weddings is so rude.

Several rows up, my aunt is sobbing and my uncle is murmuring to her. My mom looks weepy too. Me? No problem. I'm still shocked that I'm not taking nasty notes to report back to Riana and Josie. But this is a problem. I've got to have something to sidetrack them with when they ask if Nick had fun?

I take a quick look around, hoping to find something mildly interesting, something — or rather — someone catches my eye.

It's a tiny man in the back row. He's wearing a snazzy single-breasted, brown suit and glossy cowboy boots. I have a good view of the boots because he's leaning negligently back with one ankle resting on the other knee. The sun has streaked his wavy, overgrown hair so that it glows and sets off his deep tan.

Hmmmmm… Actually, he's a bit of a hottie.

Crap.

He's spotted me staring at him.

Instead of politely glancing away, his gaze lingers, talking to me as he flashes a sly grin. His perfect white teeth glimmer between his lips. 'Yeah, I know,' his eyes say, 'all the girls think that. They all want me.'

I scowl and spin away. I don't want him. I just want to find something stupid so I'll have something catty to tell my friends.

Everybody starts clapping because the couple has been united in holy matrimony. Well, some people are clapping because of that, some of us are clapping because it's over and we get to move away from the rude guys leering at us.

Nick and I turn around as the bride and groom bustle by, and I see that the miniature cowboy is still watching me. Like everyone else, he stands up as the bride and groom rush out of the door.

Nick starts chuckling and leans in to whisper, "Check him out, Hayley. He wants you."

My face flashes red. "Shut up. He does not."

"Then why is he looking at you like that?"

Because I was checking him out first? "I don't know. He just looks like that kind of guy."

Nick is laughing at my one size fits all response. "Whatever. But you better be ready to tell him why you don't want to dance with him."

I grab Nick's hand. "I'm with someone!"

"I don't think his kind of guy cares about that."

"Let's go find my brother. I bet he's got some Wild Turkey in his car."

Anxious to get away from anyone who might want to talk to me, I drag Nick through the side door. Sure enough, we find my brother sprawled against his car with Dorst, one of my other cousins. I know neither of them care at all about my wedding that didn't happen. Their heads are bobbing to Insane Clown Posse. Even though Nick casts me a why-the-hell-are-they-listening-to-that-in-the-church-parking-lot look, I'm not surprised because in my brother's case, he's unable to be polite.

I introduce Nick then — always glad to fulfill my duties as the bossy sister — ask, "Did you even go to the ceremony?"

"Yeah," he answers over the inane lyrics. "We came late so we sat at the back."

Dorst's head stops bobbing long enough for him to add, "Behind some little dude."

"Yeah, before it got started he was cleaning his fingernails with a knife."

"A pocket knife."

Like anybody cares, Dorst. Guys can be so stupid.

"Yeah," my brother says, "he looked pretty tough. I wouldn't mess with him."

Nick is looking at me out of the corner of his eye, addressing the twin idiots, "You talking about that little guy in the brown suit?"

"Yeah, you saw him?"

Nick is chuckling, so I smack him with my mini clutch. "Shut up."

Our little scenario has got the full attention of my brother and Dorst. Their glazed over gazes are fixed on Nick.

"What's up, man?" they ask in unison.

"Whatever." I wave my hands at Nick. I could get all embarrassed but decide it isn't worth the effort.

"He was checking Hayley out."

My brother is delighted. "Ohhh, Hayley..."

What losers, really.

I push my brother away from his car door and reach under his seat for the bottle of Wild Turkey that from past experience I know will be there.

"Who says?" he whines, when he spots me unscrewing the cap to take a swig of the half full fifth.

I ignore his lame protest with a smile and after drinking enough to burn my throat, pass the bottle to Nick, who uses it to salute. "Thanks, man."

Realizing he is outmatched, my brother goes along with it, like it was his idea.

We stand like that, enjoying the low budget combination of Insane Clown Posse and Wild Turkey long enough to empty the bottle. With the cheap courage of the whiskey fortifying me, Nick and I agree it's time to head back over to the lingering cluster of well-wishers and double-check the directions to the reception.

* * * *

After the mercifully uneventful buffet dinner, Nick and I pick at the cake on our plates while the farmers trade horror stories.

"Too much rain."

"Not enough rain."

"Rain isn't what it used to be."

"1982 was a good year for rain."

"Prices too high."

"Prices too low."

"Prices aren't what they used to be."

"1998 was a good year for prices."

"Kids too busy."

"Kids too lazy."

"Kids aren't what they used to be."

"1975 was a good year for kids."

Finishing up with those exciting topics, leaves a lull in the conversation. The men stare at each other and look helplessly around the room wondering where their wives are and how much longer they have to sit around in their starchy Sunday best.

One of the men zeros in on Nick. "What kind of work do you do?"

While Nick answers their questions about who he is, who he knows, where he lives, how come he never played ball, basketball, or wrestled, and why he prefers Fords over Chevys, I watch the sea-foam dresses gyrate gently as the bridesmaids and groomsmen slow dance.

There has to be a way out. I wait for one of the country folk to take a breath and cut in to ask Nick if he wants to dance.

He hops to his feet.

"Trying to rescue me from the old timers?" he asks, as he sets one hand on my waist and pulls me so close I can see the cute dimple that only shows up when he almost smiles. The weight of his body against mine makes my pulse stall, then skitter and all of a sudden I'm wondering why we haven't had sex again. Then I'm wondering when we will.

I glance up and our gazes connect. Suddenly I'm shy. More shy than when we were naked, screwing like bunnies.

"I don't need saving," he says into my ear as he settles his palm on the small of my back.

Electricity makes my skin fizzle.

Moving us toward the center of the dance floor, he whispers, "Did you hear what they were saying about using GPS for harvesting? Pretty interesting."

I have no idea what he's talking about.

I tip my head and gaze sideways at him. "Be quiet and dance. It'll keep you out of trouble for a few minutes."

"I didn't realize I was in danger of getting into trouble."

Is this the same Nick? Because all of a sudden he doesn't look, or feel, the same. Not at all.

I stare at him, and he stares back. Maybe that friends with benefits sex thing really is a myth because right then I don't feel like a friend.

When the song ends, Nick pauses to ask me if I want to go sit down. And for the first time in quite a while I'm happy with what I'm getting so I stay curved in Nick's arms and ask, "Want to keep dancing?"

His eyes flash in the glow of the rented disco lights and that dimple is back. He pulls me against him, and I melt, my soft curves matching the firm lines of his chest. We dance for most of the song in silence. The time spent wrapped in his arms gives me a chance to consider about what I want from Nick. Sex. Yes. Obviously. Friendship. Oh course. As always.

Those together require total honesty, but each on their own...maybe not.

"Tell me what you're thinking."

I don't want to think. I tip back, look into his eyes and smile. "Me too," he says.

Am I blushing? Good God.

"You want more from me than that. I know it."

I do my best to lift one eyebrow, doing what I can to look seductive and mysterious.

"Give me a chance," he says. "I'll prove it to you."

"Are you prepared for safe sex?" I ask.

He drops his hand and smacks his back pocket. "Want me to prove that to you too?"

The truth tumbles out before I have a chance to edit it, "Yes. I do."

* * * *

"Hey." Nick is kicking some dusty pieces of hay that have probably been in the hay loft since I was in middle school. "I like this place. It's pretty awesome."

I look around the hay loft of my family's barn, trying to see the planks, piles and mess through his eyes. There hasn't been much use for the loft for years, ever since my dad gave up on the idea of raising cows. Or, to be more accurate, calves. But there is enough old stuff that it looks authentic. A couple of buckets, a rake and — the hay. The moonlight is coming in through the windows at the end, stretching across the wood planks. Some ancient garden tools are piled in a corner. I suppose it might look kind of awesome. Like some country music video.

The setting might look casual and laid-back but between Nick and me there's a weird, awkward silence that kind of makes me mad. Mad for no good reason, I know. But mad still the same. I'm fighting against something I can't see or understand and somehow he is part of it.

"Why?" I ask. "Why do you like it? What is there to like?" I wave my arms and spin, looking around at everything that represents my life. Pitchforks, dust, wood, empty feed sacks, junk nobody wants and other random, country stuff.

"I like that it reminds me of you."

That is the worst thing ever.

"I don't want anything to do with any of this."

"You are this."

"No. I'm not."

The two of us are standing in the center of the hayloft, he's looking me up and down and I'm frowning as though my life depends on it. It's probably not the expression he's expecting. Maybe he thinks I should be grinning or wearing some totally sappy expression. One by one the vertebra of my spine straighten and I glare at him, challenging him to do something but I don't know what.

He shrugs off his jacket and drops it. Then he runs his fingers down the buttons of his dress shirt, loosening each one with a sharp twist of his fingers. Once it is totally unbuttoned, he tosses it aside, sending a small puff of dust upwards. Even though it's a bit chilly, he whips off his white T-shirt, creates another puff of dust when he throws it down, then grabs his belt.

His hands linger on the buckle, and I take a long look at his knuckles before lifting my gaze. Remembering how it feels to be pressed against him makes my nipples tighten and my body starts to quiver. He can make me quiver harder, I know. So hard I shake.

Heart thumping, blood pounding, I look him over. He sees me watching him and smiles as he pulls his wallet out. One of his eyebrows tips up as he slips a packet from inside it and holds it up. The gold letters on the dark square blink in the moonlight. "You still want to do the friends with benefits thing?"

"Are you asking me if I want to have sex with you? Here? In the hayloft?"

The buckle of his belt jangles faintly as he unloops it and lets it hang over his zipper. "What do you think?" he asks, the one eyebrow still cocked and a smile lingering on his lips.

"I think you want to know if I can be as hot and wild as a romance novel heroine."

"I already know the answer to that." He unzips his khakis and kicks them off. Standing in front of me in only his briefs he adds, "What if I told you I didn't want to be your friend?"

I make a point of looking down at his crotch, playing along with his game. "You sure look friendly."

That slanted smile doesn't reach his eyes. "What if I want to be your boyfriend? What would you think about that?"

The questions hang between us.

I don't want to admit it, even to myself, but I like the way he looks, standing there in my barn. It's like he belongs there. He's as rugged and strong as the wood, as solid and purposeful as the structure. He's there to do a job and right now that job is fucking me.

There have been guys who wanted to have sex, like Clifford, but Nick is looking at me like he wants to have sex with *me*. Does that make him my boyfriend? Whether we admit it aloud or not?

We could already be having sex. But he's waiting and I owe him a response. A truthful one. "I don't know what I think."

He props his foot on a wooden crate and leans forward. "I'm willing to start with what I can get." His biceps bunch up, reminding me of how his arms feel when he pins me down. "But that's not where I want to end up."

I don't want to talk, so I move forward and put my mouth on his. He kisses me back, deepening the kiss without even touching me, guiding my head back by applying pressure that makes me submit. He moves his tongue across mine. The motion is quick and simple but my whole body responds. My legs are shaky, my pussy is wet and my breasts are heavy.

When I start to pant he lifts his mouth and says, "Take your clothes off."

I slip out of my shoes, kicking them aside to stir up my own cloud of dust. While he watches, I start on my clothes. In a very matter of fact way, I undress. It only takes a few seconds for me to be standing in front of him wearing nothing but my bra and panties.

"You look perfect." He glances around us then looks up at the solid rafters in the ceiling. "Here, in this place. It's you. And you're mine."

It doesn't make sense to be mad at him for wanting me, the real me, the me who belongs in a barn, but I am.

Nick comes to me. The heat of his body warms my skin before his hands, and he reaches around to slide his fingers into my panties and grab my ass. He cups my cheeks with his fingers and pulls me to him. When I press my body against his, I feel the rigid line of his dick through the silky wet fabric. I roll my hips forward, doing what I can to get some pressure on my clit, and I take a deep breath of his familiar musky scent.

To get closer, I lift one leg and wrap it behind his back. Nick grabs my ass again, and I copy his motion and reach around to grab his too. He laughs and rocks forward a couple of times. Because I'm on one foot, I have to cling to him to keep from falling.

"Yes'm, ma'am, that's the way I like it. Grab my ass, country girl."

I don't want to laugh, but I do. "I'm not a country girl."

"Oh really?" He runs a row of kisses down my neck. "Seems to me like you're about to get busy in the hayloft. That's pretty country."

I want to smack him but the goofy look on his face makes me laugh harder. "Stop it," I manage to get out between bursts of laughter. Now is not the time to laugh but I am.

He takes my leg from behind his back and guides it to the floor. He steps back and lifts his hands. "Stop that?"

I move forward and get close enough so he can grab me again. "No. Not that."

He puts his hands on my breasts and strokes the skin above my bra cups. My nipples respond instantly, getting harder and more sensitive. "If we were boyfriend and girlfriend, would you think you could tell me what to do?"

The light caress of his fingertips is making my nerve ending skitter. I can't possibly think when he touches me. "Please stop talking and finish getting naked."

"You first." He reaches behind me and unhooks my bra. It falls to the wood planks with a soft thud. He puts his hands back on my breasts, this time lifting them so he can put his mouth over one nipple. The flick of his tongue is amazing. It makes a new wave of heat flare through me. Sure it starts where his mouth is, but it spreads through my whole body, flowing with such a crazy force I think I might forget to breathe. My muscles begin to twitch and tense.

After he moves his mouth to my other breast, I hear myself moan. He straightens and puts his hands on each side of my face.

"I like it when you lose control like that." His voice is low and rough. It's okay to lose control sometimes, Hayley. Especially when you're with me."

I'm starting to shiver but it isn't from the cold. It's from the electricity flashing through me, making my nerve endings fizzle with need. The crazed buzzing of my body keeps me from holding back the truth. I don't want to be Nick's casual fuck buddy. I want to be his girlfriend.

"Tell me what you're thinking, Hayley."

No. I can't.

He's still holding my face in his hands. I can't look away, I can't turn from the truth. But it scares me. Last time I thought I was in love, I wasn't. Not even close.

Would Nick believe me if I told him that I've never felt like this? Would I believe myself?

"Tell me," he says again and I can feel his need.

"I was thinking I want you to take your briefs off."

He lets go of my face and drops his hands. We work together to yank off his briefs. He drops to his knees and pinches the waistband between his fingers. I think he's going to pull them off, but instead he places his mouth on my stomach and kisses me so lightly I can barely feel the press of his lips. Still I weave from the roll of lust he creates. Seeing him kneeling before me, his mouth so close to my pussy, makes my legs weak. I reach for his shoulder to brace myself, and he angles back. Inch by inch he tugs off my panties, backs me up all the way to the opposite wall then presses my back to the wide, weather-worn trim around the window. The wood is smooth and solid against my back. I lift one leg and brace my foot on a low piece of trim.

Good thing he has that packet handy because my thighs are spread apart and I'm hot and wet. He looks amazingly sexy as he tears it open and covers his hard dick. Just when I think he's going to thrust into me, he pauses for a second and looks me over, his gaze soft from the rays of moonlight coming in through the opening. "You really are beautiful, Hayley."

I open my mouth to say thanks, or something similar, but he starts kissing me again and the only thing I can think about is him, his body, and the way his makes me feel like my world is spinning as he starts to slide his cock into me. But he pulls back.

"Why, Hayley?"

I can barely breath. I definitely can't think. "Why what?"

"Why is it so important to remain just friends?"

"I—I—" I grab his butt cheeks, harder this time and squeeze.

"We're going to talk about it later," he says, rubbing his cock against my clit. His cock is big and hard, and I want it inside me. "But for now..."

"Yes," I say, taking his shaft in my hand and placing his tip between my slick folds.

Bit by bit he enters me, filling me so slowly that I'm tempted to beg for more of his dick. Finally he is all the way in and for a few seconds he remains still.

I cling to him. "More," I say. "Now."

He draws back then thrusts in, going inside just a bit more until he fills me completely.

The groan that comes from deep inside him matches mine and we work together, thrusting in a frantic rhythm of back and forth, deeper and deeper, until the last of my control falls away. He holds my back to the barn wall, using the solid wood to keep me steady and upright, as he breathes in my ear and whispers my name when he manages to get his breath.

He's far and deep inside me. I can feel both his physical possession and his total acceptance of who I am. If I wasn't on the brink of coming, so hard and fast that it takes everything I have just to stay conscious, I might let myself be afraid of him getting that far inside my body and my heart.

But I can't fight it.

And just for those few seconds I don't want to fight it.

I sigh and moan and whisper his name as I come.

Chapter Thirty

New Features

Friday morning I scoot into the mini-kitchen of the clubhouse thinking of Riana who must be downing vitamins and praying that Peter has fallen and broken his leg because it is the long awaited day one of the two-day rally. I stare into the box of twenty-four donuts Mr. Hastings brought in to celebrate the day before our big day, humming and trying to decide which one I want to eat first.

"Hayley!"

It takes me a minute to figure out that Josie is calling me from the main room of the clubhouse. I grab two chocolate frosteds and make my way out to offer her one.

She is standing near my desk and takes it but doesn't smile. Even at a donut.

A black cloud drifts nearby. "What's up?" I ask.

Josie looks so serious my heart sinks. "Is... Did... Riana, is she okay?"

"Riana's fine. She's out there somewhere getting ready to pedal her ass off."

I only relax for a second. "What is it?"

"Well."

I set my donut on my desk. "Seriously, Josie. You okay?"

"Yeah. I'm okay. It's, well..." She takes a wad of newspaper out of her shoulder bag, unravels it, then hands it to me. "It's the new *Motor City*. I thought you better see it so you'd be ready."

Without waiting for her to finish, I grab the paper and flip through.

NEW FEATURE: BITCHY BOSS AWARD

Does the woman who signs your checks make your life a living hell? Is the chick who does your evaluations fit to be fried?

Nominate her for next month's bitchy boss award. If she's chosen, you'll win a day at Maxwell's Day Spa in Dearborn — so you can relax for once — and she'll get exposed — and get what she deserves for once.

Not sure if she's a true bitch or just a pain in the ass?

Compare her to this month's winner.

The Grosse Pointe Ghoul, Madeline.

The ghoul's offenses include —

Reading other employees' phone messages.

Often refusing to answer work-related questions and being rude when she does.

Disappearing for hours, leaving employees with no back up and no way to contact her.

Threatening to kill a tenant's pet

And the worst offense of all — totally stole another employee's promotional idea, took full credit for it, and was an ultra bitch about it.

Can your so-called supervisor top that? If you think so, drop me a line and maybe we'll get together.

Anger burns through me, making me wad the paper up and stuff it into my wastebasket. Maybe it isn't as bad as I think. After I steam for a few seconds, I grab it, smooth it out then read it a second time.

Josie's sister doesn't come right out and say it's Caroline from North Pointe Farms but anybody who knows Caroline and has half a brain will be able to figure it out.

Does Caroline read *Motor City*? "Is this online too?"

"Next week."

Shit. She'll know what I've been saying about her. On the record.

This turn of events can't be good for my five-year plan, whatever it is.

Sure, a month ago I would've hardly cared. Now— things are different. I've got people depending on me and in spite of myself, success has been spurring me on to—*horrors*—try to do a good job.

Josie has backed up and is standing halfway between my desk and the exit. Her expression is so overwrought, she might start crying. Even as mad as I am, I really don't want that.

I can tell by looking at the anguish in her eyes, that the damage her sister caused is even more painful than usual. This time, Josie sees the damage but has no way to do anything. She can't deny the deed or simply sweep it aside as some kind of communication problem.

"I guess it's part of her new reality series," she mumbles while looking at me from under her perfectly arched eyebrows.

Like that makes a difference? "Is she going to do a follow-up piece on the hell of job hunting?"

Josie doesn't know what to make of the scorn hanging on my words. She's frozen halfway between making a run for it and offering a tear-filled apology. But she doesn't do either.

I wish there was someone to toss the fiery ball of fault to but it glows brightly in my lap. Why didn't I listen to my instincts? Why did I ever talk to that stupid human sponge?

Those goths distracted me. Maybe that was part of her plan. I drank and talked and talked and drank while Josie's sister, sipped and listened. I sold myself out, probably giving her the idea for the story as I filled in all the blanks with my all-too-funny anecdotes about my very own boss from hell.

I am so stupid.

And that girl is such a bitch! How could she write something like that without telling me?

Who decided freedom of the press was a good idea? Benjamin Franklin? Thomas Jefferson? Why would anybody listen to those guys? Really.

My gaze meets Josie's and I know she is feeling my pain, because she has felt it before. "Stop standing there like that, looking at me that way," I grumble.

"You don't hate me?"

"I could never hate you." I smile wickedly. "I can hate her, though." My smile wilts. "Too bad my chances of getting back at her while I'm jobless and living on the street are pretty low.

"I guess I could park my stolen shopping cart in front of her office and shake my can of pennies at her every morning as she walks by."

Josie's phone rings, saving her from trying to convince me that my so-called career—the one that up until very recently I hated—isn't about to come to a screeching halt.

After talking for a minute she covers her phone and whispers, "It's Riana," then goes back to nodding and offering encouragement.

I go back to my chocolate-frosted donut and coffee while Josie is promising Riana that we'll be standing at the back entrance of North Pointe Farms to wave her on to the finish line.

Josie makes a joke about throwing herself in front of Peter but that turns out to be a bad idea because she has to follow it up with another round of gentle encouragement. "No, I was just kidding. I don't think he'll be ahead of you. Really."

After a couple more minutes, Josie drops her phone into her bag then turns to me. "I'm supposed to park at the back entrance a bit after three, right?"

"Yep. There are three more miles after that so we'll have enough time to cut through the parking lot to get to the finish line."

Josie frowns and starts staring at the carpet again. "I'm going to call my sister and tell her what a bitchy thing that was to do. You trusted her. You talked to her like she was a friend."

I wouldn't go that far but I did let down my guard. "Forget it. That's what I plan to do." As if. I shove Josie out of the door. "Three-fifteen. Don't be late."

A while after she's gone, I pick the article up, try to smooth out enough of the wrinkles then start reading it again. My blood pressure shoots up and my hands curl into fists. With a deep breath, I shove it aside.

That was nasty — tricking us all into talking about our jobs. What a sneaky witch.

I tear the article from the rest of the newspaper, slip it into the ridiculously tidy top drawer of my desk then stuff the rest of the paper into the trash. After checking to make sure there are no copies anywhere else in the clubhouse, I go back to my desk and start double-checking the last minute details for tomorrow.

Considering everything that's going on, the office is strangely quiet for the rest of the morning. I manage to get a lot done, important things like calling to confirm the stage set-up I reserved for the raffle drawing. I keep glancing at the door, expecting Caroline to come steaming in and fire me. She doesn't show. No call either.

Maybe she's outside stuffing the interior of my car with wadded-up copies of *Motor City*. Maybe her absence is some sort of strategy to make me crazy. It'll never work.

I don't think.

I do wish she'd hurry up and get here so I could stop waiting and staring at the door.

Finally, at twelve-thirty, she strolls in with Tony. Alarm bells ring in my head because, number one, I'm pretty sure he hates her as much as I do. And, number two, I want to get the ugliness over with.

He must be up to something. But what?

Caroline comes up to my desk and scans the surface, the way she always does. "Any messages?"

She's eyeing the messages for Mr. Hastings and Tony, and I know she wants to read them. I ask coolly, the same way I have each day since I got my red chair, "Messages for you?"

Her controlled scowl is delightful. It means she hasn't seen the article. Yet.

I pick up the messages and hold them halfway between us. "I'm leaving at two o'clock today."

"Whatever," she says without taking her gaze off the pink sheets of paper.

With a sly smile, I slip Tony's message out of the stack, set it on the corner of my desk, and lean around her to say, "Message here for you, Tony."

I might as well annoy her during the little time I have left because once the shit hits the fan no amount of ass-kissing will matter.

Caroline's mouth pinches tighter when she realizes I have turned the message upside down so she can't read it without being totally obvious. I smile broadly at her. "Did you want to read Mr. Hastings' messages?"

She snatches Mr. Hastings' messages and starts flipping through them while Tony comes over to get his. Because I know what his message says, I'm not surprised when he looks less than pleased.

He gawks at me. "Mrs. Klonski wants me to babysit Snickers tomorrow?"

"Yeah. I kind of told her you were trustworthy so she thinks you'll be good enough to watch her beloved pet." I smile and add, "You should be flattered."

"Why doesn't she leave the dog in her apartment?"

"She thinks someone has been stalking her little darling, getting ready to kidnap him. She's afraid to leave him alone, especially when there will be so many strangers around."

He drags his hands through his hair and groans. "I can't... I'm...busy tomorrow."

Caroline spins around and pins him with one of the ultra-bitchy looks she usually reserves for me. "You are planning on being here tomorrow aren't you?"

"Well, yeah," he says with a shrug. "But I...can't watch Snickers all day."

I sit up. "She only needs you during the raffle drawing. I'm pretty sure she plans on winning everything so she needs her hands free."

He glances at Caroline then looks back to me. "How long will that be?"

"Only about thirty minutes. From around four to four-thirty."

By this time, he's sidestepped his way to the door and is looking really uncomfortable. "Couldn't you do it, Hayley?"

"No, I'm doing the raffle." *Duh.*

"I could do the raffle," Caroline says sweetly.

Um. No, I don't even think so, you fucking bitch. "Gee thanks, Caroline. But Mr. Neville put me in charge of it so I think I better do it."

She sets Mr. Hastings' messages on the corner of my desk then heads back to her office without saying another thing.

I get up and sit on my desk. "Sorry I can't help you out but it'll only be for a few minutes and you do have to be here anyway. Look on the bright side, we're all getting overtime."

He starts picking at his fingernails. "Yeah, well, I have to be somewhere at five-thirty."

"You'll be out of here by quarter to five at the latest. I promise."

He looks so sad.

"Okay?"

He sighs and throws his hands in the air. "Whatever! I guess I don't have a choice."

"Want to come with me to watch the bike racers go past the back entrance?" I offer as a consolation prize.

"I thought the race was tomorrow?"

"It's a two-day event, this is the short day. Do you want to come?"

Looking like the puppy that always gets pushed out of the basket, he mumbles, "No thanks," then leaves.

There's no way around it. Tony is weird. Flat out weird.

Chapter Thirty-One

Bad Stuff Does Happen to Good Girls

"Anybody go by yet?" Josie calls as she trots toward me.

I step off the curb into the road to stand beside her. We squint into the sun, trying to spot anything that looks like someone on a bicycle. "Haven't seen anybody, yet."

Without talking, we move back to the curb, hoping that Riana will flash by soon and put an end to our awful waiting.

Josie smokes while I check my phone a couple of times. Has Caroline read the article yet? Is Riana going to get past Peter—literally and figuratively? About the time I think I'm going to be sick from nerves, Josie grabs my arm. "I see somebody!"

We lean forward waiting and watching the blurry dot get bigger. And Bigger.

"It's not."

Josie can't say it and I can hardly think it. Riana has a blue bike and wears a blue helmet. The bike rushing toward us is black and the rider, who is pedaling like mad, is wearing a black helmet.

That asshole Peter doesn't even glance our way when he speeds by.

I grit my teeth and resist the urge to throw a rock at his back, which is now shrinking as he zooms west, toward the finish line.

Three more bikers glide past.

"Wait, here—"

"It's her!"

We both shout and cheer as Riana rolls toward us. Her legs are pumping hard and her shoulders are low, still she manages to glance our way as she zips past. The determination slanting across her eyebrows makes my heart swell with bittersweet pride.

Josie and I shout and howl until she disappears down the road.

By that time, several other riders are streaming past so we cheer and wave them on too. Some of the other cyclists wave when we shout, "Only three more miles!"

After the next crush of riders flows past, Josie and I start jogging through North Pointe. We get about half way through the buildings, when I spot Caroline come bustling out of the clubhouse.

Usually the sight of her is simply irritating but something about the angle of her back, the way she's walking... Her face, it's not right.

I grab Josie's arm and pull her aside so we're hiding behind a bush. "Hold it."

Josie casts me a 'what's your problem' look but stays quiet. For once.

I stick my head between some branches and watch Caroline buzz around the parking lot. Her head is swiveling as fast as her legs are jerking as she struts around.

Josie gives words to my thoughts. "Who's she looking for?"

When Caroline stops and pivots on her cheap shoes, I spot a crumbled piece of newspaper gripped in her hand. The article.

"Damn that clean desk!" I groan. "We don't have time for her crap right now."

"What?"

Over my shoulder, I whisper, "She got that article your sister wrote out of my desk!"

Josie shrinks down. "Oh."

I shrink with her. "Yeah."

Caroline scans the lot with annoying thoroughness.

"I wish she'd get a clue and give up," I whisper. "We're going to miss Riana."

"Want to just go?" Josie asks. "What can she do anyway?"

"Besides fire me?" I sigh. "She'll chase me down, and dealing with her will take up time we don't have."

If the situation weren't so maddening, it would be funny. It might even be funny later, when I'll have time to laugh about it. We wait, crouching behind the bush, until Caroline marches off in the opposite direction then disappears behind the clubhouse.

I grab Josie's arm and we race through the parking lot, down the hill past Mr. Hastings' charming security booth, then stumble to a stop right next to the finish line.

There are clusters of other rider's family and friends. None of them are panting and gasping for breath the way Josie and I are. I suck in one last deep breath, then ask a woman standing near us if anybody has gone by yet.

She shakes her head and waves toward the corner with her phone. "My lookout says they'll be coming around that corner any second."

We spin and stare, like everybody else, at the empty street. The distant drone of the highway and the hum of the city settles around us. I start to dread the worst. Peter is going to beat her.

I glance at Josie. "It'll be okay," I whisper.

"If somebody else is going to come first, let it be anybody but Peter."

Just as soon as the words slip from Josie's mouth, Peter blasts around the corner and steams toward us. Long seconds tick past as he gets closer.

Damn.

I swallow against the disappointment tightening my throat and resist the urge to scream, 'You fucking fuckhead' at him as he zooms past.

Some people clap when he crosses the finish line. Josie and I turn back to spot Riana zip around the corner, pedaling like mad. Her legs are a blur, her face is glowing with pure willpower. By this time she knows that Peter has beaten her but she's still hanging in there. Two bikers cross the finish line before her.

Josie and I exchange glances. There's nothing to say so we stay quiet as we jog to the finish line. Wind whips around us as more riders stream past. The rest of the crowd is cheering and howling. Josie and I don't say a thing.

We get to the finish line in time to see Riana hobble up to Peter and offer her hand. He accepts the handshake with a broad smile that somehow doesn't ring true.

"Riana's too nice to do anything to Peter but maybe we can start a fight with his friends," Josie mutters.

I scan the crowd, looking for any other overly successful types. There are only basic Midwesterners hugging each other and looking like some made-for-TV movie about the importance of family.

When Josie and I catch up with Riana, Peter is still alone. He walks over to the timekeeper — probably to make sure he is listed as today's winner and to make sure his time is recorded correctly so that when today's time and tomorrow's time are added together, his total time will be correct. After he glances at the clipboard in the official's hands, he nods then wheels his bike toward the parking lot.

Josie is done hugging Riana so I take my turn.

Riana's face is still flushed but she's actually smiling. And her smile rings true. "It's okay," she tells us, even though we don't say anything about Peter beating her.

Like all the other cyclists, she's walking in circles and shaking her tired legs. After a while, Josie takes Riana's bike, and I help her slip her helmet off. Josie and I laugh and point at Riana's sweaty, flat hair.

"Shut up," she grumbles, making Josie and me laugh harder. Too soon, we stop chuckling and fall silent again.

All the things I want to say, 'Maybe you'll beat him tomorrow', 'You really tried', 'Who cares — he's an asshole' stick in my throat and I hate feeling tongue-tied and sad for my friend.

We meander over to the parking lot, where Riana parked her car that morning.

Riana takes her bike and helmet from us. "Thanks for coming."

Josie and I stand awkwardly, watching her slide her bike into her bike rack.

"Want to go get something to eat?" Josie asks.

Riana shakes her head. "I don't feel like eating." She tightens the straps on her bike rack then turns back to us. "I think I'll go home and get ready for tomorrow."

She straightens to find Josie and me staring at her like clueless kindergarteners.

"Really, it's okay. So he beat me." A half-smile tugs on her mouth. She swings into her car. "I'll see you guys tomorrow."

Josie tells her to get some rest then we wave as she drives off. We head to the back entrance of North Pointe so Josie can get her car.

After we cross the street, I pause by the edge of the lot and scan for Caroline. No sign of her so I jog to catch up with Josie who didn't even notice that I'd stopped.

Josie slows down after we pass the clubhouse then comes to a halt when we reach the bush we hid behind earlier. "I'm really sorry about what my sister did."

I grab her arm. "Come on. It'll be okay." But I know I'm not as strong as Riana. I won't have the nerve to shake Caroline's hand after she gives me the word.

And the idea of finding myself fired and jobless, limping my way back to the country, where God forbid, I might actually belong, pretty much scares the shit out of me. Without the intensity of the city surrounding me, exposing me to new people and news ideas, challenging me to be more than I am, I might lose the fragile new self-confidence I've struggled to build. I see now how important the past few months have been. I've gained a tiny bit of strength but that tiny bit wouldn't last if I had to spend every day looking into the faces of people who don't understand that what I want from my life is what's best for me.

After Josie gets into her car, I head to mine. Once behind the wheel, I pull out my phone and stare at it. *Text me, Nick. Text me. Call me.*

Nothing. Even though it's been days since we got back from my house.

We had super-hot, romance-novel sex in my hayloft. Isn't there some post-coital etiquette that requires him to text me? Or am I supposed to text him? My fingers hover over the screen but in the end I wimp out. I'm not ready to answer his question so I toss it back into my bag.

Chapter Thirty-Two

Basic Black

It's Saturday morning, day two of the rally and 'my big day'. A couple of hours after waving Riana off, I'm at my desk double-checking ticket stubs by making sure the names and phones numbers are legible so I don't have to mumble through a winner's name and embarrass myself. I'm regretting talking Tony into helping me, because he's sitting in the red chair, swinging his legs, drinking coffee and chattering on about how he has to decide whether or not to renew his lease.

"There's a place over on Second."

No! I live on Second! I shake my head and tell him he wouldn't like it there. "It's impossible to have people over because there's never anywhere to park."

"I guess you're right. Besides, the place I looked at smelled weird… Anyway…I could move in with this other guy. He has a great house in Indian Village. He's redoing it and he said if I help him with the drywall and refinishing the floors that I won't have to pay rent. But he's going to try and sell it next spring and then I'd have to move again and why would I want to do that?"

Would Tony notice if I snatched that cup of coffee out of his hands? Obviously, he's had quite enough. Or he is nervous about something? Intriguing. What could he possibly be nervous about? I finish looking over the ticket stubs so I start going over the prize list with the certificates I picked up from the businesses earlier in the week. Every other heartbeat I look at the door, knowing that at any second Caroline will come flying through. She'll be waving the article, ready to prove once and for all that she really is the ultimate bitchy boss by firing me on the spot.

I know it's going to happen eventually. If I can hurry up and get away from my desk, where she can't find me, I might make it through the day. I'll be damned if I'm going to let her get to me before I've finished the only major work-related task I've ever started.

"Do you think?"

Why do people have to ask me these trick questions? Like I'm supposed to be hanging on their every word? "Well," I say with pretend thoughtfulness, "is that what you think is best? I mean, you have to look at both sides."

He stops swinging his legs and frowns. Just about the time I think I'm going to have to confess that I really have no idea what he's been saying because I'm waiting for Caroline to come in with a trash bag for my desk crap, he nods thoughtfully.

"You're right. I do have to look at both sides. But if I stay where I am, well, um…"

If he stays where he is, he'll probably drive his roommate crazy. *Hey, wait a minute.* "I thought you were living with your girlfriend?"

His grimace is so intense that his mouth practically blends into his neck. "Girlfriend?"

"Yeah, you said you had to use Caroline's computer because you didn't want her to find out what you were doing on the Internet."

"Oh. Yeah. Right. That's right."

I rest my elbows on my desk. "So whatever happened with that, anyway?" I angle in closer because he looks panicky, and I'm delighted to see someone else looking the way I feel. "Why do you look...upset, Tony?" I grin evilly. "What's up?"

He starts picking at a piece of non-existent lint. "Caroline's not very good with computers, is she? I asked her about it yesterday, she wouldn't give me a straight answer. I mean, she only knows the basic stuff. Right?"

Now things are getting somewhere. "As far as I know."

"That's good."

"Out with it, Cattalioni. What have you been up to?"

He smacks his thigh. "Nothing really. Just checking that site like I said."

"So why the sudden concern for Caroline's computer skills? You going to ask her if she wants to sign up for a course at Henry Ford with you? So you two can be buddies? Maybe you want to move in with her."

"Yeah. Right. Me and Caroline a hot item." He gets to his feet. "I gotta go make sure that equipment got delivered. You know, the sound system and those tables for the pool party. What time is that thing starting anyway?"

"Caroline left a memo about it by the coffee machine. I think it goes from eleven-thirty to three-thirty. It should end a little before the riders cross the finish line. In time for the raffle."

"Okay." He smoothes back his hair and shuffles toward the door. "I'll see ya later."

"Hey, Tony?"

He spins back around and slouches at me.

"Don't forget you're supposed to babysit Snickers."

"Gee, thanks for reminding me," he says with an off-kilter scowl.

After he's gone, I start scooping up all the stuff I'll need for the day and cramming it into my backpack. My plan is to get out of the clubhouse ASAP and spend most of the day in the storage shed near the back entrance. Caroline will never find me there. The tools stored in there involve actual work.

Before I can get out of the clubhouse, Mr. Neville slips in through the side door and peeks into Caroline's sanctuary. "See her around?" he asks me.

"No, she's probably..." My reply tapers off when I notice the weird expression on his face. He looks like somebody just seriously rocked his world—and not in a good way.

"Have you seen her yet today?"

Is he going to ask me to go find her? Please, please, don't let that happen. "No, I'm sure she's right around here somewhere," I say while hoping nothing could be further from the truth.

I swing my backpack up and slowly inch toward the door. "Is there anything I can do for you, Mr. Neville?"

"No." His whole face pulls together. "I don't think so... It's about—"

"The pool party. I know." I stop moving and offer a false, reassuring smile. "Really, she must have everything under control."

He rubs his palms together then stuffs his hands into his pants pockets.

Talk about stressed. But I guess that makes sense. If the event tanks I bet he could lose his job. Good God, would they hire Caroline to replace him?

The horror.

Maybe I should ask him for a letter of reference real quick. Before somebody from Management shows up with a nasty notice in one hand and a cardboard box in the other. Probably not the best time for that though...still. "Um, Mr. Neville —"

"Have you seen her today or not?"

Can men get PMS? Because that personality flip was amazing. Lucky for both of us, I am an experienced PMS handler. "You're right. She isn't here. I haven't seen her. I don't know where she is."

"If you do see her, have her come down to the model which, thanks to you finding that new company, looks wonderful. I'll be down there with some of the guys from Regional for a while." He pauses and looks straight at me, all serious. "We're having a company dinner tonight after everything wraps up. You're an essential part of our team so you need to be there. Bring your boyfriend." Mr. Neville is smiling but I can tell he's got something on his mind. "I've invited some of the other new people who're making a difference around here. It's going to be a fun time."

Since I won't be any part of the team after Caroline shows I just nod as I inch a little farther from him and closer to the French doors. When he ducks into her office, I slip outside and hurry across the parking lot.

People from A-One Conference, the company doing the set up for the pool party and raffle drawing, are swarming all around the pool. Still no sign of

Caroline. Lucky me. I scurry between the buildings and jog to the storage shed.

The coast is clear so I dash across the drive and slip inside the shed. Tony's wide, walk-behind mower and tool chest are on the far side. Near the door are rows of chemicals and God knows what else. It doesn't matter to me what's stashed in there, because all I need is a place to plop myself down, which I find under the window that looks out on the back entrance.

As I'm slipping off my backpack, my phone starts humming. I pull it out and check the display.

"Hi, Mom."

"Have we missed anything yet? Because Sandy just called to say she's on her way. So we haven't left yet."

I shake out a blanket I'd stuffed into my backpack and spread it out, which is difficult to do one handed. "No, Mom. You know, you really don't need to come all the way here."

"Of course we're coming! This is your big day and we're so proud of you."

I drop down and stare out at the slice of world visible past the slightly open door. "Thanks, Mom, but, really you don't need to come."

"Of course we're coming. How are you, by the way? Are you going crazy, honey? Getting everything all set? You must be a nervous wreck!"

I glance at the stack of ticket stubs visible through the mesh pocket of my backpack. "I made a deal with the conference planning company. I told them they could invite their staff to the pool party if they also put up the stage I'm using for the raffle drawing. So I'm all set."

"Well! Aren't you the savvy businesswoman? Are you sure we aren't going to miss anything by not being there already?"

"Really, Mom. Things won't get going for a couple hours at least."

"You're sure we've got plenty of time? We can stop at McDonald's on the way?"

Mom and Aunt Sandy are hungover? "You guys want to stop at McDonald's?"

"We don't. Frankie does."

"Frankie? He's coming? Does he know how boring this whole thing is going to be?"

"No, honey. It won't be boring. It's your raffle. We're all so proud."

"Okay, but if you're all totally bored out of your minds, don't say I didn't warn you."

"No, if we're bored, we'll go to Greektown. Remember how much you used to love getting pizza there? Well, Frankie's never been and—oh! Here's your aunt! See you soon!"

My own mother hangs up on me.

Thinking about the busy bee workers taking care of everything for me, I get out the Grisham book Nick gave me a while ago and lean back. After about twelve pages, I realize nobody is funny, having sex, or wearing cool shoes that cost more than my entire wardrobe. I glance at the cover. Brown stuff. That should have been my clue. I like thoughtful books as much as the next girl does, but geez, couldn't there be at least one hot person?

I put the book aside, curl into my blanket and close my eyes.

* * * *

Dreams should *not* have cell phones. *Oh. It isn't part of a dream, it's my phone. Waking me up. Time?* I check my watch, sigh with relief that it's just a little before three, then answer the phone with a mumbled, "Hello."

"Hayley? Where are you?"

"Tony?"

"Yeah. Where the hell are you?"

I grin sleepily as I talk to weird Tony. "Where the hell are you?"

"Driving around trying to find a goddamn place to park my fucking car."

Bet he wishes he were having a nice nappie in the storage shed. The symphony of noise coming across the line is ridiculous. Something about it is vaguely familiar, but I can't place it. "What's all that noise?"

"People keep honking at me because I keep turning the wrong way. All the roads are fucked up because of the race and I can't park in the lot by the pool."

"Is all the parking taken?"

"No, it's just… Too hot to park there."

Too hot? What, is his car made of wax?

"Hayley!"

Whatever. I push my hair off my face as I stand up and look out of the window. "Can you get to the back entrance? I know they have it blocked off — if you go around the barrels you'll be able to park on the lawn by the storage shed."

There's a colophony of honks from the other cars and swearing from Tony, then, "I — Wait. Damn — get back in there…"

That sound. What the hell?

"Tony, do you have chickens in your car?"

"Damn it. How did you know?"

He's as surprised as I am. What the hell is he doing with chickens? "Go to the back entrance, I'll meet you there."

After a couple more 'goddamn its' and 'fuck yous', he clicks off. A few minutes later, I spot him creeping along the side of the road like he's trying to sneak in.

As he drives over the curb and rolls to a stop under a tree, I jog over to take a peek. Sure enough, he's got chickens crammed in his car. I lean in closer for a better look. A beautiful, burgundy Araucana rooster is fighting with Tony, who looks like he really could've used that nappie. The bird is hopping around inside a box while Tony is trying to stuff it back in. In the back seat, two caged birds and two more boxes with holes are clucking and crowing and making a substantial fuss.

I stare at the box on the passenger seat. "Whoever put that bird in that box didn't know what they were doing."

Tony scowls at me. "No shit," he says, trying to shove the bird back into the box. The rooster is flapping its wings and clucking like mad. Keeping one hand on the box lid, Tony turns off his car then grabs the roll of twine that's sitting on his lap.

With quick, clumsy movements, he wraps up the box, which is shaking from the bird's escape efforts.

In the back seat, a gorgeous Rhode Island Red and a huge, fat Leghorn are challenging each other with an energetic display of wing flapping. I turn back to Tony. "Are they all roosters?"

"Yeah." He throws the end of the twine down and wipes the sweat off his forehead. "That's what I needed. After I'm done here I'm taking them back. Thank God."

"Needed for what?"

"Never mind," he replies grumpily as he climbs out of his car.

I don't blame him. I'd be a little touchy if I were driving around in the heat with five stinking chickens raising hell.

"I'm only here to watch that stupid dog."

I check my phone. Two-fifty-eight. Nick should be here. In about twenty-five minutes Riana will be flashing by.

"Hayley!"

I spin away from Tony, to see my crazy cousin Frankie racing toward me. His smile is so wide, I grin back and even give him a hug when he collides with me.

He returns the hug, then jumps back, his eyes wide.

"Hey. Whatcha doin' with those roosters?" he asks, as soon I as I finish introducing him to Tony.

Tony glances quickly at me then shrugs. "Nothin'."

I tap Frankie's shoulder. "How did you find me?"

"I've just been wandering around, you know. This place is pretty cool. It's huge! Eww!" he wrinkles his nose. "I met that Caroline. You're right. Her hair doesn't move." He holds his palms a few inches away from his ears and chuckles. "It's like a helmet."

"Was she at the pool?"

"Yeah. I ate three hot dogs. I would've eaten four but Mom wouldn't let me. She said that would be disgusting."

Tony starts unrolling the windows of his car and the noise from the roosters gets louder. "I guess I gotta go find Mrs. Klonski," he says.

I glance at my phone again. Three-o-three. Tony finishes opening his windows then slams the last door shut on his mobile chicken farm. "Hey, Frankie. You going to be around for a while?"

"Yeah."

"Want to earn some money?"

"Yeah?" Frankie gazes around — being a country boy he's probably looking for a shovel or pitchfork. "Doin' what?"

"Keeping an eye on these chickens. Making sure they don't get out of their boxes."

"Seriously?" Frankie eyes the car. "Just standing around? How much?"

"Ten dollars?"

"Yeah?" Frankie glances at me. "Think it'd be okay?"

"Sure, as long as you stay here. Do not wander off. Okay?"

After he nods, I point toward the pool and clubhouse and add, "I'll tell your mom what you're doing when I go up."

After he nods, I head to the road.

Tony hollers his reluctant goodbye then wanders off to find Mrs. Klonski.

As I jog over to the curb, I spot Nick strolling toward me, with his usual long strides. "Parking was insane," he says when he reaches me.

From up on the hill, Frankie starts yelling, "Over here, Nick! Hey!" He takes a few steps forward but must have remembered his promise because he backs up and touches the hood of Tony's car.

Nick waves up to Frankie, grabs my hand and pulls me over for a quick but yummy kiss on the mouth.

"It's, um..." I grip his fingers tightly and swing his arm between us, trying to find a way to make my request sound reasonable.

"What's up?"

Still swinging his arm and this time avoiding his gaze, I add, "Can we um, not let on to my mom and Aunt Sandy that we're...we're...a thing?"

He stiffens his arm and frowns. "That's what we are? A thing?"

I try to soften him with a smile.

"You're being ridiculous, you know that, right? Because I bet they sort of caught on when we danced for an hour straight then disappeared after the reception."

He's right and I know it. "I'm not ready to talk to my mom about it. Not yet."

"Why?"

"I'll explain it all later. I promise."

Still frowning, he nods. "Okay but only for now."

"I really will explain later." Then I spot Josie crossing the road so I let go of his hand and whisper thanks. Smiling and waving, she hops up onto the curb.

Josie slows and jogs the last twenty feet. "Anybody...go by...yet?"

"Nope." Josie and Nick stare at the chickens in Tony's car at the same time but their probable question, 'What the hell is going on?' gets cut off by the sight of Riana flanked by several other riders speeding toward us.

She's doing it! She's in the first pack!

We all start screaming and jumping up and down, bumping into each other. The grin on Riana's face as she zips past is picture-perfect.

Nick wraps his arm behind me then we grab Josie and shake her. I bet even the roosters are excited.

"Hey" — I poke Josie — "where's your sister?"

After Nick finishes howling at Riana's back, Josie says, "I dropped her off by the finish line. She's walking around doing on-site interviews."

Nick is pulling us away from the road because more riders are streaming by. "Where's the asshole?"

Josie and I scan the riders. Peter is nowhere to be seen. The crush of racers thins and they start passing us in single file. Still no ex-boyfriend.

The peaceful whiz and whirr of bicycle wheels is broken by the throaty crow of a rooster. Josie, Nick and I swing around in unison.

"Frankie," I scream, running over to where he's trying to shoo the Rhode Island Red back into his cage. "What are you doing?"

"Trying to get this thing back in his cage."

I glance at the road, then back to him. "Why did you let him out?"

Frankie is waving his palms at the bird, the rooster is not about to go back into that tiny cage. "He looked so sad. I wanted to pet him."

"A sad chicken?" I glance at the road again, still wondering what happened to Peter, then turn back to my cousin. "You wanted to pet him?"

He casts me a defensive look. "Your dad pets his chickens."

I sigh. "Those are hens."

Frankie stops waving his arms and pops head first into the open car window. His dangling legs wiggle back and forth as he starts yelling, "Get back in there. No! Bad chickens! Stop that! Hayley! The other one is getting out!"

The flurry of feathers tells me there's going to be more trouble. Before I can get to Tony's car, the Araucana hops up and perches on the passenger door, flapping its wings and flipping its beautiful, burgundy head.

Nick and Josie step away from the road toward Tony's car. There isn't time to explain what's going on because one of the other birds, a flashy, Old English Bantam has got out of its box and is hopping around the back seat, trying to get the better of the Rhode Island Red that is still fighting with Frankie.

The Araucana is still posturing and showing off.

So far, the Leghorn and whatever else is in the other box are still out of the fray.

There's a reason why people pay money to see roosters fight. They don't mess around—with each other or with anything or anybody that gets in their way.

First things first, I reach in and haul Frankie out.

He's moaning with frustration and I have to hold him back from going after the birds that are hopping out of the car and chasing each other around the grass.

Getting those birds contained is not a job for one eleven-year-old boy. "Go get my mom. Explain what happened." I spin him around and tell him the quickest route to the pool. He stays frozen, staring at the birds as they challenge each other by bobbing their heads and spreading their wings. I hurry him to the top of the hill, point to the clubhouse and give him a push.

Once he starts racing across the hill, I run back to get my backpack and tell Josie and Nick I have to go do the raffle but stop short when I see Peter.

He's limping alongside his bicycle—right toward the Old English Bantam. Nick and Josie are darting around the grass, trying to keep the other three birds close to the car, so they don't see Peter. Even if they did, they probably wouldn't realize that what he's doing is really, really stupid.

A rooster who's flapping his wings and puffing up his chest isn't to be messed with. Of course Peter doesn't know that. That must be why he's swearing and kicking at the bird. Taking one's frustrations out on a rooster, no matter how small, is a bad *idea*.

A couple of riders slow down briefly to watch Peter stomp toward the bird but they turn away and pedal on.

Curving around Josie, Nick, and the loose birds, which they will never get rounded up, I run toward the road but don't get there in time to chase Peter away from that rooster.

After crowing once last time, the rooster turns into a flurry of feathers as it hops straight up and swipes Peter's arm with its spur. A bright red gash glows all the way from his elbow to his wrist. The bird isn't done. It's hopping around, getting ready to fly at him again.

I know. We all hate Peter. Still—I can't stand there and watch him get attacked by the rooster. When I reach the road I give the bird three swift kicks. The thing topples over, rights itself then runs off to hide in a bush and regroup.

A cluster of bikes speed past Peter who is holding his arm and whimpering, "Oh my God! That bird is fucking insane!"

"You okay?"

Josie and Nick come racing up to ask him if he's okay too. Over in the grass, the other roosters run off to take shelter in the bushes. Everything falls quiet.

"Hayley!" Josie turns to me. "That was awesome. You totally saved him!"

Crap. The raffle. I check my phone. Three-fifty.

Riana!

Josie slips past Nick, takes Peter's bike then looks at me. "He needs to get cleaned up right?"

My amazing skill impressed her so much that she assumes I know these things about rooster scratches. I do, so I nod then add, "With some serious soap."

"I'll take him up to the clubhouse. Okay?"

But that means Josie will miss Riana's big finish. "You sure?"

Josie glances at the angry gash already swelling on Peter's arm and shrugs. "Yeah."

I dart over to grab my backpack out of the storage shed. "There's a first-aid kit in the bathroom."

Peter tries to look indignant as he clutches his swelling arm. "I don't need help."

I look at him with sharp eyes. "Check out that scratch. Where do you think that thing's feet have been all day? Can you say infection? You want a huge scar?"

He studies his arm, which is getting worse by the second, shoots a glance at the road, then looks at me. "Um, did you see —"

"Riana?" I nearly bark at him, stupid pain in the ass that he is. "Yes. I did see her. She was one of the first to go by."

Without saying anything to Peter, Josie wheels his bike toward the hill. Still holding his arm, Peter shuffles after her. The last thing I see before Nick and I hurry over to the parking lot and toward the finish line is the flutter of feathers.

"Are those stupid birds going to follow us?" Nick looks worried, probably wondering if the birds have a thing against guys.

"Probably. Come on."

Chapter Thirty-Three

Too Cocky

"I told you someone was trying to steal him!"

Why is Mrs. Klonski staring at me with teary, bloodshot eyes? I scan the crowd for Frankie, my mom or my aunt. *Where's Riana? Did she win?* I take Mrs. Klonski's arm and guide her through the mob of sweaty, bike riders and festive spectators as I make my way to the small, square podium that's been set up just past Mr. Hastings' security booth. "It's time for the raffle, Mrs. Klonski. Don't you want to see what you won?"

The old lady squares herself in front of me. "What about Snickers?"

"Tony has him." I slip around her and climb up the low steps. "Right?"

"No!" Mrs. Klonski follows me halfway up the steps and points over my shoulder toward the clubhouse. "Tony said he was going to keep Snickers right by the pool, until I got back. I just saw him go inside and he didn't have Snickers. Something's happened. I know it."

The mob around the podium starts to press closer. Frantically, I dig through my backpack for the raffle tickets and prize certificates. "Dogs aren't allowed inside, remember? Maybe Tony had to…go…to the bathroom. He left Snickers with somebody else. Did you go up to the clubhouse and check on him?"

Her face pulls together. "No. I came to find you. You said Tony would take very good care of my little man."

"I did?"

"Yes, you did. Don't you remember?"

Sometimes I need to keep my mouth shut.

All four sides of the podium are packed with people who are staring at me. Bikers holding their helmets mingle with residents who've eaten too many hot dogs. Their eyes say, 'We're hot, sweaty and tired. We want our prizes.'

Riana and Nick appear at the back of the crowd. He's pointing to her head and she's grinning like, well, like she just showed up her hyper-competitive ex-boyfriend, which is awesome.

I notice Josie going into the clubhouse with Peter. I point at them, but Riana and Nick don't get it. They probably think I'm being an excited idiot so they don't turn around.

"Hayley dear? Is it time for the raffle? What about Snickers?"

I'm back to 'Hayley dear'?

Obviously she's having a hard time dealing with the conflict here. Precious Pooch versus Prizes. She'll be my second rescue for the day. "Go check on Snickers. Any prizes you win, I'll set aside."

"You sure?" She starts digging through her pocketbook. "You need my tickets."

"No, I don't. You wrote your name on all the stubs, remember?"

She totters off as quickly as her feet will carry her.

If Tony did something stupid with that dog I'm going to kick his ass. I pick up the microphone and get started.

* * * *

"What do you mean you lost the dog?"

The raffle drawing was a huge success and after passing out the last of the prizes, I've come into the air-conditioned clubhouse to find Tony holding Snickers' cowboy hat but not looking very sad that he's misplaced the beloved pup. "I left him out by the pool and when I got back he was gone."

How stupid is this. "You didn't tie him up?"

"I had to check on something. You don't seem to get that I'm in the middle of something today." He shoves the hat in my backpack. "I've got to go, Hayley. You promised I could leave."

I didn't know men could whine like that. Too bad things are about to get even worse for him. "Your roosters kind of —"

The shriek from outside cuts me off. I throw down my backpack and race outside. Snickers, still sporting his red, white and blue sweater is chasing the Old English Bantam around the poolside tables. The Rhode Island Red, feathers fluffed and ready for action, is perched on the fence.

Oh! There's Caroline. The party's over and she's all alone, tiptoeing around in bright pink, high-heeled sandals. Now I know that she was the one who screamed because she's screaming again.

Urgh. It's an awful sound.

She glares at me. "Get that thing out of here."

Me?

It's Tony's fault the dog is knocking over plants and dragging down tablecloths. I spin around to see Tony dash off in the direction of the storage shed and disappear between some buildings. Well, he's about to get a surprise.

"There's my little sweetie! Oh, thank heavens!" It's Mrs. Klonski weaving her way to nowhere. "Come to Mommy, darling."

But Snickers is on a mission. He nips at the rooster and chases it around the corner. Mrs. Klonski huffs after them calling, "I won't let those nasty birds hurt you."

"Caroline?" Mr. Neville. Where did he come from? "Caroline. Would you please come to the office with me."

Hmmmm. He didn't say that like a question.

Caroline's opens her mouth then snaps it shut. She really looks like she wants to say something to me — *gee, I wonder what that could be* — but Mr. Neville has asked her, again, to go with him to the office.

The office.

Not *your* office.

"The chickens!" It's Tony again and he is so distraught I feel sorry for him. "I have to have the chickens!"

He gazes at me with big eyes. "Really, Hayley," he's pleading now. "I have to have those birds back or...I'm going to be in big trouble."

"Why is this my problem?"

"That Frankie kid, he's with your mom."

I throw my hands in the air. Those damn familial ties. "How many are still out?"

"Just these two." Even through his distress I can see the confusion swirling in his face. "Your friends were kind of helping, but it was your mom that caught the others."

The panic in his eyes sends me into action.

"Give me your shirt," I say.

He sighs, peels it off, and exposes a chest so evenly tan it looks plastic. "She used it too."

After he hands the T-shirt over, I shake it out then sidestep my way to the Rhode Island Red. Careful not to look the bird in the eye, I slide steadily closer until — *zip* — I've got it covered with the shirt.

Careful of its spurs, I hand it over to Tony.

His smile is crooked. "I guess I could've done that."

I reach for the bird. "I'll take that one to your car if you want to go after the bantam."

He backs up. "No, um, I'll go put this one in the car. Back in the box."

"Hey, Hayley." Frankie is sauntering toward us, and I can tell by the flash of color on Tony's face that he isn't too happy with my cousin.

Frankie flashes a contrite grin our way. "Hi, Tony. Sorry about the roosters thing." With that nasty business out of the way, he smiles wide at me. "Mom said I have to ask you if I can check out the microphone that you used for the raffle."

Holding the bird out as far away from himself as he can, Tony scowls at Frankie then hurries off.

Frankie swings around so he's in front of me. "Your friends said they'd be up here in a minute, that they went to put that girl's bike away. So can I? Check the mic out?"

"Sure," I mumble as I head around the far corner of the clubhouse, toward Snickers' yip. I see the dog dart back around the other side then disappear. Mrs. Klonski is chattering to her precious pet and it is totally ignoring her.

I cross behind the clubhouse, then pause outside the slightly ajar side door when I hear Mr. Neville.

"Thoroughly embarrassing. That sort of thing is inexcusable."

After a few beats of silence Caroline says, "There must be some misunderstanding. I'm sure —"

"My daughter showed me this!" The rustle of newspaper shifts through the air. "I had no idea this sort of thing was going on."

"That article is crap, um, Mr. Neville. I can explain, um…"

Not now, Snickers! I dive for him as he dashes past, hot on the trail of the small rooster. The pooch slips through my grasp and chases the bantam right into Caroline's office.

As I scramble in after them, Tony appears and holds out his shirt, which I grab and shake out. Caroline's steely gaze rakes over Tony's fake 'n bake chest. Mr. Neville does nothing but stand there looking damn surprised.

The chicken hops onto Caroline's desk then skitters across to her computer workstation. Its feet click across the keyboard. When it steps on her mouse and starts to slip, I toss the shirt over it and scoop it up. Seeing the bird out of his reach, Snickers barks twice then zips back out the way he came in.

When I turn around to hand Tony his bird he is so amazed by my skill that his mouth is hanging open. So is Mr. Neville's. That's one way to impress people on the last day at work.

But they aren't staring at me. They're looking at Caroline's computer screen.

I spin around. *Holy shit.* Right there on Caroline's computer in gorgeous, vibrant color is the very bird Tony's holding. And that Araucana. And a naked man with a huge erection. Bright red words scroll across the bottom—

COCK OF THE WALK. INTRO PEEK $4.99 COCK OF THE WALK. ALL MAJOR CREDIT CARDS ACCEPTED.

Josie's sister's voice comes from just outside the door. "Shit. Josie, are you sure this is her office?"

I spin back around to see Josie and her sister standing in the doorway with Nick and Riana looming behind. They're all staring at the screen too.

"Is there a problem?" Caroline is asking.

Stupid Caroline. She's marching forward as though she weren't in the middle of being totally embarrassed. Nobody is paying any attention to her because they're all staring at the roosters strutting across her computer screen. They might be looking at the very tan naked man too. Maybe. Me? I'm watching Tony slip out of the clubhouse through the front door for a change.

"You poor thing," Josie's sister is saying to me. "If I'd known she was this freaked out I would've got you a better prize. You need more than a day at the spa."

Caroline's face flashes red. "You got her the prize?"

"Yes. And I wrote the article."

For once I'm glad that Josie's sister is a power bitch because I will never ever forget the crazy mixture of embarrassment and rage swimming across Caroline's face. In fact, I'm still admiring it when I realize that she's streaking toward Josie's sister with both fists swinging. The snarling string of curses tumbling from her mouth would've impressed both Kid Rock and Eminem.

It's delicious.

We all step back. Some of us are shocked. The rest of us are delighted as Caroline and Josie's sister tumble around the office like second-rate stunt doubles. Papers are flying, files are spilling, and for a few seconds everyone not in motion is stunned silent. About the time Caroline's shirt is getting torn, Mr. Neville breaks them up. Josie grabs her sister, and Nick and I duck out of the door. Outside, I give Riana a huge hug and tell her how proud of her I am, and we all laugh about Caroline and Josie's sister.

Nick mumbles something about Mr. Neville breaking it up just when it was getting good so I smack him. "You're an idiot."

"I know," he says softly and our gazes hook up and something snaps between us. It's simple and obvious and I wonder why I didn't figure it out sooner. I'm in love with one of my best friends. He sets his hand on my hip and I know he feels the same thing.

Caroline is loitering in the doorway clutching her purse and pushing around her stiff hair. Mr. Neville is stepping toward us, calling my name. "Please step inside when you have a minute, Hayley." Without waiting for an answer, he goes back inside then closes the door.

"You okay?" Riana asks Josie's sister who has just come out of the clubhouse. I have to admit for a girl who was trading jabs a minute ago she looks pretty good.

For a tense minute I think she's going to say something totally bitchy. She doesn't. Instead, she and

Josie glance at each other and break out laughing. It's a crazy, wild, silly laugh and pretty soon Riana, Nick and I are laughing with them.

Still laughing, Josie's sister looks at me and says, "Hayley, we need to talk about the chickens."

My laughter dies in my throat. "What about them?"

"We want you to teach us how to raise them," Riana says.

I'm stunned. "What are you talking about?"

Josie kicks sharply at nothing then holds out her hands, carrying an invisible bird. "That stuff you did to rescue Asshole Peter and the maintenance guy was amazing. And those roosters are awesome. We want some."

"The city changed the laws. Lots of people are raising chickens in their backyards and I want to do a piece on it," Josie's sister says, using her know-it-all voice, which suddenly I find a tiny bit less annoying. "I'll call you. We'll set something up." Then she waves, calling out goodbye as she heads to the parking lot.

Josie and Riana are grinning and shaking each other like little kids. "We want chickens!"

I frown because they are being weird beyond belief.

Josie stops shaking Riana. "You teach us about the chickens and we'll be even for me saving your hair and showing you all the best places to buy clothes and helping you pick stuff out."

"I — I — " But what can I say? She did save me.

"Don't look like that!" Riana says. "We love that you're from the country. Especially now." She and Josie are hopping up and down again as she finishes with, "Because you're going to get us some chickens!"

I catch Nick's eye and see he's smiling and I'm smiling too because they are so excited and crazy.

"You can have hens. Not roosters. You saw what they can do!"

Riana isn't giving up. "Can we have just one rooster?"

"Maybe. We'll see how you do with the hens first."

Nick wraps his arm behind me and we all laugh until a low thumping beat bumps through the air. Nick nudges me and points to the podium where Frankie is standing, holding the mic in one hand and waving out at an imaginary audience with the other.

He taps the mic again, making it thump, then clears his throat and giggles.

"There once was a boy named Bart,
With great delight he did fart.
The gas he would pass,
Came out of his ass,
Until his butthole would smart."
Good God.

I guess I won't have to discuss the dangers of limericks and microphones with him after all because he's running from his mom and I bet when she catches up to him she's going to take care of that herself.

For the first time ever, I'm actually excited to go talk to Mr. Neville. So I'm smiling as I head into the clubhouse.

Chapter Thirty-Four

Then This Happened

Nick and I are sitting around a table in a private dining room with Mr. Neville and the guys from Regional. We're at a hip restaurant on Woodward and 'the guys' from Regional have turned out to be a mix of guys and women, and are actually pretty cool. We all got drinks from the bar and turned into best friends while waiting for the table. Holding my glass of wine, I bend down and give Nick a kiss. It's quick and sweet but means everything.

"That was pretty amazing, what you did with the chickens," he says as I slide into the chair next to him.

I say, "No big deal." But secretly I'm glad he noticed. That girl, the one who can handle chickens, is also this girl, the one who's been invited to this celebration dinner. And for the first time, that's feeling totally all right.

I lean over, kiss Nick on the cheek then actually giggle. It's a bit embarrassing but right then I don't care. Call me giddy.

Right after I'm seated, Ollie places himself at the head of the table and raises his drink. He waits until everyone around the table falls silent. "First thing, we need a round of applause for Hayley, who has just moments ago accepted the promotion to complex manager."

A polite round of clapping rises and fades. The people from Regional are cool, but wild would not be a word used to describe them. They are calm and collected. They've probably been to a bunch of these promotion dinners. But not me, I'm still smiling when Ollie raises his glass again. "A promotion well deserved, I must say. Not only did she do an amazing job with the celebration, she also solved one of our biggest and most expensive problems when she found our new painting company, Midtown Improvements. And I'm so impressed by their work that I've invited them to join us. Please welcome them when they arrive, but until then enjoy yourselves and—" He waves his glass toward the door of the private room. "Wonderful timing guys, come join us."

And in walks Waylon Walker.

Six-feet-two, two hundred pounds of brown-eyed country boy. He's impossible to miss in his shirt embroidered with his name and his company's logo. I realize what Todd was trying to tell me back at the bar then again at the dance—Waylon had started a new company, the very one that I'd initiated the contracts with for the complex, and he'd moved to Detroit.

Score one for Todd for trying to fill me in.

If I hadn't been so caught up in my own crap I would've listened.

But I had been caught up in my crap and so here I am—totally blindsided.

Waylon is shaking hands with Mr. Neville and saying hi to everyone from Regional. Everything is going as okay as it possibly can, considering the man I had promised my life to then changed my mind about at the last minute just walked in while I was sitting next to my new boyfriend. While my world is spinning, Ollie brings me into the introductions and says something implying that Waylon and I already know each other.

Needless to say, it's horrible.

I stand up, and when my gaze connects with Waylon's I lift my shaky arm and stutter, "Hello."

Waylon takes my hand and pumps it up and down three times then lets go and steps back. He doesn't say anything while we stare at each other.

I feel like I'm going to throw up or pass out or start crying. Nick stands and offers his hand to Waylon. "I'm Nick," as though that means something to Waylon.

"Waylon." My ex-fiancé takes my boyfriend's hand and they shake, each kind of wincing from the pressure the other puts into the grip.

Then they both look at me, and I have absolutely no idea what to say.

So I say nothing and continue saying nothing until some of the guys Waylon came in with start goofing around, smacking each other like twelve year olds. I spot Chip Patterson, a guy from back home, and he comes over to say hi. He's all smiles and silliness until Waylon tells him to sit down. Waylon finishes staring down Nick, backs off then goes to sit in one of the chairs at the other end of the table.

I drop myself down into my chair then Nick does the same.

"Anything you want to tell me?" he asks in my ear.

I shake my head then he leans away from me. I feel the distance between us as intensely as I'd felt our closeness moments ago.

For the first time ever I appreciate Oliver Neville's social cluelessness. He's smacking people on the back, laughing and making so much noise about how amazing the new 'players on our success team' are that I can get away with not saying anything to anyone. Cheers and laughs float around like a soundtrack.

The server comes by, passes out menus and people start ordering. "I'll have the Jamison burger and a salad with oil and vinegar," Nick says. "Hayley?"

It takes me a second to understand he's prompting me to order. "I'll have the same," I say, even though I don't remember what he ordered.

After the server leaves, all the people around me, except Nick, start talking. I pretend to listen. Eventually my heart stops thundering and I'm able to talk. Occasionally the sound of Waylon's laugh makes my stomach twist but each time I feel like I'm going to run from the table, I dive into one of the conversations around me. Tigers baseball. City politics. Police brutality horror stories. I don't care what people are talking about, I jump in only to lose focus within seconds. Nick saves me each time and I find myself gulping for air, trying to remember what I was just talking about. Hearing his voice, feeling him beside me, it's a constant reminder of what I kept from him and what will now be even harder to admit.

Minute by minute I alternately dread and welcome the end of the meal. When it finally arrives, Nick thanks everyone and shakes Mr. Neville's hand.

"Thank you, Mr. Neville," I say, reaching out my hand.

"You really ought to call me Oliver now," he says.

I force an appreciative smile and call goodbye to everyone from Regional. I wave at Chip. He waves back. I half-heartedly wave at the other guys from Waylon's company and ignore Waylon completely. He ignores me back.

Outside, Nick sets his hand on the small of my back and says, "You're going to tell me now, right?" His touch is light, not possessive but reassuring.

"Okay." Even though he's right next to me, I can't feel his body heat because my blood is chilled.

Nick responds to my lame reply. "Okay isn't the same as yes."

We walk toward his truck which is parked about two blocks down on Woodward. Light from the bowling alley across the street flickers, casting a lemony glow over the traffic rumbling past.

I'm hoping Nick will take my hand, lace his fingers between mine and make everything okay. He doesn't. I don't blame him. I keep wanting it but I know it's up to me to make things right. I blurt out, "I was engaged to him. Waylon. Back home. I was supposed to marry him last spring."

The neon glow of the city shadows his face when he looks over at me. "And?"

"We planned the wedding." It actually feels good to say it aloud so the rest tumbles out. "We sent invitations. I bought a dress."

Nick and I reach his truck and climb in. I snap on my seatbelt. He snaps on his. But he doesn't start the engine. He's waiting for me to say more.

"I had the dress fitted. My mom has pictures of me all covered in pins, wearing flip flops and drinking a Diet Coke."

He's not getting the significance of the dress. "I took pictures *with her* while I was wearing the dress. My wedding dress. She posted them on Facebook. And Instagram. Everyone was excited—my family, his family, all our friends. But I— I—" The reflection in the window stares back at me, and I see the face of a girl who everyone said walked away from the best thing she ever had. All these months later, I know they were wrong and I'm proud of myself for doing what I had to do, but I still feel the weight of their judgment and the gravity of my actions. Finally, I get the last words out, "I canceled it the night before. At the rehearsal dinner."

He sets his hand on my thigh. I look over. No more words come out of my mouth but tears do come out of my eyes.

The corner of his mouth quirks. "Your mom's on Instagram?"

I sigh. "We had a hashtag. HayleynWaylongethitched."

He shifts in his seat and lifts an eyebrow. "Seriously?"

My mouth twitches into a smile and the tears slow up. "Kind of stupid, huh?"

He laughs lightly but stops when I turn toward the window. He lifts his hand and I'm alone again.

This time I concentrate on not seeing my reflection and look out at the battered concrete of Woodward, the broken facades of the run-down shops and fast-food bags rolling like tumbleweeds on the sidewalk. This is the place I'd come to mend my spirit. This place of broken down dreams and newfound hope. Only here in this city can those two impossibilities live together and make sense.

I look in the direction of the river, wanting to see the restored parts of the city and remember how great I felt when I first arrived. But I can't. I keep remembering the expressions on everyone's faces when I walked out of the rehearsal dinner. Even worse than that was the argument with Waylon the next day when I told him about the bank account I'd opened with his grandfather's gift. In the end, I'd given in to the weight of my guilt and agreed to Waylon's demand. I wince, thinking about the still unfinished piece of business and how I have regretted giving in ever since.

"Hayley?" Nick is staring at me, his hands on the steering wheel even though the engine is still off.

The last of his smile fades and he asks, "Is that it? Is there anything else?"

"I called a wedding off at the last minute. Isn't that enough?"

"You did what you had to do." He drops his hands and the keys hanging from the ignition rattle when he smacks them.

"Can you take me to my car?"

"There's more, Hayley. It's obvious."

He's right. There is more. That part stays tight in my chest.

I open my window and let the night air into the cab as he drives me back to the complex. The night guy is in Mr. Hasting' booth so I have to tell him who I am, show ID and wait while he looks me up. He waves us on. The lot in front of the clubhouse is empty except for my car. The only sign of the celebration is the beaten down grass from where everyone was walking.

Nick pulls up beside my car and cuts the engine of his truck.

He doesn't say anything.

I don't want to sit there in silence, feeling his judgment on top of the judgment of all the others. Without any more prompting, I tell him about Waylon's grandpa and how he gave me some money a couple of days before the wedding. He'd wanted me to have my own nest egg, separate from the savings Waylon and I would have. He'd told me to save it for something important. I'd tried to say no, but he'd insisted, telling me that women always need a little money of their own. So he'd given me the money in secret. I finish with, "I still have the money."

"Why didn't you give it back?"

"He doesn't know what happened."

"He thinks you two are married?"

I nod.

"His whole family is lying to him?" He makes a face. "That's messed up, Hayley."

"I know." My voice is so small even I have a hard time hearing myself. "He was in the hospice wing of his nursing home. They wanted him to die thinking Waylon was settled. They told me not to tell him. So I didn't." I sigh and unbuckle my seatbelt so I can turn to face Nick. "He didn't die. He got better. Now he's in the residential section of the home, still very much alive."

"But they're still lying to him?"

I nod. "I asked my mom." A security guy buzzes by on a golf cart. I wave, pretending everything is fine. "If I give the money back, they'll all hate me."

"He didn't give the money to them. He gave the money to you."

He's right. I already know that.

Question is, am I ready to do something about it?

Chapter Thirty-Five

At Last

I hand my photo ID to the woman seated behind the counter of Green Acres and wait while she types my name into her keyboard. After the drive out, it feels good to stand up, but my legs are shaky from nerves so I lean over the counter. Behind the woman busy checking her screen is a welcoming display of staff photographs. I look them over and wonder if they know the truth about me.

Disturbed by that thought, that the family may have pulled them into the lie as well, I move my gaze around the reception area. It looks about the same as it did when I came to visit him the last time. Silk flowers, cozy chairs and some abstract art from local artists. That last visit would have been about a year ago.

About the time I start wondering what Waylon's grandpa thought about me disappearing from his life so suddenly, the woman looks up with a super bright smile. "Family or friend?"

One more lie, just to make things faster. "Family."

"Oh yes, I see you on the list." She hands my driver's license back. "Do you want to speak to a doctor or nurse as part of your visit today?"

I shake my head, worrying again what I might leave in my wake. Again.

"All righty. I'll just go check on him, make sure he's ready for a guest and be right back." She says something to the woman seated beside her, pops to her feet then scoots off with a swish of her floral skirt.

The remaining woman behind the counter smiles at me, looking as though she's about to ask how my day is so I turn away from her and stare at the glass double doors leading to the parking lot. The hood of Nick's truck is visible at the edge of the lot. Still no sign of Waylon. I'm not surprised. Just still hoping. He hadn't responded to any of my texts, including the final one I sent a couple of hours ago, letting him know I was headed back home to see his grandpa.

"He's excited to see you, Hayley," the woman in the floral skirt is saying as she strolls back from the hall. "Head on down to the lounge. Third door on the left."

"Thanks." I fake an easy-going smile and head to the room. Before going in, I pull the envelope of cash from my purse, take a deep breath.

I spot him right away because he's on his feet heading in my direction. For a man who was supposed to die last spring, he looks great. His beard is trimmed and his hair is slicked back and up in some swanky old style. He pulls me into a hug, kisses me on the cheek then takes my hand and guides me to a couch beside a window that looks out over a pond.

"If you weren't so pretty I'd be mad at you for not coming sooner," he says, waiting while I sit then easing himself down to sit beside me.

As soon as he's settled, I hold out the envelope. "I brought this for you."

He takes the envelope, looks inside and makes a harrumph noise.

"I didn't spend any of it—I wanted to tell you the truth about Waylon and me sooner but everyone...well, they asked me not to. I'm so sorry, I—" I take a deep breath and dive in again, "I should have...I should've—"

He waves his hand and cuts me off. "Exactly what are you sorry for?"

I lean forward and touch his shoulder. "Lying to you."

He tucks the envelope into the pocket of his gray and black plaid shirt. "You're not sorry about walking out on my grandson?"

I look into his face and remind myself, the truth only. "No, Sir. I'm not."

He nods then stuns me by smiling.

Something isn't right. I drop my hand from his shoulder. "You understand what I'm saying? Waylon and I didn't get married."

He leans back and grunts. "I know that." Pointing to himself, he adds, "You think a man gets this old and doesn't know when people are lying to him? You think I don't know how to find out the truth?"

"I—I—"

"Don't be so shocked." He pats my knee and that smile comes back. This turn of events is almost worse. I want to know how long he knew but then again I don't. Not really.

"I'm sorry I was part of that."

"I'm sorry too, Grandpa." It's Waylon talking. Leave it to him to arrive after the hard part is over.

"Are you still single?" His grandfather asks him.

Waylon blinks and takes a step back. Finally, he replies, "Yeah."

"We'll be having a talk about this later." The old man shoves himself to his feet. "But right now, I want you to come out in the hall. There's a gal here I want you to meet."

"What? I don't want you to introduce me to anyone."

"Obviously you need help, son." He takes a couple of steps then turns back and says over his shoulder, "I'm not going to introduce you. I'm going to pretend to have a heart attack. You introduce yourself." Then to me he adds, "You better get on out of here. You don't want to be part of this new small-town scandal."

And just like that, it's over.

It may seem quick, but I'm well aware that quick moment was months in the making.

* * * *

Outside, Nick is leaning against the hood of his truck, arms folded across his chest and warm rays of early summer sun slanting across him.

"I saw Waylon go in," he says, dropping his arms and stepping toward me.

I nod. "Yeah. After I gave the money back."

"Things go okay?"

Thinking about Waylon's feisty grandpa who at that very moment is probably lying on the floor, clutching his heart and practicing his acting skills, I say, "I think Waylon's grandpa is kind of annoyed about being lied to."

"Oh yeah?" Despite the situation, Nick actually looks worried for poor Waylon.

"He's also annoyed that Waylon's still single."

The concern falls from Nick's face and he takes both my hands and swings me around so my back is pressed against the truck cab. Smiling down at me, he says, "Waylon who?"

"Exactly."

There's no need to say any more because Nick starts kissing me in the perfect way that only a true boyfriend can.

About the Author

Thrill-seeking risk takers, heroes with the dark past, sexy locales, untamed women! Isabelle Drake writes stories featuring men and women who aren't afraid to go after what they want. An avid traveller, she'll go just about anywhere—at least once—to meet people and get story ideas.

Isabelle Drake loves to hear from readers. You can find her contact information, website details and author profile page at http://www.totallybound.com.

Totally Bound Publishing

Home of Erotic Romance

Made in the USA
Lexington, KY
30 March 2017